this year's
passion
will be...

asked

PRAISE FOR THE AUTHORS

JENNIFER BLAKE

"Jennifer Blake touches the hearts of her audience…"
—*Rendezvous*

Jennifer Blake will "thoroughly please."
—*Publishers Weekly*

"Blake…consistently produces compelling stories…"
—*Library Journal*

JANET DAILEY

Janet Dailey is "a winner in any genre…"
—*Affaire de Coeur*

Janet Dailey is "a master storyteller of romantic tales…"
—*Leisure Magazine*

ELIZABETH GAGE

"Gage writes with amazing intensity…"
—*San Jose Mercury News*

"Gage proves herself a shrewd chronicler of the rich and rotten."
—*New York Daily News*

"…Gage is a writer of style and intelligence.…"
—*Chicago Tribune*

Unmasked

JENNIFER BLAKE

JANET DAILEY

ELIZABETH GAGE

MIRA BOOKS

MIRA

ISBN 1-55166-272-8

UNMASKED
Copyright © 1997 by MIRA Books.

LOVE IN THREE-QUARTER TIME
Copyright © 1997 by Patricia Maxwell.

THE TAMING OF KATHARINA
Copyright © 1997 by Janet Dailey and Sonja Massie.

TAPESTRY
Copyright © 1997 by Gage Productions, Ltd.

Printed in U.S.A.

CONTENTS

LOVE IN THREE-QUARTER TIME
by Jennifer Blake

One

The ballroom of the old Garden District mansion was like something straight out of the antebellum era, Adrienne O'Banyon thought as she made a slow circuit of the empty, echoing space. She appreciated its beauty, but the true appeal was to her imagination. How many courtships had begun and ended here? How many dreams had unfolded or been shattered? Would the ghosts from past balls be on hand tonight, watching from the shadowed corners as modern couples danced during this twenty-fifth annual Mardi Gras ball at Sans Souci?

"A closet romantic, that's what you are," she accused herself in soft derision. "Next thing you know, you'll be looking around for Prince Charming."

All the same, she couldn't help smiling with the pleasure that bubbled inside her like party champagne. It should be quite an evening, with wonderful music and seriously good food and drink. That she was a part of this particular New Orleans tradition might be as unbelievable as the hoop-skirted dress she wore and the mask that dangled from her wrist, but she could still enjoy the excitement of it.

The stage had been carefully set. Real wax candles filled the holders of the French crystal chandeliers that marched down the ceiling of the long room. Their soft glow picked out the gilding on the room's cornice and the tall Corinthian columns at the archways inset in the open space and made shimmering pools of liquid gold on the polished cypress floor. Fires burned brightly in the twin black marble fireplaces, doing their bit to take away the coolness of the winter evening. The taint of wood smoke blended with the scents of the enormous spring bouquets gracing the mantels. Behind the flowers, gilt-framed mirrors doubled their profusion and reflected the sea-foam brocade on the walls and pale green draperies lined with pink, which framed a series of French windows.

In the music room, located through great pocket doors at the rear of the ballroom, the musicians hired for the evening were setting up their sound equipment with low-voiced comments and an occasional thumping clatter. They were the only other people nearby since it was a good half hour before the guests should begin arriving. Even the host and hostess for the evening, Charles and Millicent Duchaise, were still upstairs getting dressed.

The caterers could be heard shouting back and forth in the direction of the kitchen at the back of the mansion. Waiters in black-tie were setting out drink mixers and opening champagne with noisy competence in the butler's pantry. The security personnel hired for the evening were gathered in the main hall, with its black-and-white marble squares, where they were receiving last-minute instructions from their boss who had decked himself out as the butler.

Adrienne could hear the rumbling bass commands of Captain Byran "B.B." O'Banyon, lately of the NOPD. Her dad was in his element. A smile of gladness tilted her lips as she listened. It had been so long since he had sounded that positive, that cheerful.

Just then, a movement beyond the tall French doors overlooking the ballroom's terrace and the dark street that fronted the house caught Adrienne's attention. She turned in time to see a low-slung sports car pull up to the curb in front of the house next door. The headlights blinked out, then a man unfolded himself from behind the wheel and emerged onto the dimly lit street.

As the new arrival started around the car's hood, one of the parking valets hired for the ball hailed him, apparently asking if he needed his car parked while he attended the Duchaise party. It seemed a reasonable question, since the man was wearing fairly elaborate evening dress. But the newcomer answered with a negative shake of his head, then strode up the walk of the neighboring residence.

The parking attendant turned away. Adrienne's attention wavered also. Then, from the corner of her eye, she glimpsed the man from the sports car veering toward the Victorian iron fence that separated the grounds of Sans Souci from the other property. He reached it in a few long strides. Placing his hand on an ornate post, he vaulted the fence in a lithe, athletic movement, landing on his feet in the Duchaise side garden. He settled his evening jacket back in place, then wound his way toward the house through the thick shrubbery.

A frown creased the skin between Adrienne's eyes. She lifted her wide skirts and skimmed toward the French doors to keep the man in sight. She could just see his wide-shouldered form and dark head as he skirted the terrace, moving with the easy grace of a man comfortable with the power of his body and certain of where he was headed.

Her quick movement behind the glass must have attracted his attention, however, because he paused and swung his head in her direction. For a single instant they stared at each other through moving shadows created by security lamps gleaming through ancient, wind-tossed live oaks. The light from inside the house highlighted his face in its mellow glow.

His gaze was dark, intent in its appraisal. His even features had a hawklike cast that gave him a predatory look. Alert and balanced on the balls of his feet, he assessed the situation with unsmiling concentration.

Awareness tingled along Adrienne's nerves. It was immediate, compelling, like an atavistic acknowledgment she could not accept with her conscious mind. She stopped breathing and stood perfectly composed with her fingertips just touching the cool glass before her. In its mirror polish with the night behind it, she could see her own parted lips, her pale shoulders, the brown-gold glint of her eyes, and the aureole of blazing light around her head that was her untamed auburn hair.

Abruptly, the man looked away, walked on. Bare seconds later, he disappeared in the darkness toward the back of the mansion.

Adrienne let out her breath on a low laugh that was part nerves, part astonishment. In soft tones, she said, "And just where do you think you're going, my man?"

There was no way to tell, of course, not that she was too concerned. He hadn't seemed the burglar type. In fact, she had a distinct impression of the kind of confidence that went with money. Maybe he was an old family friend used to making himself at home. Or possibly he lived next door and had decided to show up for the ball through a side entrance she knew nothing about.

Regardless, she would have to tell B.B. It was his job to check these things out.

As Adrienne swung back toward the middle of the room, a spray of dogwood shifted in the bouquet above the nearest fireplace and a white petal fluttered to the hearth. She moved forward, her skirts whispering around her feet. Kneeling in a wide, spreading pool of white silk, she picked up the petal. With it in her fingers, she turned around, putting her back to the crackling fire.

"Careful there, *acushla,* or you'll be sending that dress of yours up in flames."

Adrienne glanced up, startled. For a man pushing sixty, and a large one at that, B.B. O'Banyon had a disconcerting ability to move without making a sound. He also had an uncanny way of fitting into any setting. In the formal wear he had rented for the job tonight, he looked as dignified and pompous as any real butler.

"No great loss, if you ask me," she said, relaxing as she glanced down at the gown she wore with its tight bodice, capped sleeves and acres of spreading skirt.

"Not even if it takes your pretty backside with it?" her father said as he moved to join her.

A quick look over her shoulder showed that she really hadn't allowed enough room for the wide sweep of her hoop. She took a hasty step forward. "You may have a point there!"

"Trust your dear old dad," he said, strolling forward. "You'll find a use for it one day."

She eyed him with suspicion. "The costume?"

"No, love," he said fondly, "not the costume. Though now you put me in mind of it, I don't see what you've got against it."

"Oh, nothing at all," she said, her smile and her tone overly affable. "Except that it's only slightly more respectable than going topless."

He glanced at her bodice. "It isn't that bad, about like what most of the females are wearing in the pictures on the walls of this place."

"You try it," she recommended. "Though not if you expect to breathe at the same time. Or did you think that might be a mere detail?"

"Now, don't be blaming me, Adrienne, me heart. It was Duchaise's doing entirely. The theme for this bash is Legendary Lovers, and you're supposed to be the Lady of the Camellias.''

Adrienne tipped her auburn head with its heavy weight of high-piled auburn curls. "What, like Garbo in that old movie?"

"La Dame aux camélias," he answered with a rueful shrug, "though Duchaise, being the cultured type, mentioned *La Traviata* and something about Dumas *fils.* Violetta, I think he named you."

"A consumptive call girl, I might have known," Adrienne moaned. "And you okayed this getup?"

"Didn't get the chance," her father answered. "First I saw of it was when Duchaise handed the whole shebang over just before you got here. Oh, I knew he was lining up something, since I'd told him I wanted you on the job, but he said leave it to him."

"Couldn't you have at least suggested a shawl? I haven't exposed this much cleavage since the last time I tried on a string bikini. I'll probably come down with consumption for real, not to mention pneumonia."

A dubious look strayed across her father's strong, fleshy face. "I do see your point, but it's not really that cold. Anyway, nobody will know who you are."

"I'll know, you big Irish lummox! And I can tell you right now that walking around half-naked wasn't part of this arrangement."

"Be reasonable, love. It's a Mardi Gras ball, not a picnic. And I have to say, you look grand." Softness edged the clear blue of his eyes, and his voice took on a low note of pride. "You're more like your mother than I've seen you in a long time."

Adrienne was touched against her will by the sadness behind his words. His grief for the early death of her mother, the only woman he had ever loved, was real and deep, even if he was perfectly capable of using it to get what he wanted.

She might be like her mother with her typical redhead's brown eyes and pale, easily freckled skin, but she was not in the least like poor, fragile Violetta, the Parisian courtesan who sacrificed all for love. The only thing the two of them had in common was a narrow waistline, and that was mainly because of a bug Adrienne had picked up on her last archaeological dig in the Yucatán. Khaki shorts and a backpack were more her style than silk and satin. And she was nobody's mistress except her own.

"You wouldn't be thinking of running out on me, now, would you?" B.B. gave a doubtful tip to his big head.

She looked at him a long moment, then she sighed. "No, of course not."

"Good. You had me worried. I'd be in over my head without you, love."

"That's blarney, and you know it." Her gaze held affection in spite of the sardonic note in her voice.

"No way," he said, turning down the corners of his mouth. "I'm fine with the legwork and keeping an eye on things behind the scenes, but talking the fancy talk and mingling with the ritzy crowd is beyond me. For you, now, it's natural. You're used to wining and dining with bigwigs who pass out grants and sit on museum boards.''

"Maybe," she said dubiously, "but I still can't see what you expect me to discover that you couldn't get just as well some other way. Say with a nice wiretap?"

"That's illegal," he said in pained protest.

She laughed. "Since when did that stop you?"

"Since I left the force and became a private citizen."

"Private eye, you mean. Not that I believe a word of it. And I'm not fooled about why you want me here, either. You just hope I'll run into a man who can take me away from jungle expeditions and scrounging for skeletons."

"I'll admit I'd like to see you interested in jumping on the bones of a man who hasn't been dead for a thousand years."

"B.B. O'Banyon!" she cried.

"You're my one hope of ever being a grandfather," he said with a guileless look in the clear blue of his eyes. "I deserve to be one, I want to be one. And soon. Before I'm too old to enjoy it."

"You're not that old and neither am I. There's plenty of time for all that."

"You never know what's going to happen," he muttered, looking away from her.

He was thinking of his involuntary retirement, she knew. He hadn't intended to leave the force so soon, but there had been cutbacks in his department, and he had been put out to pasture. It galled him that all his experience meant nothing compared to the drawback of his age. That was why it was so important that he succeed with this job. He needed to prove that he could do it. He needed that as much or more than he needed the money or the referral from a man of Charles Duchaise's position and connections.

Adrienne was going to do her best to see that her father got what he needed. The two of them were close, even if she did call him B.B. instead of father or dad. He had brought her up the best he knew how. after her mother died. The sacrifices he had made to see that she had all the things young girls want, to put her through school and help launch her career had been many, and Adrienne knew them, every one. Whatever it took to make this evening turn out right for him, she would do. Even if it meant going stark naked.

"At least I have my mask." She twirled the scrap of white satin sewn with pearls, iridescent sequins and feathers by its silk-covered elastic cord.

"You aren't going to wear that thing?"

She gave him a jaundiced stare. "It is a masked ball, right? Everyone else will be in costume."

Her father nodded. "Otherwise they don't get in the door. Duchaise's orders."

"Count me among the incognito, then," she said, slipping the mask into place and winking at him through the eye slits. "I have a reputation to protect."

"You're covering up one of your best assets," he complained.

"You're prejudiced. Anyway, just think of what's left uncovered." Her smile was crooked.

B.B. grunted. "Make sure you stay where there are plenty of people and no dark corners, okay?"

"You can bet on it."

"Good. Everything should be fine, then."

He was reassuring himself as much as he was her, Adrienne thought. He wasn't quite as comfortable with the idea of her snooping around as he pretended. It made her feel better.

After a pause, she said in a businesslike tone, "So, all right, boss man, you promised to tell me what's going down as soon as I got dressed. What am I suppose to be looking for? What desperate case are we on that requires me to rub elbows with the rich and famous?"

"Not so loud," he protested, glancing toward the door again. "This is no joke."

"Sorry," she said, lowering her voice to a near whisper. "What is it, then?"

"A case of adultery."

She stared at him through the almond-shaped holes of her mask. "You mean... Are you saying all this dressing up is to catch some guy in the act?"

"No, it is not to catch some guy in the act," he said with pained emphasis. "It's to catch some woman in the—that is, it's to discover who the lady of the house has on the side."

Adrienne shook her head in disbelief. "This is

the special job Duchaise called you in on, the one he's paying a fortune for, not to mention putting out a bundle on a costume for me?''

''Besides keeping out gate-crashers and protecting the family silver, yes.'' B.B. shrugged. ''Duchaise loves his wife and can't believe she's cheating on him, so he wants to keep it confidential. He'll be just as happy if we prove she's innocent.''

''But he wants to know, one way or the other.'' It was disturbingly sordid when compared to the promised grandeur of the evening. Which just went to show how close she had been to succumbing to the romance of it all.

B.B. nodded, watching her with lively apprehension.

''And then what?''

''Who knows? I guess he'll divorce her. That part's not our business.''

There was something so depressing about the whole thing, Adrienne thought, staring around her at the fine house with its air of quiet good taste, its unmistakable evidence of old family, old money. If prominent people like Charles and Millie Duchaise couldn't be content without sneaking around, then who could?

As the image behind her train of thought triggered a memory, she frowned. ''I don't know for sure,'' she said slowly, ''but I just may have seen your man.''

B.B. was instantly alert. ''My darling dear, I knew having you on hand as an extra pair of eyes would be a grand thing.''

"Maybe. This guy could have nothing whatever to do with Duchaise's wife."

"Tell your old dad about him, and I'll be for deciding."

She did as he asked, then stood waiting while he thought about it. When he made no comment, she said, "Well?"

He sighed. "I guess it wouldn't be proper to go barging into the lady's boudoir while she's dressing, but I'll bet my old uniform buttons that's where your man is right now."

"It would be a bit daring, don't you think?"

"Indeed, it would, but I hear that's what the ladies like."

Adrienne couldn't deny it, though such behavior didn't stand high on her own list. She said after a moment, "Just how old is Millie Duchaise?"

"Fifties, maybe," her father said with a shrug. "Why?"

"I thought she might be, from seeing her and her husband in the papers from time to time. But I don't believe the guy I saw outside was quite that old."

"He's not supposed to be." B.B.'s expression was sardonic as he spoke.

Her eyes widened. "You mean...?"

"A younger man, right. Duchaise's wife has found herself a boy-toy. At least that's what Duchaise thinks."

"I'm impressed." Hard on the words, she frowned.

"What?" Her father waited, watching her with narrow-eyed interest.

She shook her head. "I don't know. I just have a hard time connecting the man I saw with this situation."

"People do things for a lot of reasons, Adrienne, love, not all of them easy or simple. Or nice."

"Hmm," she agreed. "Then there's Charles Duchaise. He's such a distinguished figure, so respected around town, that I have trouble with the idea of him hiring somebody to check up on his wife."

"It's not a matter of social standing, *acushla*," her father said, "but of feelings."

"I suppose," Adrienne said on a sigh. "So just what is it I'm supposed to do to help get the goods on the lady?"

Two

As it turned out, B.B.'s instructions were easy to follow. Adrienne had only to keep her eyes open. She was to take note of Millie Duchaise's activities, such as when she left the ballroom and with whom, and watch to see if she made contact with the man who had leaped the garden fence. Other than that, Adrienne was free to mingle or dance as she pleased. If she heard any juicy rumors or picked up a lead in the course of conversation, her dear old dad said, that would be all to the good. But she wasn't to go snooping on her own, should take no chances.

Adrienne was restless, feeling at loose ends as the ballroom slowly began to fill. She wandered here and there, trying to look as if she belonged. It wasn't easy, since most of the guests were arriving as matched pairs of lovers: Lancelot and Guinevere, Romeo and Juliet, Andrew Jackson and his Rachel, and so on. A Casanova did show up alone in a lavender satin coat and white wig, but he soon melted into a group that included Pocahontas with John Smith, as well as Abraham and Mary Todd Lincoln, both in funeral black.

No other single women arrived, however, which

made Adrienne feel horribly conspicuous. The urge
to yank up her skirts and make a run for it grew
so strong it took all her considerable willpower to
fight it. But she couldn't let B.B. down, darn it all.
She finally located a secluded spot, where she stood
making her heavy skirts sway like a bell to the old-
fashioned waltz the band was playing as it warmed
up for a more modern tempo.

It was interesting to see how the other half entertained themselves, to watch the glitter of jewels,
the swirl of silk, satin and velvet, and to inhale the
designer fragrances that floated on the air like a
miasma. The elite of New Orleans were certainly
on hand, decked out in the richest and most unique
costumes to be had, as well as the most fantastic
masks. The majority had commissioned their party
wear from the specialists who made a good living
at such things in the Mardi Gras-mad city, but some
had imported creations from Paris or Milan.

The theme of the ball had been printed on the
bottom of the invitations from the year before, just
as the one for next year's ball was engraved on the
cards for this evening. New Orleanians knew exactly how to do these things for the greatest convenience. And why not? They had been at it for
more than two hundred and fifty years.

Nevertheless, Adrienne thought she had seen
more animation at an Irish wake. It was the effect,
no doubt, of all the pomp and dignity of the occasion. The level of conviviality would likely rise
once the host and hostess abandoned their receiving
positions at the door, or else as the champagne be-

ing circulated by the waiters began to take effect.
She had to admire the aplomb of Charles and Millie
Duchaise, however, as they greeted their guests.
They were a perfect team, helping each other with
names as they moved people along. To watch
them—Duchaise slight of stature but silver-haired
and suave, his wife bright-eyed and vivacious with
her artfully burnished gold curls—it was difficult
to believe they had ever exchanged a cross word
in their lives.

"Is this a private corner you have staked out
here, or may I join you?"

The deep baritone at her shoulder startled Adrienne so that she swung in a whirl of skirts. The
movement sent the plastic hoop of her crinoline
knocking into the ankles of the man behind her. He
stepped back, at the same time moving the glass of
champagne he held well away from the sea of silk
that engulfed his feet.

"Oh, excuse me," she exclaimed with only the
briefest of glances before snatching the excess material out of the way. "I'm not quite used to all
this, I'm afraid. How women used to manage is
beyond me."

"With practice, I would imagine," he answered
in a drawl laced with appreciative humor, "helped
by the knowledge that the style has certain com-
pensations."

As she realized who the man was, noticed the
direction of his brief glance, her amusement died.
A flush began in the region of her navel, traveling
like a flash fire to heat the gentle valley of her

cleavage. She felt it climb to her hairline and was intensely grateful for the mask that covered the upper part of her face.

She'd known her dress was revealing, but she had not expected she'd have anyone comment on it. Certainly, she had not thought she'd hear about it from the handsome stranger she had seen from the ballroom window earlier.

It was the same man. There was no doubt about it, in spite of the black velvet half mask he now wore across his eyes. Did he also recognize her? It seemed likely. Even if he had not been able to make out her face through the glass, the draped fullness of her white skirts would have been hard to miss.

There was no reason he should think she knew anything about him, of course. Nor was there anything to prove that he was having a hot affair with Duchaise's wife. Still, it seemed unlikely it was a coincidence that he had sought her out.

"Yes, well," she said on a brittle laugh as she tried for composure, "no doubt that was the whole point, for a Victorian courtesan." She touched the heavy white flowers pinned at the lowest point of her neckline. "I'm supposed to be the Lady of the Camellias, you know."

"I'm glad you told me," he answered, the words dry.

"What? You didn't recognize me? For shame."

"My apologies," he said. "I suppose it's because you don't look the type to die for love."

Adrienne was well aware that she lacked the

simpering chocolate-box prettiness usually associated with the past century. Her features were too angular, her skin less than perfect, her hair impossible. These things had been the bane of her existence as a teenager, but that was some time ago.

"Ah, well," she said, fluttering her lashes, "dying for love is a bit extreme. Living for it is so much better."

His gaze narrowed behind its covering, darkening as he watched her. "Is that what you do? Live for love?"

She almost laughed. Mostly, she lived for pieces of ancient pots, bits of bone and chunks of corroded silver. It was love of a sort, just not the variety this guy apparently had in mind. Stringing him along might not be particularly nice, but then he shouldn't make it so inviting.

"You might say so," she murmured, her gaze teasing yet a little cool.

Hunter Sutherland watched the amusement that lay in the Lady of the Camellias' eyes, swirling in their golden brown depths like fine old brandy. It was so refreshingly expressive, yet so heady, that his mind was clouded by sudden doubt. She wasn't at all as she'd been described to him.

She was beautiful, yes, with fascinating angles to her face under high cheekbones, and a pure, disarming attraction far different from the hard-edged, artificial perfection he'd imagined. She seemed natural and unaffected with her wild tumble of auburn curls and the dusting of freckles on her milk-white skin, which reminded him of pale gold snowflakes.

The need to reach out and touch a finger to them was so strong he had to push his hands into his pockets to prevent it.

More than that, the fiery warmth and sensitivity to his moods that he sensed inside her came as a definite surprise. And the delicate flush that lay on her skin, like the blush sometimes seen on a white rose petal, was the last thing he had expected. The very last.

Of course, he only had Millie's impressions to go by, and they weren't the most reliable. Especially now. He could almost think she had steered him wrong.

Or maybe his impressions were colored by his memory of the woman in white he had seen at the ballroom window earlier. She had seemed so pure and cool, yet so burningly brilliant, that she had beckoned like some distant, untouchable star.

As he glanced toward where Millie Duchaise stood with her husband, the woman beside him followed his gaze. With a slight nod in that direction, he asked evenly, "Have you known our host and hostess long?"

"Not really."

That told him exactly nothing. He might have guessed. He said, "I understand Duchaise's wife was originally from Texas."

"So I've heard, though she's been here so many years, and done so much for various charities, that it seems New Orleans has forgiven her the lapse."

"Of birth, you mean?" He could not quite hide his aversion to the idea.

Her eyes seemed appraising as she surveyed him from the concealment of her mask. Still, her voice was pleasant as she answered. "It's an insular town, especially among people like the Duchaises. Money is fine, but it's the ancestors perching on the limbs of the family tree that are really important."

"I've noticed." His lips curled at one corner with his scorn for the attitude.

"Of course, Millie Duchaise gives a mean party, and that makes up for a lot. A few sticklers may remember she isn't one of them, but you won't see them staying away because of it."

"I'm surprised she ever got a foot in the door."

"Oh, well, she did start out right."

"How was that?" Hunter asked, uneasily aware of the tightness in his reply.

The stare the woman in white gave him was pitying. "She married Charles Duchaise, of course. His family goes back to martyrs killed by the infamous Bloody O'Reilly on his mother's side, and to a marriage between one of the Bienville's casket girls and a younger son of a count from Normandy on the other. Blood doesn't come much bluer in New Orleans."

"On top of which, Duchaise is a powerful man."

"There is that," she agreed with a small shrug.

"And is that what you like best about him?" Hunter asked softly.

Her glance was astringent as she said, "Maybe I like him because he's what people call a gentleman."

"Meaning I'm not." He gave a short laugh as he accepted the reprimand.

"I didn't say that."

"You don't have to, since I'm a fair hand at reading between the lines." He paused. "Would you care for a drink?"

Adrienne gave a brief nod. It was enough. With swift efficiency, the dark-haired man beside her snagged a champagne flute from the tray of a passing waiter and pressed it into her hand. She took a sip of the golden liquid without taking her eyes from the couple near the ballroom entrance.

The Duchaises, though unmasked since they would be recognized, anyway, as host and hostess, were richly dressed as Napoléon and Josephine. It was Millie's choice, no doubt; Duchaise seemed the type to prefer something less obvious. He would almost certainly have chosen a costume that did not call attention to the fact that he was an inch shorter than his wife. Still, he bore his part with good grace, making the small stiff bows appropriate to his military uniform while passing off graceful quips that created ripples of laughter around him.

Toward his wife, Duchaise was courteous and a little proprietorial. If there was strain in the smiles he turned on her as their time on duty lengthened, no one seemed to notice. Just as no one seemed aware of Millie Duchaise's quick, nervous gestures or the quiver of impending hysteria in her breathless voice.

Adrienne glanced at the man who stood at her

own side. It was easy to see why Millie might risk so much for an affair with him. It was less easy to understand his attraction to the older woman, she thought, which very likely showed her own unexpected prejudice toward an age difference that was the reverse of what was generally accepted.

She said, "I recognize you from your unusual entry, in case you're wondering."

The only sign that she had startled him was his fixed gaze, though that lasted only an instant before his lashes came down to screen his expression. "You think that's why I came over to talk to you?"

"Isn't it?"

"I'd say it was more because I recognize you."

Neat, she thought in reluctant appreciation for the riposte, even if she didn't believe it. "You must know the house well to come in the back way."

"Actually, no. I was early, so decided to sit in the back garden until a decent time to show up. I can't say I expected anyone to be on the scene already."

The last was a polite inquiry, she thought, one that might become more insistent if her answer wasn't acceptable. She lifted a shoulder, her smile a little crooked as she held his gaze. "I'm one of those compulsive people who always arrives ahead of time out of fear I'll be late. If I had known there was a back garden I might have joined you."

The tune being played by the band ended. Immediately afterward came the introduction to the "Anniversary Waltz." Adrienne saw Charles Duchaise speak to his wife, then lead her away from their receiving post and out onto the floor. To-gether, the older couple circled the polished cypress planking, moving in and out of the shining pools of yellow candlelight.

The waltz was in honor of the twenty-fifth an-niversary of the ball, of course. Yet it was such a potent reminder of the enduring nature of love that Adrienne felt sad for the marital troubles of the two people out on the floor. They moved so well to-gether, were so easy in each other's arms. What a shame that it was all for show.

Adrienne felt it when the gaze of the man who stood so near returned to her face. That concen-trated attention made her uneasy. She drank a large swallow of her champagne as she hunted around in her mind for something to use as a distraction.

"So," she said, running a quick glance over the dark blue velvet jacket that covered his wide shoul-ders and the white cravat wrapped and tied around his throat. "Just who are you masquerading as to-night? Anyone in particular?"

"A Romantic poet, I believe," he said with a flash of caustic humor in the black glitter of his eyes behind his mask. "As to which one, take your pick."

Adrienne was willing to play along, at least for the moment. "Not Byron, I think, nor Keats. Shel-ley, maybe?"

"If you say so." He smiled, his gaze specula-tive. "Of course, I could be any Victorian gentle-man, even whoever is the match for the costume you have on."

"Alfredo? Oh, I doubt that!"

"Why not?" He watched her over the rim of his glass as he took a sip of his champagne.

"With all the high passion and deathless devotion? Come on." The words were scathing, though she took refuge from his direct gaze by drinking more of her own wine.

"You don't think I'm capable of it?"

A prickle of uneasiness moved over her skin. It made her cautious. "Not that exactly, but I doubt you would care for it. Not many men do."

"You might be surprised," he said, the words clipped. Taking her empty glass and setting it on a table along with his own, he turned back to offer his hand. "Dance?"

It was a perfectly acceptable offer. The host and hostess had made a complete circle of the floor and were now motioning for others to join them. Adrienne could think of no good reason to refuse and several for agreeing, including the fact that she might be able to learn something of benefit to B.B. Regardless, she had no intention of making it easy for the man beside her.

Tilting her head with its heavy curls, she said, "I don't know who you are."

"No," he answered as a smile quirked his mouth. "I thought that was the purpose of a masked ball."

"For some, maybe."

"But not you? Are you ready to unmask, then?"

She looked at him from under her lashes, disturbed by the hint of double meaning behind his words. "I don't think so." After a moment, she added, "I suppose I could make do with calling myself Violetta until after the midnight unmasking. But where does that leave you?"

"Alfredo will do. Unless you have some other objection?"

"No, why should I?" she said as she put her hand in his and allowed him to lead her out onto the floor. But even she could tell that she didn't sound too certain.

Three

Dancing was something Hunter did because it was expected, rather than because he enjoyed it. He led the woman calling herself Violetta out on the floor only as an excuse to extend their time together. That was the sole benefit he expected from it. Or so he told himself.

He should have known better.

It was the dress—at least in part. He could feel the graduated levels of the hoop skirt pressing against him with every movement she made. It was a hidden and incredibly erotic enticement, like feeling her bones under her soft skin. The great width of her skirt made her seem fragile by contrast, as if she might be breakable, yet the warmth of her body beneath the delicate silk gave him an insane urge to smooth his palms over every inch of her. The way her shoulders and the curves of her breasts rose out of the top of her dress made him think she might come out of it completely with just a little help from him. And giving her a hand seemed like one of the best impulses he'd had in years.

He needed something to use as a distraction, and he needed it now. Snatching at the first thing that came to mind, he said, "The song they're playing now sounds familiar. Recognize it?"

Her eyes were bright behind her mask. "The theme from *Romeo and Juliet*. Millie Duchaise doesn't miss a trick, does she?"

"Sign of a good hostess, I suppose. Have you known her long?"

"Not really."

He tested the guarded sound of that in his mind before he said, "I expect you're a friend of her husband's?"

"Actually, it's my father who knows him. What about you?"

"Millie and I have a couple of charities in common, Boys Clubs, St. Jude's. We're both on the board for historic preservation in the city."

"You're a philanthropist, then?"

"Oh, I wouldn't say that. Helping out here and there is just a sideline. Keeps me busy when I'm not working."

Her stare said she wasn't convinced, but she didn't press it. Instead, she asked, "What line of work?"

"Can't tell you that," he said with a shake of his head. "It might give me away."

"And that would never do, would it? Only, what are we going to talk about?"

It was an effort not to stare at the curves of her lips. They really had the most enticing shape. "You," he answered. "Tell me why you're here alone."

"What makes you think I'm alone?"

"I don't see any other Alfredo hovering protectively."

"And why should I need protecting?" she queried lightly.

With the lift of a brow, he nodded at one of the tall pier glasses that stood between the French doors not far away. "Have you seen yourself?"

She turned her head to look, and for a single instant he met her gaze in the reflection. The two of them were a perfect pair in the soft glow given off by the candles in the chandeliers overhead, male and female, dark and light, yin and yang, a matched set in height and shape and mystery, separate parts of a whole. Playing the eternal game of hide-and-seek behind their masks.

God, he was losing it. This was no time to get soft, especially not with this woman. The last thing he needed was to forget who she was, or why he was at Sans Souci.

"Of course," he said, "maybe there's somebody here somewhere? Whoever paid for the dress you have on, for instance?"

She stiffened in his arms. "What makes you think anybody did?"

"Simple deduction. It's exactly the kind of thing a man might buy to show off a woman, so long as she wasn't his wife."

"You would know, I imagine," she said, anger going off like fireworks in her eyes.

"Not really. I'd prefer to keep my woman to myself."

"How intriguing. Locked up, I suppose!"

"I'd be tempted, if she looked the way you do." The words were grim. He meant them.

"I'd like to remind you that Violetta is supposed to be a—a lady of the evening!"

"And all for love, I suppose, instead of money?"

"What are you trying to say?" she demanded, meeting his gaze in hot suspicion.

"I think you know." Funny, but he was reluctant to lay it out in plain words. It didn't feel right in his mind, regardless of the facts as he knew them.

"I don't believe I do. If you are trying to suggest that I am—that Violetta and I have more in common than a dress, I don't appreciate the idea."

"You're the one who mentioned love and making a living in the same breath." If he pushed hard enough, she might tell him plainly that what he had been led to believe wasn't so.

"It was a joke!"

"Was it? I happen to know who paid for the costume you have on."

She stumbled, and he was forced to catch her, pulling her closer against him. He closed his eyes, assailed by her warm softness, the faint scent of jungle flowers in her hair, the gentle tickle of a curl that brushed his face. His heart shifted inside him and he held his breath.

She pushed away at once to the length of his arms. A pulse beat in the fragile line of her neck, and her face was white. The look in her eyes was searching and entirely too conscious. She knew exactly what he meant. He hated it, he really did.

She parted her lips and said, "Millie Duchaise told you."

"Who else?" he answered with scant inflection.

"Then that means—" She stopped short, and the expression on her face became indecipherable.

As she remained silent, he said deliberately, "It means the smartest thing you can do right now is get out of here. Before it gets embarrassing."

The music was coming to an end, and they were not far from the corner where they had begun. He swung her in an easy turn, then released her and stepped back.

She met his gaze for a scorching instant, then she lifted her chin. Brushing past him, she walked quickly away.

He stood watching her progress; he just couldn't help it. She glided with the grace of a queen, managing the full skirts that swept the floor around her as if she had been doing it all her life. There was nothing coquettish, nothing come-hither in any way about her movements.

She was heading toward the door into the hallway. Apparently she was leaving as he had suggested. He should have been happy. Instead, his gaze rested on her straight shoulders and the regally outraged set of her head with brooding intensity. Had he made a mistake? It seemed distinctly possible. The thought made him feel cold to the bone. And suddenly alone. He was used to the latter, but this was different. This, he had brought on himself.

* * *

Adrienne found B.B. in the central hallway. He was stationed near the front door, ready to admit guests in his role as butler. He started forward as he saw her, but she motioned him to remain where he was, away from the racket coming from the butler's pantry at the opposite end of the long marble-floored passage.

"Is something wrong, *acushla?*" he asked as she came closer. His craggy features turned wary as he studied her set face.

"You might say so," she answered, "though I'm not quite sure what it is. I've been dancing with Millie Duchaise's lover."

He nodded. "I suspected he was the guy when I looked in just now. That was fast work."

"It might have been, if it was any of my doing," she said. "The truth is, he came to me. I think he's on to us."

"Now, how would that be?"

She told him, omitting nothing. "Besides that," she finished, "he seems to be confusing what I am with what I look like, since he suggested some man paid for this dress."

Her father pursed his lips before saying reasonably, "Well, some man did."

"Yes, but if Millie told him, then she knows we're watching her."

"Then why the devil didn't she ask her boyfriend to stay away?"

"Maybe she did, and he paid no attention. He seems the type, and it would account for him sneaking around to see her before the party started." Adrienne could hear the tightness in her voice, but couldn't prevent it.

"Might be at that."

"But if that's it, he has a lot of nerve making slighting remarks about anyone else. I can't imagine what he thinks gives him the right."

B.B., watching her with a shrewd light in the clear blue of his eyes, said, "What's more to the point, love, is why you care?"

She glared at him. "I care because I'm not what he thinks, not in any way, shape or form!"

"What difference does that make? You'll probably never see him again."

Adrienne stared at her father, recognizing the craftiness in his voice. "True," she said in abrupt agreement. "He's just another man, and a dumb one at that. I don't care for straight up what he thinks."

B.B. tilted his head. "Not even a little?"

"Not at all." She set her lips in a grim line and gave her skirts a shake, as if her dance partner was dust she could dislodge with a gesture.

"What makes you think he's dumb?"

Her glance was scathing as she heard the thoughtful tone of her father's voice. "He's involved with Millie Duchaise, isn't he?"

B.B. lifted his hand, rubbing a finger along the bridge of his nose. "That just it, we don't know for sure. And I guess we won't find out if you are going to go tearing off every time he says something you don't like."

"What are you suggesting?"

"Well, I can't dance with him, love, now can I? Come on, be a professional."

"It's not my profession," she said incisively. "It's yours."

"But you agreed to help. You were more than anxious to do your part less than an hour ago."

B.B. was up to something, Adrienne could tell. She just wasn't sure what it was. "That's not fair. I didn't know I'd have to take on Millie's partner in adultery single-handedly."

"And no more will you, dear heart. What do you think he can do with me right here on duty? All I'm suggesting is that you talk to the guy a little more, find out exactly what's going on between him and the lady of the house. Hey, it may not have a thing in the world to do with S-E-X."

"Oh, Dad," she said, rolling her eyes in the same gesture of exasperation she had used as a teenager.

"Anyway, you're not the only one working, you know. While you were having a good time dancing and drinking champagne, I was checking out your partner."

Her head came around. "You discovered who he is?"

"Nothing to discover, once I got a good look at him. When you're a cop, you learn to remember what the bigwigs in town look like."

"And?" she said impatiently when he paused as if to gauge how badly she wanted to know what he had to say.

"The name Hunter Sutherland mean anything to you?"

"What? It can't be!"

"Promise." His nod carried conviction.

"Sutherland Construction," she said slowly.

"Nouveau riche, as far as such things go in New Orleans, but respectable. Hunter's grandfather, Axel Sutherland, founded the company back before World War II—he's the Sutherland who saw the future for offshore drilling rigs and started building the things. His son David is the one who made a habit of giving away the money the old man made, so developed the rep as a do-gooder. Hunter took over both the business and the charity work as the next Sutherland in line when his dad died maybe ten years ago. Sutherland Construction has increased in size at the rate of ten or twelve percent every year since, and the Sutherland Foundation has become a major source of funding for special programs in the city."

"I know," she said dryly. "The foundation financed the last dig for the university's archaeology department."

A blue glint shone in her father's narrowed eyes. "You've met him, then?"

She shook her head. "It was handled very quietly. I wouldn't have heard about it except that—well, I was involved with the man who was head of the department at the time. I helped him put together the proposal to present to the foundation."

B.B. grunted, an indication of his lack of enthusiasm for the professor-type she had just mentioned. Her father had been pleased when that particular relationship died a natural death during the last dig. Now he said, "Sutherland doesn't have many friends, seldom shows up on the social scene, at least not since his mother passed away a few years back. Some seem to think he's a mystery man."

"And what do you think?"

"Don't know enough about him to tell." Her father's innocence was carefully done. "I was hoping you could clue me in."

She glanced back toward the ballroom. Through the open doors, she could see Hunter dancing with Millie. From all appearances, they were in close conversation. Thinking of the traps he had set for her during their brief dance, and also of the assessing darkness of his eyes, she said slowly, "You're asking what I think? I don't really know, except I'd hate to have to face him across a negotiating table."

"What about a breakfast table?"

Her brows snapped together as she turned on her father. "Don't be ridiculous. If I thought for one moment that you had some idea of—"

"Hold on, *acushla*," he said, flinging up his hands. "I was only interested in the feminine point of view, wondering what it might be that attracts Duchaise's wife."

"That's pretty obvious, isn't it? Hunter Sutherland's your typical dark and devastating hunk, and secretive to boot. How could any woman resist, especially one of—how do they put it?—a certain age?''

''Or of your age?'' he said, tipping his head in a sly gesture.

She almost snorted. ''He isn't my type, thank you very much. I prefer someone considerably more easygoing, a guy who's comfortable in hiking boots. Hunter Sutherland doesn't come close. He's the intense, driven sort, never happy unless he's stirring things up or making trouble for somebody. Just thinking about it gives me a headache.''

''In that case,'' her father said with seraphic calm, ''you won't be in any danger of falling for him while you ask him a few more questions. Now, will you?''

She opened her mouth to tell him what she thought of his machinations. Then she closed it. B.B. was right. She didn't know why she was so reluctant to face Hunter again.

''What about Duchaise?'' she asked after a moment. ''When will you report what we've found out?''

''We haven't found out anything, not yet. All we have are suspicions.''

''Same thing,'' she said, even as she acknowledged a fleeting admiration for her father's fairness.

''Maybe, maybe not,'' B.B. said. ''Anyway, I agree too much is happening too fast to keep him in the dark. I don't think he's the kind to make a stink over it in public.''

''Thank God for small mercies.''

B.B. nodded, his expression brooding. ''Of

course, you never can tell what a man will do when it comes to this sort of thing.''

''What do you mean?''

''Love, hate, jealousy, it can get out of hand. That's why they write tragedies about it.''

Adrienne gave him a sharp look. ''Let's hope it doesn't come to that!''

''Aye, love, let's do that.'' B.B.'s smile was crooked. ''It never hurts to hope.''

The candles were burning lower in the chandeliers when Adrienne returned to the ballroom. Their soft light cast prism gleams among the drapings of crystal ropes and in the dangling lusters. The iridescent colors danced on the ceilings and the walls and played over the heads of the shifting, dancing guests, making them appear almost mystical in their bright costumes and fantastic masks. The heat wafting at ceiling height swayed the lusters so they touched with the soft chiming of crystal. Mingling with the sound was the music of the dance, as well as the subdued roar of the crowd as their spirits began to expand with the advancing evening.

Adrienne noticed these things with only a fraction of her attention as she skirted the dance floor. Her mind was occupied with how, in the name of heaven, she was going to approach Hunter Sutherland again after leaving him in such high dudgeon. She could march up to him and tell him she wanted to talk, of course, but a direct, frontal attack had never been her style, and she wasn't sure she could carry it off. It would be much more subtle to stroll nonchalantly past him to see if he had any interest in finding out why she had not left as he suggested. But if he didn't rise to the bait, then she didn't know if she would be able to drum up the courage to try again.

"Miss O'Banyon? May I take a few minutes of your time?"

She turned to face Charles Duchaise, recognizing his voice even before she saw him. "By all means," she said with a strained smile. "I've been wanting to tell you how much I appreciate the costume you provided."

"My pleasure, of course," he said, his somber features lightened by the glimmer of a smile, "though I take no credit. I only called the shop where my wife gets her costumes and told them what I required. I must say, however, that the results are very becoming."

"Thank you." His grave courtesy made it extremely easy to say the polite thing in return.

He cleared his throat. "I don't like to impose, but it might be best if we stepped outside on the terrace for our chat. That is, if you don't think you will be too cool."

"I'm sure it will be fine," she answered, and turned in that direction.

In all truth, the ballroom had grown rather warm with the press of people. The fires burning under the marble mantels were more for atmosphere than for effect; there was a highly efficient central heating system somewhere that was doing a better-than-average job of heating the cavernous space. The fresh coolness of the terrace was welcome, even with the gusting wind that blew across the flagstones now and then, rustling a stray leaf across the weathered slate surface.

Charles led her away from the windows, toward the stone balustrades that flanked the wide steps down into the garden. As he paused, he scanned the night sky and the waving branches of the big live oaks where the wind sighed among the leaves. "Looks like we may have rain before the night is over."

"Could be," she agreed as she followed his gaze.

"Millie won't like that. She hates rain."

"I rather like it, myself." Adrienne, identifying the talk about the weather as a minor diversion, waited for her host to come to the point.

"So do I." The older man gave her a faint, almost melancholy smile that faded even before he looked away. "I spoke briefly with your father, a quick word in passing. He said you have something to tell me concerning my case."

"Did he, now?" she said in annoyance. What did he mean, she wondered, leaving her with the touchy explanation? Just wait until she got her hands on him.

"If you'd rather not go into it, I will certainly understand. I know this is not your usual occupation. I can wait, I suppose, until such time as I can speak to your father without arousing suspicion. But you must realize how anxious I am for answers."

"Yes, I can see that. And I don't suppose it really matters who gives them," she said, sighing before she launched into a description of what she had seen and what happened afterward.

Duchaise heard her out in silence with his hands braced on the balustrade railing. When she had finished, he looked up at the dark clouds moving overhead while his chest rose and fell. His throat moved with a swallowing sound before he finally spoke. "I saw you dancing with Hunter. That must have been when you had your conversation with him."

She nodded. "I didn't know his name at the time, of course."

"Yes." Charles Duchaise passed a hand over his face. "You have been very quick at putting one to him. It's my turn to be grateful."

"I was lucky," she said uneasily. "Anyway, there may be nothing to it."

"I quite agree, but the situation is peculiar. Certainly it merits closer investigation. Extremely discreet investigation."

She could only nod.

He gave her a measuring look. "I feel I owe you an apology, regardless. It can't have been pleasant to be accused of—in short, I'm sorry if Sutherland mistook your involvement with this affair."

"It doesn't matter." To spare the older man's feelings she didn't look at him but turned to stare into the shadowed garden below.

"It matters to me," he said. "All the same, I will admit that I'm happy to hear you weren't too upset."

As she glanced at him, a car passed in the street that lay beyond them. The bright light of the head-lamps moved across his aristocratic features, revealing a set, determined expression. Warily, she said, "That's very kind."

"You may not think so when you've heard me out." He smiled with a slight twist to his mouth. "I don't quite know how to put what I am about to say—the last thing I want is for you to take it the wrong way. But I really would be most grateful, Miss O'Banyon, if…"

"What?" she asked as he came to a halt.

He searched her face in the flickering candlelight from inside. "Forget I mentioned it, if you please. I can see that it's quite impossible."

She tilted her head, intrigued in spite of herself. "What's impossible?"

"You aren't the kind of young woman one sends on the errand I had in mind. I'm appalled that I came so close to asking it of you."

"It sounds important," she said, her attention snagged by the despair underlying the words he spoke.

"It's a question of my life, since my wife means everything to me. That is my sole excuse. But it isn't your problem, even if you are perhaps the only person who might succeed."

"At what?" It wouldn't hurt to hear it, at least.

"No—really." He looked away, his face bleak.

"It's something to do with Hunter Sutherland, I expect, since we were discussing him." In a feeble attempt to relieve the tension, she added, "Did you want me to get rid of him, to take him out for you, as they say in the movies?''

"Don't tempt me," he said with a hollow sound that was part laugh, part groan. "No, I only thought you might—I don't know exactly how to say it. Play up to Hunter? Engage his interest, perhaps?"

"You, too?"

"I'm not sure what you mean. I was only trying to say that Hunter seems to be attracted to you, so it should not be difficult for you to, that is…"

"You want me to find out the details of his—his association with your wife," she said as he floundered to find the right word. "Dad was just suggesting the same thing a few minutes ago."

Charles Duchaise looked away as if unable to sustain her clear gaze. "Actually, I had in mind something a bit more personal. I don't mean," he added hastily, "that I want you to—to do anything you'd rather not. But surely you need not, that is, you wouldn't have to sleep with the man, or anything like that, in order to entice him away from my wife. You are a young and beautiful woman of greater than average intelligence. It shouldn't be that hard."

She was shocked, though she tried hard not to show it. She could not quite grasp this idea everyone seemed to have of herself as a femme fatale. "That's…all very flattering," she said slowly, "but if he cares for her, then I don't know…"

"I'm afraid he may be using her."

It had cost him something to say that, she thought. His pride and anger was in every line of his body, in every muscle of his lean, patrician face.

"Then I'm not sure what I can do," she said. "I mean, what difference will it make if I'm able to keep him with me an hour or two, when he may have an entirely different program where your wife is concerned?"

"You can give Millie cause to think about what she's doing, maybe make her see that it isn't her he cares about. My wife is a lovely woman, and I love her dearly. She still makes my heart beat faster after all these years. But surely she must realize that a man at least sixteen or seventeen years younger wants something from her that has nothing to do with the finer emotions."

"Maybe she knows it already and doesn't care," Adrienne suggested in low tones, since he was speaking so plainly.

A spasm of pain contorted his face as he swung around so the candlelight gleamed across his taut features. "She doesn't have to settle for that. Not when she has me."

Those quiet words touched Adrienne as no amount of reasoning or pleading ever could. Against her will, she found herself considering what he had said. It was a simple thing he was asking, when all was said and done. Wasn't it?

On a deep drawn breath, she said, "There's no guarantee that I can distract Hunter, but I suppose I could try. I'll be talking to him, anyway."

"You won't regret it," Charles Duchaise said, the strain in his features easing a fraction as he inhaled deeply and let it out again. "It would be crass beyond words to suggest that there is any way I can repay your generosity, but if there is anything I can do you have only to say so."

She shook her head. "You've already done it by giving B.B. a chance here tonight. I'm grateful, which is one of the reasons I would like to help."

"You can be sure I won't forget it." He touched her arm, then brushed his hand over her cool flesh in an aimless gesture of gratitude. "I do have a certain influence, if I may say so without sounding too pompous. It would give me pleasure to put it to use on your father's behalf."

It was the way things were done in New Orleans, the delicate exchange of favors. She said gravely, "I'm sure he would appreciate that."

"Good. Then we understand each other."

She thought they did, hoped they did. Yet as he took her arm and they turned to move back toward the ballroom, she wasn't entirely certain of it.

Four

"**D**id you see him take that girl out onto the terrace?" Millie wailed. "Did you? And in front of all our friends! It is too humiliating. I can't stand it. I can't!"

"Not so loud," Hunter cautioned, as he put a hand on the older woman's arm. "Calm down. They're just talking."

He moved to shield her from view of the other dancers. They stood near the French doors at one end of the ballroom. That the position offered him an excellent view through the glass of Charles Duchaise and his Violetta was no accident. Hunter was more than a little interested in what the two were doing out there.

"This isn't like Charles. He always swore to me he would never so much as look at another woman. And now just see how he flaunts this one in my face!" Tears rose in her eyes, threatening her artful makeup. She blotted them with the back of her forefinger. "I can't believe it. Why? What have I done?"

"You haven't done anything," Hunter said soothingly. "It's nothing against you. She's just a beautiful woman, and—"

"And young!" Millie moaned. "So young. Do you have any idea how that makes me feel?" She clasped her hands, holding them tightly together in front of the Empire waist of her gown, over which was draped a red cloak embroidered with gold Napoléonic bees.

"Don't think about it," he said, hurting for her. "You can talk it out with Charles later. More than likely, you'll find there's nothing to it."

"Nothing to it? I saw the bill for that fancy dress she has on with my own eyes! A man doesn't buy clothes for a woman unless there's something going on between them, not a man like Charles. He's crazy, mad in love with her. He has to be!"

Hunter could see the logic of that, especially when he looked at the woman on the terrace. "If it's any consolation," he said, "I don't think she's the type to be an older man's darling."

"Don't say that," Millie begged. "If she won't have him any other way, he'll want a divorce. He'll marry her and I'll be left all alone. What am I going to do, Hunter? What am I going to do?"

"Get hold of yourself, for one thing," he said, catching her hands, trying to calm her and make her feel better by sheer force of will. "Creating a public spectacle isn't going to help."

"Maybe not, but it would help me. I feel like crying and screaming, yes, and going out there and tearing the dress my husband—mine!—bought right off the back of that scheming little—"

"No!" Hunter said in rough tones, his scalp

prickling at the very thought, in spite of his concern. "You couldn't do such a thing."

She gave him a taut look and jutted out her chin. "You don't think so? Then you don't know me."

She was right, he didn't know her. But he was going to, in spite of everything; he needed that with every fiber of his being. The knowledge carried a certain responsibility, and because of that, he said, almost reluctantly, "I noticed Charles's lady friend having a heart-to-heart with your butler a few minutes ago. It looked a bit odd."

"That man is no butler of mine," Millie declared with a scornful laugh. "He's in charge of security, if you can believe such a thing. Charles hired him for tonight, though I've never heard of his company, and neither has anyone else that I can discover. Really, it goes with all the rest. Charles used to discuss such things with me, but not anymore." She shook her head, misery showing in her red-rimmed eyes.

Suspicion was a weight in Hunter's chest. "You think there's something fishy about the man?"

"It wouldn't surprise me at all. I've heard him using the most atrocious Irish accent, one he puts on when it pleases him. Wouldn't it just crown everything if we wake up in the morning and find out we've been royally ripped off? The way things are going, I wouldn't be at all surprised!"

"If this Violetta was part of it," he said, "the whole thing might make more sense."

Millie's eyes widened. "You mean you think she

could be leading him on just to—oh, no, poor Charles!''

"Poor Charles?" he said, thunderstruck by her about-face. "Idiot Charles, you mean."

"But just think how miserable he'll feel if he's really in love with her and she's only using him," Millie said, her fingers shaking as they tightened on his. "We can't let her do that to him!"

He shook his head, his lips compressed in a thin line. "There's not much anyone can do if a man is determined to make a fool of himself."

He might as well not have spoken for all the attention she gave him. "We have to get her away from Charles, some way, somehow. We could—could find out if she has a police record and have her arrested. Or maybe hire someone to kidnap her— Don't look at me like that!"

"Then don't talk like a crazy woman." The words were as blunt as he could make them.

"But I am crazy, absolutely insane with what's happening. Help me, Hunter. How can we get rid of this girl? Oh, if only some other man would come along, someone young, rich, t-taller. If only—Hunter!" Her gaze moved over his features and along his shoulders in quick, avid appraisal.

Alarm zinged through him. He wasn't sure exactly what she had in mind, but the light beginning to glow in her hazel eyes was enough to put him on his guard.

"Now, Millie," he began.

"You could do it, I know you could."

"What are you suggesting?" He was afraid he

knew, but intended to put off admitting it until the last possible moment.

"You're handsome, wealthy, everything a woman could wish. I know you've escorted some of the most gorgeous females around, though somehow you've managed to escape their clutches."

"I have no time for serious entanglement, just as I have no time for whatever you're cooking up in your head. I came here tonight because—"

"I know why you came, but don't you see this changes everything? How can I possibly go to Charles with what you want when he may already be thinking of ending our marriage. He'll divorce me and never look back!"

Hunter clasped her arms in a firm hold, trying to stem her rising hysteria. "Charles isn't going to do that, not if he's half the man you claim."

"You just don't know," she moaned. "He has these standards, high ones, so much higher than most."

"Oh, yes," Hunter said in grim sarcasm as he glanced briefly toward Charles Duchaise and the woman in white. "I can see that."

"You can't go by this lapse—really, you can't," Millie said, her eyes wild with pain as she turned her head to look also. "It's never happened before in all the years we've been married. Oh, if I can only get him away from that little hussy, this whole thing may turn out to be a blessing in disguise, since he won't be able to judge me quite so hard. But if speaking to him about you is only going to drive him into the arms of that—that girl, then I can't risk it. Don't you see?''

There was peculiar kind of logic in what she said, as much as he hated to admit it. ''So what am I suppose to do in the meantime?''

''Seduce her.''

''Millie!'' He felt the impact of the suggestion in the pit of his stomach, even as he searched her face in disbelief.

''I mean it,'' she insisted with a defensive stare and a quick nod of her golden head. ''Oh, you don't have to take her to bed or anything like that if you don't want to, but if you could just make her think you're interested, convince her she has a chance to be Mrs. Hunter Sutherland, I'm sure she'll fall into your arms.''

He would love to take the lady in white to bed. Or anywhere else he could find that was quiet and private. The effect of the mere suggestion on his lower body was an inevitable and uncomfortable indication of how much he would love it. Hunter clamped his mind down on the image in an effort to subdue his rampaging hormones.

Voice flat, he said, ''As flattered as I am by your faith in me, I have to tell you that your Charles is not the only one with standards.''

''You're too high-and-mighty to come on to her?'' Millie jerked free of his hold.

''I would feel too low if I succeeded,'' he said softly.

''If she's all she should be, if she cares anything at all for Charles, then you won't succeed. Have you thought of that? But if she is after him because of some scam, then distracting her is more important than your scruples.''

"To you, maybe.''

She searched his face a long moment before she looked away. Lips quivering, she said, ''You think it's terrible of me to even suggest it, don't you?''

"I think it's desperation talking, not you. You can't really expect me to consider stalking that woman out there.''

"Can't I? You don't think she deserves it?''

"It seems unlikely.'' The words were concise.

"You may be right, and yet—'' She stopped, her eyes holding his. Then horror dawned in her face. "Oh, Hunter,'' she whispered, ''I see what it is. You want to think the best of her. That means you're attracted to her, too.''

"Am I?''

"I can't stand it,'' Millie cried, pressing her hands to her face. ''Both of you. It's too much!''

"Don't,'' he said, catching her arms, giving her a small shake. ''Don't talk like that. Get hold of yourself.''

"Help me, Hunter, please,'' she said, her eyes haggard. Her words were quieter and her whole body trembling as she stepped nearer. ''It's such a small thing that I'm asking.''

Outside on the terrace, he saw Charles Duchaise take the arm of the woman who called herself Violetta. The older man chafed the pale, smooth skin in a brief gesture, as if in dismay at its coolness.

Turning together, the two moved back toward the ballroom.

Voice abrupt, Hunter said, "You're right. It can't hurt anything if she's innocent."

"Oh, Hunter, you won't regret it," Millie said with tears rising to drown the hazel irises of her eyes. "I promise you won't."

He hoped she was right. But he didn't want to bet on it.

The couple outside were coming closer, had almost reached the French doors farther down the room from where Hunter and Millie stood. Millie squeezed his hands, then moved away with jerky strides and a stiff smile to speak to a pair of guests dressed as Tristan and Isolde. She looked around vaguely as Charles and the Lady of the Camellias came through the door. It was a blatant attempt to appear uncaring, if not unnoticing. It seemed to work, for a grim look appeared on Charles's face as he glanced toward where his wife stood in apparent animated conversation. The older man murmured something to the woman beside him, then moved away.

Hunter walked forward, coming up behind Violetta in white under the cover of the noise and the music. For an instant he inhaled her mind-stopping scent, stood close enough to touch the tender curve of the back of her neck, sink his fingers into the springing fire of her hair. Instead, he caught a single curl, wrapping it around his finger, absorbing its warmth and tensile strength.

She was turning to face him; he could tell by the

feel of her hoop gliding across the top of his foot in a long, sensual caress. He released her hair, schooling his expression to one of rueful apology even as his senses went spinning out of control.

Seduce this woman? God, if he only could. To lay her down somewhere and strip away the layers of clothes, releasing her from their confinement, was a burning enticement in his mind. He could spend hours holding her close in naked captivity while he explored all the places where her soft skin carried the delicate gold freckles that dusted her face and the tops of her shoulders. To kiss them one by one was a goal he could spend years achieving.

He met her brandy-gold gaze, willing the heat from his voice, trying to sound sincere as he spoke. "If I offended you earlier, Violetta, I'm sorry. Will you dance with me again while we talk about it?"

Adrienne faced him with her heart pounding in her chest. The fact that she needed to charm him was so strong in her mind it seemed almost impossible that he couldn't tell. To have him come to her of his own accord made it seem he might.

At the same time, the fact that he had approached her, removing the awful need to make him notice her again so she could carry out her agreement with Duchaise, was a tremendous relief. Her smile was warmer than it might have been for that reason alone.

"I suppose," she said, "though I'm not sure what we have to discuss."

"I was way out of line," he said, gazing down at her from behind the screen of his lashes as he took her hand and led her out onto the floor. "What you do is no affair of mine."

"Now, that would certainly be true," she said, falsely demure. "If I were doing anything."

He smiled, and the fan-shaped crinkles around his eyes were fascinating to behold. "I think I need safer ground before I find myself in over my head again. If your normal line of work is not as a courtesan to French nobility, then what do you do?"

She told him in one or two succinct phrases. At the same time, she was painfully aware of the hard muscles of his arms beneath the velvet of his coat, and of the easy strength with which he guided her around the floor to the vibrant strains of a fast Cajun waltz. Something about him had changed since the last time he had held her. Whatever it was made the fine hair at the back of her neck rise in disturbance.

In the midst of a fast turn, her attention was diverted by a movement at the doorway. B.B. had paused there to give her a discreet thumbs-up. She frowned with a minute shake of her head.

"Something wrong?" Hunter glanced over his shoulder in the direction she had been looking.

Thankfully, B.B. had disappeared. "No, not at all," she said in quick answer.

He returned his regard to her flushed face, studying it. After a moment, he said, "So you're an archaeologist? I have a hard time with the idea of you grubbing in the dirt, or maybe sitting up nights marking pottery shards by lantern light and slapping at mosquitoes.''

"Why is that?" she demanded. "I not only enjoy it, I'm good at it.''

"I don't doubt that—you obviously have plenty of brain power. What I want to know is why some man hasn't taken you away from it all?''

"To do what? Keep house and have babies?''

He lifted a brow. "Something wrong with that?''

"Not if it's a couple's rational and joint decision. But you make it sound as if I should be doing it instead of working in the field.''

"I happen to think it's a higher calling. If that makes me a chauvinist, then so be it.''

"It's certainly a fine calling,'' she told him pointedly, "but only if it's for the right reason. Getting married and having babies because it's expected makes about as much sense as a man going hunting because it's the macho thing to do.''

Ignoring her somewhat heated analogy, he said, "And just what, in your opinion, would be the right reason?''

"Love, for a start. Then mutual commitment to having a family. A husband who respects the role of the mother in making a home, and who understands the importance of being a good father to whatever children might be produced. Someone who would realize that we both would have to give up something to make it happen as it should.''

"You seem to have given it a lot of thought.''

"I was engaged once,'' she said without quite looking at him.

"So what happened?" There was real interest in his voice.

"It didn't work out."

"Because he expected you to forget about going on digs and concentrate on being a housewife?"

She shook her head so that the curling auburn wisps around her face brushed her cheeks. "He thought the two of us made a perfect field team, with him as the great leader, of course. A permanent home and family weren't high on his agenda. If I insisted on having children, he expected me to leave them with a nanny while we spent months in the jungle."

"And that didn't sit well with you."

She gave him a straight look. "My mother died when I was three. My father buried himself in his work to forget it. I was brought up piecemeal by a series of housekeepers and more or less ran wild until I was in my teens. It wasn't anybody's fault, not really, but I didn't much care for it."

"Understandable," he commented, then drew her closer as he executed a quick, complicated step.

Adrienne followed the lead of the man who held her, but just barely. The feel of his hands on her sent a shiver along the surface of her skin. The close embrace, his concentrated attention and the hint of something very like sympathy in his eyes as she spoke of her childhood made her heart beat with shuddering strokes. At the same time, the knowledge that she needed to hold his interest gave her such a feeling of strain that she could feel a headache forming in the front of her skull. She searched her mind for something light and fascinating to say, something, anything, to keep the conversation going between them.

Drawing back to see his face a moment later, she said, "What about you?"

"What about me?" he said, the words unencouraging.

"Is there some reason you don't have a family?"

His expression remained closed. "My experience with home life hasn't exactly made me want to jump into it with both feet."

"Oh?" She didn't try to disguise her curiosity.

He stared at her a long moment, as if debating the wisdom of what he meant to say. A muscle hardened in his jaw before he answered. "I grew up in foster homes, seven or eight of them by the time I was nine. The only reason I was adopted was because I happened to look like somebody else."

Her face went blank with amazement; she could feel it. At the same time, she could hear in his voice the stifled echoes of old pain, old loneliness, old rejection. She searched the taut lines of his face as she said in confusion, "But you are—" She stopped, fighting the need to speak his name, which she was not supposed to know. Finally, she said, "Your adopted family seems to have been well-off. Surely they chose you because they wanted you."

"You think so? The woman who took me in picked me the same way you might choose a puppy from a litter. She was big on charities, spent a lot of time touring children's homes. When she saw me, she was floored by how much I looked like her brother as a boy and, not incidentally, her own son who had died in infancy.''

"But you had an adoptive father, I suppose," she said. "What about him?"

"He wasn't bad, but his health was poor and he was used to letting his wife do as she pleased. He was glad to have company, I think, but he died before I was twenty."

At least she had always had B.B. and his boundless, unabashed affection. To ease the moment, Adrienne said, "They must have given you so much."

"Everything, in fact—food, clothes, education, background, future, inheritance—the whole shooting match down to the last penny. Everything except love."

Her heart ached for the boy he had been, the one she could just glimpse behind his words. "Oh, but surely—"

"No," he said, his eyes dark and voice definite, "not for me. I was my foster mother's pet and her plaything and the answer to her prayer. She dressed me up and paraded me around with her, but she didn't love me, wouldn't let me love her. Somewhere in her mind I was never myself but her son who had come back to her. She loved the idea of me, but never who I really was, or what I was inside. As long as she kept me at a distance, she never had to see and accept the difference."

Was this why he was known as a mystery man, Adrienne wondered, why no one seemed to know much about him? Was it the reason he stood apart, watching people instead of joining them? And did it, just possibly, have some bearing on why he was involved with an older woman like Millie Duchaise, an older woman who might give him the love he had missed?

Adrienne could understand his pain, but there was an underlying hardness about it that disturbed her. In some confusion, she said, "Your attitude is rather—unforgiving, isn't it?"

"I'm not a very forgiving man," he said grimly, "not when it comes to love." His smile was wintery. "And especially not when there is any kind of pretense."

Five

"Walk with me?" Hunter said as the music ended and he was forced to release her. The room had become uncomfortably crowded in the last half hour as latecomers swelled the number. There was hardly room to move, much less dance. More than that, a few of the new arrivals had come from other parties where they had already been drinking. Their bottle-induced conviviality was perfectly normal for the Mardi Gras season, but nonetheless irritating.

The woman beside him took the arm he offered in acceptance of his suggestion. The two of them made their way from the ballroom and into the central hall. There was little relief to be found, however. The back portion of the long space had been taken over as a male refuge. A dozen men had gathered, relaxing in the collection of club chairs, or else holding up the walls with their shoulders while they nursed their drinks and talked in low mumbles about football and politics and business. Beyond them, through transomed, double French doors, lay the back gallery, which had apparently become the unofficial smoking room.

Hunter crossed the hall, heading toward a wide

arched opening that led off at a right angle from the main hallway. This was the hall where the great staircase—one of Sans Souci's glories—swirled upward in dizzying curves to the belvedere that crowned the roof.

The stair hall was deserted for the moment, though voices could be heard echoing down from upstairs where a couple of bedrooms and their connecting baths had been set aside as powder rooms. Someone also seemed to be in the open belvedere, probably inspecting its stained glass windows by Tiffany, which made the climb worthwhile. The voices had a hollow, disembodied ring as they vibrated against the glass and traveled downward.

To one side of the stairwell was a low rosewood settee covered in green velvet. Hunter seated his companion on it, with the half-formed intention of dropping down beside her for a few minutes. That was before he watched her maneuver her hoop and settle her wide skirts into place.

"I see now why the men in pictures of Victorian, life are always standing next to their women with their hands behind their backs," he said in mock disgust. "There was no place left for them to sit."

She gave him a quick grin as she swept aside a portion of her skirts. "It's not as hopeless as it looks."

"Never mind. I wouldn't want to wrinkle all your pristine perfection." He had discovered another advantage to standing over her that involved her rather daring neckline, one that he thought it best not to share. Her skin, he saw, was milk white and blue veined where the sun had never touched it.

"Hardly pristine anymore," she said.

No, he conceded with silent regret, not if she was having an affair with Charles Duchaise. He was startled in the next moment to find out how deeply the idea cut.

He wished he could see her face. He didn't like this business of masks; they got in the way, hid expressions, came between him and the truth. But, then, that was the idea behind them, wasn't it? He was wearing a mask of his own.

Seduce her, Millie had said. Just how in the hell was he supposed to go about it? His past relationships had been relatively open, involving women with a high degree of self-awareness and sophistication. It was assumed from the beginning that they could end up in bed with each other. The woman usually came straight out with what she wanted, or at least gave him some sign of what was on her mind.

Not this one. This time, he was on his own.

He was also in dangerous territory. He couldn't imagine why he had mentioned his adoption; it wasn't something he talked about as a rule. Yet he had looked into the intoxicating brandy-colored eyes of this particular woman and found himself spouting off like a loose-lipped drunk. It had seemed vitally important that she understand certain things about him, and the only way to make sure she did was to tell her.

What had happened to his carefully constructed

plans for this evening? How had everything gone so wrong? And just who did he think he was kidding with all his reluctance and scruples when it came to the woman who sat before him? He should be delighted Millie had asked him to seduce her, because it gave him an excuse. If she hadn't he might have had to find a reason for himself because there was no way he was going to let Charles Duchaise have her without a fight.

Now what? He would smile and he would talk and he would touch her when he could, whatever it took to draw her to him. Tonight, tomorrow or next week; it made no difference. He wasn't the most patient man in the world, but he was tenacious.

Adrienne, glancing up at the man who stood over her, took in the heat in his gaze and felt a shiver of mingled alarm and pleasure slide down her spine. It was so unexpected that she caught her breath. In the next instant, his lashes came down and she was left to wonder if she had imagined his intense interest.

She sat on the soft cushions of the settee with her back straight, her ankles crossed under her skirts, and her hands placed demurely in her lap. It wasn't that she intended to assume such a classic pose, but rather that she had no choice. The back of the settee bulged in a curve that made it impossible to sit comfortably. More than that, the plastic bones of her corset were as unyielding as a back brace, and the width of her skirts left her no place to rest her arms without dragging her bodice lower than it was already. It was a revelation concerning nineteenth-century female posture. It was also a darned nuisance.

How on earth was she supposed to entice Hunter Sutherland when she could barely move without stepping on her own hem or knocking into everything within a seven-foot radius? It was impossible. She felt as helpless as a bird in a cage.

Yet some of the greatest courtesans of all time had captured men of nobility, wit and wealth while wearing costumes very similar. How had it been done? What could they possibly have used? If her past reading was any guideline, it must have been their eyes, and possibly their hands. Yes, and above all, their minds.

She lowered her lashes, then tilted her head to glance up at the man above her. Her smile tentative, she said, "I think men in Victorian times must have been much shorter than you are. If I have to look up at you for long, I'll have a crick in my neck. Won't you sit down? Please?"

"Since you put it that way," he said on a low laugh as he moved to sweep the folds of her dress to one side and drop down beside her. "Better?"

"Much."

Her answer was steady and even, but it was a lie. She had not realized quite how close he would be on the antique settee. His knee was pressed against hers as he sat turned toward her. The mossy woodland scent of his aftershave drifted to her, along with the smells of champagne and warm male. They seemed to encompass her, drawing her toward him. Barely breathing, she played with a silk fold of her skirt, pleating it like a fan. After a moment, something B.B. had once said about how to talk to people came to her aid. Everyone's favorite subject, he always said, was themselves.

She smoothed her skirt, then folded her hands again. Keeping in mind that Hunter had refused earlier to talk about his work, she said, "What do you do when you're not donating time to charity? How do you entertain yourself?"

He mentioned a cabin cruiser he kept at a Lake Pontchartrain marina, and she drew him out to talk about fishing and shrimping on the lake and in the gulf, which opened from it. Once he let slip a brief mention of taking the boat out to escort a newly built offshore oil platform into place. She let it pass, concentrating instead on the sun-glazed planes and angles of his face, the dark arches of his brows and straight line of his nose. There was such strength in his features, such firm indication of character. They had a certain roughness at their edges, but tenderness was present, too, in the curves of his mouth and in the midnight depths of his eyes.

"But enough about me," he said after some minutes. Taking one of her hands, he played with the slender fingers. "What about you? You have calluses in your palms, especially here at your ring finger. Is that from a shovel?"

The callus he mentioned was a leftover from wearing an engagement ring all summer, one she had removed several months ago. She told him about it in a few brief sentences.

"A nice arrangement," he said, "the two of you sharing the same work. So what happened exactly, other than disagreeing about children?"

"I'm not sure," she answered, looking away as she removed her hand. "It turned out, more or less, that he wasn't the same man on the dig as he was off it—kind of a Jekyll and Hyde thing. He ordered me around during the day as if I hadn't a brain in my head, then at night was all lovey-dovey affection and expected me to be happy and accommodating."

"Typical, I imagine," he said, his gaze intent on her face. "But you didn't feel accommodating?"

"The opposite." She hadn't wanted to be touched at all, certainly hadn't wanted to share the same tent.

"And he didn't understand."

Her lips curled. "You could say that. He seemed to think the problem was my libido. I thought it was his ego. We agreed there was no room in the arrangement for two such opposites."

"But you stayed on the dig?"

She nodded. "The work was fascinating. We were discovering such amazing things." She went on to tell him about the Mayan burial chamber she had helped locate and enter. Somewhere in the middle of her account, she forgot that she was supposed to be trying to be alluring. That was, until he fell silent, watching her as he stroked her palms, trailing his touch along her fingers to the tips.

"You love it, don't you?" he said quietly.

"I suppose so." She kept her gaze lowered, unwilling to share the extent of her passion for it with him.

"It must be great to care that much about something."

She hadn't really thought about it in that light. "I suppose it's a little like marriage. You have to care a lot, otherwise the difficulties of adjustment would be too much."

He smiled at the comparison and asked for details. She supplied them, laughing about camping out for months on end in stifling heat and with biting, stinging insects, rough food and inadequate bathing facilities.

The time slipped away, becoming a half hour, an hour. Every time she turned the subject back to him, he waited a few minutes then reversed it again until it became a game between them, like a mental pas de deux. She found the exercise exhilarating, perhaps too much so. It made her careless.

They had been speaking of the Make a Wish program, which arranged special excursions for children with potentially terminal illnesses. She had been involved with a scuba diving expedition for the group the year before, one to which he had contributed. On impulse, she said, "Children's programs like this one are so worthwhile. It must make you feel good to be a part of them. But then, I can see where you're coming from, given your background."

"There is that." His gaze remained on her fingers, which still lay cradled in his hand, while a dark wash of color surfaced under his skin.

She had not meant to embarrass him. To smooth it over, she said, "Of course, I'm particularly grateful for your contributions to the university. I doubt there would have been a dig this year without them, in the Yucatán or anywhere else."

His grasp tightened while his dark eyes turned slowly to obsidian. "I don't think," he said, "that I mentioned that particular interest."

"I—you must have said something that gave me the idea," she answered, stumbling over the words.

"No." The contradiction was soft. "But if you are aware of it, then you must have some idea of who I am. How is that, when I've been able to learn so little about you?"

Panic, as vivid as it was unreasonable, rose inside her. It constricted her voice as she said quickly, "Oh, all right, I just put two and two together. There aren't many people who have a reason to visit an offshore rig as you described a while ago, and everybody knows about the Sutherland Foundation."

"I don't think so," he said with a slow shake of his head as his gaze bored into hers. "I think somebody told you. And I have a feeling it may, just possibly, have been Duchaise's butler."

She moistened her lips as thoughts skidded through her head at warp speed. If he had seen her with B.B., it couldn't hurt to admit talking to him. "O'Banyon?" she said with a quick smile. "People like him know everything, don't they? Putting names and faces together is a part of his job. And you're a prominent man, whether you like it or not."

"If I asked him about you, what do you think he would tell me?"

"Very little," she said with a private smile for the truth of that statement. "I have no claim to fame."

"How is it that you and this butler know each other?"

Just what was his interest? Could it be a test? Did he know that she was B.B.'s daughter and did he want to see if she would deny it? But no one was suppose to be aware of that except Charles Duchaise.

"Oh, New Orleans is like a small town," she said vaguely. "If you move in certain circles, you keep running into the same people."

"And do you? Move in certain circles, that is?"

"From time to time."

"Why is it, then," he said deliberately, "that we've never met?"

Why, indeed? She wished that they had, that they could have come together without masks or suspicions or false pretense between them. But it was too late for that.

"Who knows why?" she answered with as much artlessness as she could manage. "I guess it's one of the mysteries of life."

"One too many where you're concerned," he murmured, his gaze slumberous as he circled her palm over and over with his warm thumb. "I think I'm going to have to investigate them."

Her breath caught in her chest as she heard the trace of a threat in his voice. Her hand tingled to her elbow, while a melting sensation like caramel dissolving over a slow fire was taking place in the pit of her stomach. Her defenses, she was uneasily aware, were all too likely to do the same thing.

Disentangling herself, she rose to her feet. The words not quite even, she said, "We had better get back to the others, don't you think? They'll be wondering what became of us."

"They who?" he asked as he rose to his feet with lithe strength. "I thought you were here alone."

"Yes, but you aren't, not really, are you?" she said, turning to attack out of sheer self-protection. "Didn't I see you with Millie?"

"Well, she is my hostess." He stepped aside to allow her to move toward the arched opening that led back to the main hall.

"Have you known her long?" Adrienne asked, slanting him a quick look from the corners of her eyes. She had the feeling they were fencing now, rather than dancing around each other with words, and it was a match that could become lethal at any moment.

"Long enough." His words were clipped, his gaze trenchant.

"Yes, of course," she murmured. "All that charity work. And historical preservation, I think you said. I'd have thought it more likely that you'd have met Charles that way, since he's the one with the enthusiasm for old houses.''

"Is that how the two of you came together, out of a passion for old things? Say, yours for older men?'' His comment was slicing.

She turned her head sharply to stare at him. "I like old stones and bits of pottery, but I prefer men of my own generation.''

"Do you, now?'' he said, his gaze challenging. "What would it take to encourage you to look into my qualifications?''

He couldn't mean it. It was something to say to trip her up again, or else some way of getting to her for a reason she couldn't quite grasp.

"Don't be ridiculous,'' she snapped in abrupt irritation. "How can you have any interest in me when you've never seen my face?''

A low laugh left him. "Easy. Don't you know imagination is ninety-nine percent of fascination?''

He reached out and caught her wrist. She halted, turned toward him and was snared in the black shadows of his eyes behind his mask. She moistened her lips, a movement he followed with care. "But you aren't fascinated.''

"No?'' The single word was a caress.

A shiver snaked down her spine. Her skin glowed with heat. Her heart thudded against her chest with hard, suffocating beats that shivered the silk of her bodice and pounded with feather strokes in her ears.

Things were moving too fast. She didn't know quite how it had happened, had no idea what she had done to bring it about. All she knew was she couldn't handle it. She needed time to regroup and calm her jangled nerves before she went a single step farther.

At that moment, a man appeared at the end of the stair hall. He smiled and started toward them, his manner relaxed and his stride assured. It was Charles Duchaise.

"My dear Violetta, so this is where you got off to," he said when he was close enough to be heard. "You promised me a dance if I'm not mistaken, and I'll claim it now, before you forget again."

"Oh, I didn't forget," Adrienne said, playing up to his concocted tale with genuine gratitude as she took the arm he offered. "I would never do that."

Hunter didn't want to release his hold on her arm. The struggle it took to force himself to do it was an unpleasant surprise. Male instinct, that was all, he told himself, the age-old urge to isolate an attractive female and keep her for his own. Possessiveness carried to the max. It had nothing to do with anything more tender or longer lasting. How could it? He didn't know the woman behind that damned scrap of white silk.

No, he didn't know her, but he was beginning to feel as if he did. Her scent, the satin smoothness of her skin, the warmth of her body wove a quiet spell. He had begun to watch for the way her lips twitched when she was trying not to smile. For the sudden deep breath she drew and held when she was disturbed. The way she tilted her head with its soft, heavy weight of hair as she puzzled over something he had said. The rich color of her eyes. That incredibly seductive white cleft between the gentle globes of her breasts.

Yes, the last. God, the last.

She was beginning to get to him, and he didn't like it. He didn't like it at all. It was supposed to be the other way around.

Wasn't it?

Six

"I apologize if my timing was inconvenient," Charles Duchaise said in quiet, conspiratorial tones as they entered the ballroom. "Your father sent me to find you. It seems he saw you with Sutherland and his policeman's instincts—or perhaps his fatherly instincts—warned him you might need rescuing. Naturally, he couldn't come and demand to know what was going on."

"It should have been obvious," she said, her mind still on Hunter and the way they had left him standing in the hall. The look on his face as she walked away, its odd mixture of condemnation and loss, bothered her. She almost felt she had abandoned him.

"It certainly is to me, at any rate," Duchaise answered, "and I'm more grateful than I can say. I'd hardly dared hope Sutherland would turn around and chase after you so easily."

She gave the silver-haired man in his Napoléon costume a startled look, not at all sure she liked the idea of herself as Hunter's new quarry. "I suppose B.B. doesn't like it?"

The older man's smile was singularly attractive.

"His view is more personal, of course. I think he wants to discuss it with you."

"He would," she said with resignation. "Where is he?"

"In the pantry. You can join him there, but after we've had our dance, if you don't mind. Mustn't allow Sutherland to suspect anything."

"I hate to tell you, but he already does."

"You mean he realizes that you are related?"

"No, not that," she said quickly. "Rather, he seems to have the idea that B.B. and I have something going on."

The dark eyes of her host widened. "But why on earth would he think that?"

"I can't imagine." Her smile was wry. "Maybe he'll switch his attention back to you, now that you've rescued me from his clutches."

"Ridiculous!" Duchaise snorted. "At my age, too. He must think I'm a fool."

She shook her head. "No, only that I'm a gold digger, or worse, if I read things correctly."

"I've a good mind to punch him in the nose!"

The idea of Charles Duchaise, courteous, erudite and a good eight inches shorter, squaring off against Hunter should have been funny. It wasn't. Hastily, Adrienne said, "I'm not sure that's such a good idea."

"Oh, it's a fine idea," he corrected her in grim tones, "just not very practical. Though I would dearly love to try."

They had reached the ballroom. Duchaise led her into the sea of color and glitter on the dance floor,

making a small space for the two of them among
the crowd. It was impossible to do more than shuf-
fle a few steps this way and that, but it didn't matter
since the music was a fast rock piece and everyone
was doing their own thing. Watching them jump
and gyrate to the beat while dressed in the costumes of other eras was comical. It was also a bit
saddening in its lack of dignity.

The older man was quiet, probably because the
clash of drums and keyboard effects was too loud
for anything else, but also as though his mind was
occupied with his problems. Once Adrienne saw
him glance around to locate his wife, where she
was dancing with a tall and lanky Harlequin. He
watched her for a long moment before he sighed
and looked away.

As the hard rock moved into the slower pace of
a country two-step, Duchaise escorted her toward
the back of the ballroom and the music room that
opened from it. If she slipped through there, he
said, past the band, she could make her way out
onto the back gallery, then enter the house again
through the kitchen on her way to the butler's pantry. That should throw Hunter off the scent long
enough for her to talk to her father.

It seemed a workable arrangement. Adrienne
thanked him, and he gave her a small bow that
would not have been out of place when Sans Souci
was built. In honor of it, she dropped a curtsey.
Then, feeling more than a little cloak-and-dag-
gerish, she went in search of her father.

B.B. flung her a quick glance as she appeared in

the pantry doorway, then turned at once toward the
two waiters who were helping mix drinks at the
long cabinet set against one wall. ''Go peddle
champagne or something for a minute, will you,
guys? I need to talk to my daughter.''

It was a credit to B.B.'s personality, as well as
to his unconscious air of command, that the two
men did as he said. Adrienne moved farther into
the room and waited for her father to start. He
didn't seem in any particular hurry as he busied
himself at the cabinet, sweeping ice from the coun-
tertop into the sink, then wiping up the water. The
tips of his ears were red, she saw, a sure indication
that he was either embarrassed or in a rage. She
strongly suspected it just might be the first.

Taking pity on him, she said finally, ''So spit it
out. What did you want to say?''

He swung on her as he burst out, ''What's going
on with you and Sutherland? He's ignoring Duchaise's wife and following you around like a rut-
ting buck after a doe.''

She reached up and pulled off her mask as she
tried to control her irritation. Voice tight, she said,
''That's a terrible way to put it!''

''Accurate, you mean. Well?''

''Isn't it what you wanted?''

''Not by a long shot!'' he growled. ''What made
you think it might be?''

''But you said—'' She stopped. Moving toward
the nearest cabinet, she turned to lean her back
against it. With her gaze on the flattened bell of

her skirt, she muttered, "No, I guess that wasn't you, was it?"

Voice a low growl, he said, "What wasn't me?"

Her father had only wanted her to talk to Hunter, ask him a few questions about his association with Millie. It had been Duchaise's idea that she distract him. She dangled her mask from her fingers, watching the light dance on its silk and beading as she explained in a few careful phrases.

B.B. stared at her with his mouth set in a grim line before he demanded, "And you agreed to this scheme?"

"It wasn't exactly a scheme, only a suggestion." She looked at him, then away again. "Besides, Charles Duchaise had helped you by giving you this job, and he was desperate. He looked like he might even...cry."

"I don't care if he was bawling in his beer! Nothing is worth you getting into something you might not be able to get out of."

"I was supposed to talk to Hunter for you, anyway. Besides, I really didn't expect it to work."

"You're young and you look blooming fantastic tonight," her father said in tones of disgust. "Why the devil not?"

She shrugged, as disturbed by the tribute as she was by his censure. "It's only a little flirtation."

"You'll get in too deep if you aren't careful." The warning was grim.

"I realize that, and I'm being careful, believe me."

B.B. stared at her from under his bushy white

brows, then pushed his splayed fingers through his hair so it stood on end. "I don't know, *acushla*. I keep thinking about how you took chances as a kid. You were always sneaking away from your sitter while I was working, roaming the streets, riding your bike down to the docks. You knew no fear, never had a decent sense of self-protection. And you haven't changed much now you're grown, either. Just look at the way you keep going off to that South American jungle and living with snakes and other lowlife like that professor."

"Mexican jungle," she corrected him without troubling with the rest.

"Whatever. The point is you don't have a proper sense of self-preservation—something I should have remembered before I brought you along on this thing. I think maybe you should stay away from Sutherland."

"Isn't it a little late for that?" She spun her mask around her finger without looking at him.

He reached out to stop her, his gaze steely. "Meaning?"

"That I'm in it now and see no way out short of cutting and running like Cinderella."

"Good idea," he said with a short laugh. "Do it."

"I was joking!"

"I'm not. As I said before, triangles like this one between Sutherland and Duchaise and his wife can get messy, real messy. Especially when somebody makes a quadrangle out it."

She flung off his hold with an impatient gesture.

"Don't be so melodramatic. It isn't going to come to that."

He stared at her a long moment before he said, "You're enjoying the whole thing, aren't you?"

"In a way. Maybe," she admitted in low caution. Having the interest of Hunter Sutherland was exciting, she had to admit. So was helping her father, being a part of his job for a change, after years of being kept out of it.

"You had better watch yourself, then, dear heart. This guy you're fooling with came up in a hard school. I've been checking some more, and it seems he was shipped around from pillar to post as a kid, hung out on the streets before he knew how to read. He may have a layer of Sutherland refinement, but it's only skin-deep. He plays for keeps and takes all the marbles home. You could wind up hurt."

Adrienne felt her heart shift with love as she heard the underlying concern in every syllable her father spoke. Her smile was a little tremulous as she reached out to give him a swift hug. "Don't worry," she said with a reassuring smile. "I'm a big girl, I can take care of myself."

"I know you're a big girl," he growled, his face red. "That's what bothers me."

She didn't ask what he meant. She wasn't too sure she wanted to know.

Hunter watched Adrienne from the terrace where he sat with one thigh propped on the balustrade, letting the rising, moisture-laden wind ruffle through his hair and slap the ends of his loose cravat against his jawbone. She came from the rear of the house, strolling from out of the deeper darkness. In her white dress, she looked as if she were floating over the ground, drifting toward him like a lovely ghost. Or else like a flower as fragile and easily crushed as any of the fallen camellia blossoms that littered the ground under the tall shrubs along the garden path.

The skin on the back of his neck prickled and goose bumps ran down the lengths of his arms. For a single instant, he clasped his knit fingers together so tightly that the muscles of his arms and shoulders stood out in solid ridges. Then with a single, swift movement, he pushed erect. Swinging toward the wide steps, he went to meet her.

She looked up. He could tell the instant she recognized him, for she fumbled with her mask she carried, slipping it on as if it might provide some kind of protection. She also stopped where she was in the darkness beyond the reach of the light falling through the French doors of the ballroom.

"I wondered where you got off to," he said, his voice even as he moved closer, "especially since I saw Duchaise inside."

"I just...felt like a little fresh air."

Her voice was low and not quite steady, exactly what might be expected if she were lying. And she was, as he knew very well. He had seen her slip off to the pantry to talk to the butler. She must have left the house afterward by way of the kitchen, then circled around to this side garden. Certainly, she had not come from the ballroom because he had been on watch on the terrace for what seemed like hours.

Anger flowed in his veins like acid. It had begun when Duchaise had come to take her away. The sight of the older man's hand on the pale skin of her arm had twisted his gut. The thought of the two of them together was a slow-burning fire in his mind. Seeing the relief on her face as she walked away from him had made his chest feel as if it were in a vise. There had been nothing to do except follow the two of them.

He had been able to handle it as long as they were really dancing. Then he had seen this woman he knew only as Violetta slip away to join the butler.

He hated scams and swindles. The only way to stop them was to put whoever was behind them out of business, no excuses, no exceptions. This Lady of the Camellias was playing both ends against the middle, involved with Duchaise yet also up to her pretty neck in some deep game with the butler behind Duchaise's back.

God, she was beautiful, though, a perfect jewel glowing against the black velvet of the night. The darkness had deepened with the gathering cloud cover, intensifying the light of the street lamps. Their glow through the trees cast shadows that danced like loving wraiths across the white of her skirts. The moistness of rain hovered in the air, a fine mist that touched them now and then with a minuscule drop of coolness.

He couldn't permit her to win, yet he didn't want to scare her away, not now. He had an idea of how to take her out of this game for good. It would involve some hard and smart negotiating, he thought, but that was his specialty. Anyway, what did he have to lose?

"So have you had enough? Air, that is," he added quickly, trying for easy familiarity as he reached for her hand and tucked it into the bend of his arm.

"I suppose." She glanced up at him with inquiry in the angle of her head, though she moved beside him readily enough as he swung back toward the terrace.

"Seeing you just now was a surprise. I'd about decided you had gone home."

"No. Why?"

"You vanished," he said with the lift of a shoulder. "Anyway, the Sans Souci ball is elegant and all that, but it's not exactly the most scintillating affair of the season. The younger crowd considers it boring." He was talking almost at random, distracted by the warmth and scent of her so close to him, and the damnable way her silk-covered hoop nudged him as she walked at his side.

"Actually, I thought it was getting fairly racy. I saw a few odd goings-on back there." She nodded toward the dark garden behind the house.

"It happens," he said, then added as he cast a glance at the lowering sky, "though they had better bring it back inside if they don't want to get wet."

She inclined her head in close accord. "I suppose it's a wonder there aren't more incidents, all things considered. Masks tend to give people ideas, which is probably the reason this is one of the only real costume balls held any more.''

He agreed. There were many Mardi Gras parties during the season, but the real balls were staid affairs held by the Mardi Gras krewes, and mainly black-tie only, with the exception of the royal court. ''Did you know,'' he added solemnly, ''that more men actually own tuxedos here than in any other city in the United States?''

She gave a low laugh. ''Who says so?''

''The companies who sell them. It isn't called a party town for nothing.''

''The Big Easy? We do like our titles, don't we,'' she said readily, ''even when Hollywood bestows them on us.''

''It's an attitude. Pleasure before all else. Laugh and be merry, because tomorrow—well, tomorrow may never come. There is a point to it.'' He stopped, swung to face her. ''And because there is, I have this nearly uncontrollable urge.''

''To do what?'' She came to a halt, poised on her toes as if for flight.

''This,'' he said, his voice turning suddenly husky. He reached for her, closing his hands around her slender waist. As his fingertips came close to meeting over her backbone, he made a low sound in his throat. She was so fragile, so tender, yet such a pulse-pounding siren. He didn't know whether he wanted to hold her safe like a piece of fine crystal or carry her off into the dark and lay her down in the circle of her wide skirts.

Her lips were soft, so soft, as he bent his head and touched them with his own. The edges were sweet, the corners moist and beguiling. For a single instant, she stood perfectly still, then she sighed and leaned into him, against him.

He took that surrender, pulling her closer while hot, rampant need shuddered through him. God, but he was on fire. He had never felt anything like it, as if he were flammable tinder and she was the spark that could send them both up in smoke.

He needed more of her, had to have it. As her lips parted under his onslaught, he delved deep, abrading the nubbed smoothness of her tongue with his own, twining around it, inciting her to do the same. The full breath of gratification he drew took her scent and heat into his lungs, filled his heart and mind with it so it sent his senses reeling.

She was magic and mystery and sweet, sweet longing. And he wanted to hold every inch of her, to kiss every square centimeter of her flesh while she writhed under him, begging to be taken. And he would fill her, sheath himself in her hot, pulsing flesh and make her his before he drove them both mad. Before he sent them both careering over the edge.

Madness. Yes.

He lifted his head, striving for control. He had never in his life been so close to losing it, and all for nothing more than a kiss. What would it be like to actually have her naked and pliant under him? He couldn't wait to find out.

He held her close against him, rocking her slowly as he whispered, "I have an idea, Lady of the Camellias. Why don't we go somewhere and take off our masks?"

A shiver shook her, for he felt it. Slowly, she drew back, as if trying to see his face. "What? What did you say?"

"I'm suggesting that you forget Duchaise and come with me. Right now. I can give you more than he ever could, and I will. You won't regret it, and you can take that as a promise."

"Go with you? You want me to..."

"I want you any way I can have you, for as long as you will allow it. But I warn you, I don't share."

She drew back, pushing against his chest with firm hands and more strength than he would have imagined. Her voice tight, she said, "Neither do I."

"Fine. Then, what are we waiting for? My car is parked just over there. We can—"

"No!" She pulled away from him, stepped back as if he were contaminated. The lower part of her face was taut and as pale as the silk mask that covered her cheekbones and the bridge of her nose.

He stepped toward her with his hand outstretched. "I don't understand."

"Then let me make it clear," she said in breathless contempt. "I am not going to be taken anywhere. Not now, not ever. I don't need any promises from you."

He couldn't think for the blood that still throbbed in the lower part of his body, pulsing with the hard pound of his heart. Or maybe it was just that he didn't want to think because it might mean he would comprehend too well. He let his hand fall to his side as he said, "Why?"

Her laugh was choked as she backed away, then turned in a swirl of skirts. "Because I'm not what you seem to believe. But you turned out to be exactly what I figured!"

"Wait!" he said, taking a swift step after her.

She didn't answer, but broke into a run for the terrace. She skimmed up the steps, her white skirts sailing around her like the plumed wings of an egret in flight. An instant later, she was through the door. Then it slammed shut.

Seven

The ballroom was crowded and stiflingly hot after the outside coolness. Adrienne did not pause, but made her way through it and into the hall. Even then, she kept going, gliding into the stair hall and up the winding staircase with the hem of her skirts trailing behind her on the Oriental runner that centered the mahogany treads. Refuge, a place to catch her breath and sort out the chaos of her thoughts; that was what she needed.

She had a vague idea of slipping into the upstairs powder room, but two women were standing outside the door, and more voices could be heard from inside. Adrienne barely paused at the second-floor landing before continuing upward toward the dim isolation of the belvedere.

It was empty and cool at the top of the house. It was also relatively quiet, in spite of the rumble of the party below, which funneled up the curving staircase as if it were coming from a giant speaking trumpet. The belvedere was foursquare, the size of a small room, with the stair opening in the middle fenced off by the final circle of the railing. Dim gleams from the mercury street lights and security lamps filtered through the stained glass windows, falling across the floor in muted shades of turquoise and purple, pink and green, yellow and blue. Against that discreet glow, the patterns of wisteria and willow and lotus with water, earth and sky formed in the glass could be seen primarily in silhouette, though in sunlight they were probably glorious.

Banquettes were built under the windows, wide and soft seats scattered with thick brocade cushions in jewel colors. Adrienne sank down gratefully on the one nearest the stairs. Clasping her arms around her in sudden internal chill, she leaned back and closed her eyes.

She was so confused. She had been trying to entice Hunter, yes, but somewhere in her mind it had seemed so unlikely he would respond that she had treated it as a game. Even B.B.'s warning hadn't made much of an impression, not really. Oh, she had understood the danger on an intellectual level, but not on the emotional one, where it counted. That had been stupid.

Now she had refused Hunter's kiss and his offer of more, running away like a scared rabbit. That meant it was over. All over.

She hated it.

She hated it because Hunter had made her feel things she had never felt before, startling, wonderful, unbelievable things. She hated it because he had, for long moments, caused her to forget her loyalty to her father and her agreement with Charles Duchaise, to forget why she was trying to get close to him. She hated it because he had made her want to fling everything to the four winds and go with him, be whatever he wanted, for however long he wanted.

Dear God, but she was still shaking with the violence of the need he had aroused in her. How had he done that with a single kiss? How?

Yet it wasn't just the kiss so much as all that had gone before, she thought. The smiles, the warmth of his touch, the interest in his dark eyes and the way he listened when she spoke.

Yes, and it was the way he looked, the angles and surfaces of his face beneath his mask, the thick waves of his hair, the intensity of his gaze. Oh, and the shape and strength of his hands, the width of his shoulders and the hard feel of his body under his clothes. These were impressions that nothing could ever erase.

Then there was the mystery. What woman could resist that?

She was half in love with the man, and she had hardly seen his face except in the dimmest light. It was incredible. It was wild. It was crazy.

Still, it was also wrong to say she knew nothing about him. She did know; she had been told by both Duchaise and her father. She had been told repeatedly, and she hadn't listened.

Pain rose inside her without warning. It began near her heart and flooded her chest, aching as it spread. It hurt in her throat like an embedded thorn, burned in the back of her nose, swelled behind her eyes. She clenched her teeth against it, fighting back the tears. It hurt, oh, it hurt, a deep and intolerable ache that had a bitter rind of betrayal.

He wanted her in his bed, though not in his life. He thought she was easy, a woman to take for a night or a month or even a year, but not forever. Never forever.

It was her own fault. What else was he to think, considering the way she was dressed and what he knew of her, the little she had allowed him to know? Yes, and there was the way she had behaved. If a woman acted free and easy, she had no right to be distressed at being seen the same way.

But she was, oh, she was.

She also resented it. Beneath her pain was simmering anger. Anger at Hunter, yes, but also at B.B. and Charles and Millie Duchaise, and at herself. Most of all, herself. She had walked so blithely and blindly into this, lured by problems not her own. Now there was no way out without being hurt, because there was no way out without loss.

The low, rough note of a masculine voice drifted up to her from below. She stiffened, then sat up. It was Hunter. His voice was a permanent part of her memory now, a sound that would echo in her dreams as it was echoing up the stairwell. For an instant, she thought that he was coming after her. Then she heard the clear, carrying tones of Millie Duchaise.

Adrienne rose to her feet and stepped to the railing. She leaned over to glance down, gripping the banister with quick strength as she saw the deep, dizzying spiral of the stairwell. At the bottom, she could glimpse a portion of the long red cloak with its gold embroidery that Millie wore as Josephine, and also the glint of her lightened hair. She was standing near the foot of the stairs, not far from the settee where Adrienne and Hunter had talked earlier. Hunter had one hand on the newel post and a foot on the bottom tread, as if the older woman had caught him just heading up. Their voices, one sharp and feminine, the other a masculine rumble, were amplified by the staircase.

"I asked you where you are going." Millie was saying in strident insistence. "This is my house, after all."

"Upstairs, if you must know, though I'd say it's pretty obvious." Hunter's reply was impatient, barely polite.

"Nothing is obvious with you," the older woman exclaimed. "Is she upstairs, Charles's lady in white? Or perhaps I should say yours now?"

Adrienne straightened as she heard herself mentioned, then stood perfectly still with her hands clasped at her waist as she listened. It was crass to eavesdrop; even the idea of it made her feel uncomfortable. Yet she was incapable of moving away out of hearing distance.

"What if she is?" Hunter's words were clipped short.

"First Charles, and now you," Millie cried. "What is it about her?"

"I couldn't begin to tell you."

"Or you won't" came the instant reply. "I had

no idea that you, of all people, would be so susceptible.''

"Neither did I.''

Adrienne had to strain to hear that last low-voiced comment. She still could not be sure of it, for it made little sense. Did it signal a change in the relationship between the other two? Had she really supplanted Millie as Hunter's female interest of the moment? At least Charles should be happy.

"When you find her,'' Millie said, her voice hopeful, ''will you take her away? Tonight?''

That didn't sound at all like the suggestion of a woman spurned, Adrienne thought. Then such speculation vanished from her mind as Hunter's voice came again.

"Not without confronting Charles.''

Millie laughed, a brittle noise. "That's not likely to happen. I mean, how can you and I face him? What you are planning will make it completely impossible.''

"Then you will have to talk to him, tell him yourself. It's what you should have done as soon as it came up.''

"Don't you see that this changes everything?'' the older woman said in shrill demand. "How can you expect him to be reasonable? He's kind and understanding, but he's no saint!''

"Neither,'' Hunter said softly, "am I. Something you might remember.''

"What on earth do you mean?''

"I've had enough. It isn't going to get any better by waiting. It's been too long already.''

"Oh, Hunter," Millie said, her voice cracking. "When did you get to be so hard?"

"You know when, and how, though that has nothing to do with here and now. I want this over, so I can start a new phase of my life. If you won't do what it takes, or can't, then I will."

"Don't threaten me, Hunter," Millie warned. "I won't stand for it."

His voice was edged with steel as he said, "You won't have to if you don't keep me waiting."

There was a small silence broken only by the sound of Millie's strangled breathing. Finally she said, "But if you are leaving..."

"We can reschedule the meeting for one day next week, but that's it. If you don't come through, then you'll be out of time. I'll take matters into my own hands."

Quiet fell again. Adrienne stood staring at the stained glass window in front of her as she tried to make sense of what she had heard. The colors of the glass had turned watery and blurred, caused by the rain that had finally begun to fall as it often did in New Orleans in winter. No lightning, no thunder, just the heavy increase of moisture until it turned to globular drops that fell endlessly from a leaden sky. Now the rain hitting the glass washed down it in long, wet streaks like the tears of silent grief.

The exchange below had not sounded at all like a disagreement between lovers. It seemed, rather, that Hunter had the upper hand in some peculiar arrangement between himself and the older woman. Millie had something he wanted, or rather could get for him from her husband. For some reason not made plain, she was reluctant to ask. Hunter, with the relentless pressure of his personality, was forcing her to do it, anyway. At the same time, he was delivering the threat of more drastic measures if necessary.

It seemed Duchaise was right, after all. Hunter was using Millie. A shudder rippled down Adrienne's spine. What in God's name had B.B. gotten her into? And how was she going to get out of it?

Down below, Millie spoke again, a brief comment that Adrienne did not catch in her concentration. Immediately afterward, there came the click of high heels retreating along the marble floor of the stair hall. A distant voice called out some sally, perhaps as Millie made her way back toward the ballroom. Then all was quiet.

A frisson of unreasonable fear, like a presentiment of danger, moved over Adrienne. She swung away from the stairwell so quickly that her skirts made a soft, fluttering noise as they swept along the banisters of the railing. Walking to the banquette, she put her knee on its thick cushion and leaned close to the glass to stare out.

Thrashing treetops, rain-slick roofs and wet streets were all that she could see. The glass held the night coolness, however, and she pressed her hot forehead against it. It made the ache behind her eyes feel a little better. Still, as she lowered her lashes and squeezed them shut, salty wetness seeped out to catch in their thick tangle.

"So I was right," Hunter said from the stairwell

behind her. "I thought I saw a scrap of white silk shining over the edge up here. I should have known you would be wherever it was dark, safe and far away from everyone. Including me."

She pressed her eyelids tight again, then opened them. Lifting her head, she turned with slow deliberation. "Congratulations," she said, keeping her voice even with supreme effort. "You were absolutely right."

"I would rather have been wrong. I'd much rather you hadn't run away."

"There was no reason to stay."

"No? I thought there was."

He was mounting the last steps of the stairs, coming closer with every word he spoke. His face in the uncertain light appeared grim, implacable. She lifted her chin. "You could have saved yourself the trouble of coming after me. I'm going nowhere with you."

"Then I'll stay here."

"Fine. You can have it to yourself," she said through tight lips. Gathering her skirts, she made as if to brush past him.

He reached out, a casual, almost negligent gesture, but his fingers closed fast and firm around her wrist. She was dragged to a halt. A slight tug, and she stumbled, dropping her skirts as she came up against him.

"What are you doing?" she demanded, and was embarrassed to hear the breathlessness of her voice.

"Making sure you don't run away again." He gazed down at her, his face calm.

He was not hurting her, yet she could not stand to be held against her will. With a swift, upward jerk, she broke his grasp, then stepped back. He did not stalk her as she half expected, but only took a swift step to one side, a movement that blocked her access to the stairs.

"You will leave here when I permit it," he said. "Or you can leave through me."

She wanted to defy him, to pick up something, anything, and lash out at him until she fought her way free. She had no weapon, however, even if she had the strength to use it against him. All she had to protect herself were her wits and willpower, and she was far from sure they were equal to the job.

"Let me by," she said, narrowing her eyes, "or I'll scream the house down."

"Will you? I'd have said you weren't the screaming type, but go ahead if you think it will help."

"It'll bring B.B. running."

"Who is—? Oh, let me guess. The butler."

It was on the tip of her tongue to answer with the truth, but she bit back the impulse. It might be best not to use all her weapons at one time. "As it happens, yes."

"Let him come, if you don't care if he gets hurt."

Her heart beat into her throat, choking her as she said, "Why would you want to do that?"

"I don't," he said with a quick negative gesture. "But I will if he interferes before I get some answers."

"What makes you think you have any right to ask questions?"

He was quiet a moment, then his lips firmed. "Your smiles, a shared dance, the way you look at me. A kiss in the dark. Can you honestly tell me," he added roughly, "that none of it meant anything, or that it doesn't count now?"

She whirled from him, clenching her hands at her waist as she walked away, circling the enclosing railing. He prowled after her, far enough away not to be a threat yet close enough to prevent any sudden dash for the stairs.

"So what do I need to tell you?" she asked in scathing self-defense. "Where is the big mystery in a woman who refuses you?"

"Who are you?"

To give him her name might well reveal that she was related to B.B. "What does that have to do with anything?"

"Don't answer a question with a question—it isn't polite. Or informative. Of course, if you want to stay up here all night…" He paused suggestively.

"Hardly," she flung at him over her shoulder.

"Too bad. I can't think of anything I'd like more. In fact, I can think of little else, period."

"Am I supposed to be flattered?"

A low laugh sounded in his throat. "No, but you might be sympathetic."

"I can't imagine why you think so."

"Because you're pacing as if you feel the same way."

She stopped abruptly, then turned to face him. It was a serious error, for it allowed her to see the look that burned in his eyes.

"I'm not," she said, the denial hoarse as she squeezed it through the tightness in her throat. "I don't."

"Liar." The word held strained certainty.

They watched each other there in the watery dusk with the rain-washed shades of blue and purple lying across their faces. The silence that stretched between them sang with repressed hope and virulent desire.

Then from the second-floor landing below came the mellow, musical chiming of a grandfather clock. It rang out six or seven times before it was joined by ragged, chanting voices.

They were counting down the seconds to the hour as if it were New Year's Eve, though it wasn't, not at all. *Eight. Seven. Six. Five.*

Hunter smiled, a slow, sensual movement of his lips below his mask.

Four. Three. Two!

Adrienne's pulse throbbed in her ears, almost deafening her. She caught her breath on a silent gasp.

One!

Twelve o'clock!

The last was a shout, one that rang full-throated and hectic with gaiety as it spiraled up the stairs.

"Midnight," he said, the word shadowed with rich satisfaction.

Midnight.

Hunter lifted his hand toward the black velvet that covered his face. "Time," he said, "for the unmasking."

Rogue of the Night Jennifer Blake

Hunter licked his mind against the house before, *it* as a defini...te of the distance. "Hugh ... to...co...the instance.

Eight

For an endless, suspended instant, Hunter thought she was not going to remove her disguise. Then she reached up in a quick, defiant gesture and stripped the white silk away.

The sight of her face was like a hard, stunning punch to the heart. She was lovely, yes, but there was more to it than that. Clarity was there, and frankness, also pride and accusation and a kind of angry innocence that touched his soul. This was not the kind of female a man took for a night or a week, or even for a year. She was a forever woman.

He had miscalculated—seriously—based on faulty evidence. He had suspected it in the garden, which was why he'd followed so close behind her. Now he was sure of it.

Fear poured over him like a cold shower. He could feel his features set with it, feel it stiffen his neck and shoulders. He was afraid he had gone too far, afraid there was no way to correct what he had done.

"I'm sorry," he said, the words ragged at the edges as they were torn from him.

She met his gaze for a long, tremulous second. There was a splash of gold across her face from the street lamp's gleam through the stained glass. It gilded her cheekbones, the bridge of her nose, the delicate ridges of her collarbones. In it, her eyes looked like those of some ancient marble statue: austere, unseeing, pitiless.

For a long moment, they stared at each other. Then he saw the moment when she recognized she now held the advantage. She blinked as if awakening, then lowered her lashes and stepped forward. Brushing past him in a sweep of full skirts, she glided toward the stairs. She was almost running by the time she reached them.

She was running away from him. Again. That abrupt knowledge released his paralysis.

"Wait!"

She did not pause or look back. Her skirts belled around her feet as she skimmed down the staircase. He leaped after her, driving downward two and three steps at the time. She glanced over her shoulder, her eyes wild with alarm and resentment. Then she reached the bottom tread at the second-floor landing. Snatching up her skirts, she darted out of the stairwell and fled down the hall toward the bedroom set off as the ladies' powder room.

The hallway was empty. Hunter registered that salient fact with fierce satisfaction. Apparently everyone had hurried downstairs to catch the grand unmasking ceremony.

He leaped down the last steps, sprinted forward. She must have heard him coming, because she plunged for the powder room's half-open door.

Swinging around it, she twisted to slam it behind her.

Her skirts got in the way. Hunter snatched the door edge, thrust hard against it. As she stumbled back, he stepped inside.

She retreated from him with dismay and a shadow of regret in her eyes. Her hand shook as she held it out as if to ward him off. The low timbre of her voice raked along his nerves as she said, "Don't. Please."

His own anger rose as he realized she really thought him capable of hurting her. His fault, of course. Yet if he could see her worth, why couldn't she do the same with him? Why didn't she recognize him for what he was inside, and also for what he was not? His need to make her see beat up into his head in such powerful waves that he felt sick with it.

He couldn't do it here, not in this too-public room where anyone might show up at any time. But there were other places, other bedrooms.

Face set in grim lines, he bore down on her. She cried out, a soft sound of despair as he snaked an arm around her waist. He thrust an arm under her knees and lifted her. She stiffened, then doubled her fist and struck out at him. He ducked away from the blows as he carried her from the powder room and into the hall. Once in that open space, he hefted her, then loosened his hold as if he meant to let her fall.

She gasped and clutched at his jacket. He took advantage of that brief respite to stride toward the bedrooms on the far end. As he neared the door, he felt her draw breath to scream.

"I wouldn't advise it," he said, "unless you want to be thoroughly kissed."

She hesitated; he felt it. A flashing thought went through his mind that she might be weighing the risk, might even be considering calling his bluff. There was no time to find out for certain, for he was at the doorway of the last bedroom. Lowering a shoulder, he shoved inside, then kicked the door shut behind him.

The sudden darkness brought him to a halt. The bedroom was on the back side of the house away from the streetlights and had thick draperies drawn across the windows. It was only as his eyes adjusted to the gloom that he saw the bed.

The sight sent desire driving like a white-hot spear deep inside him. He closed his eyes while he fought it. At the same time, he lowered the woman in his arms, letting her slide downward over his body, slipping with the silky crush of her skirts until she stood pressed against him, the ribs of her hoop caught between them like the bars of a cage. He could feel her slender curves conforming to his hard body in a perfect fit. The sweet, half-wild, totally unforgettable scent of her rose around him in warm enticement.

God, he wanted her. It was a madness beating against the hot cauldron of his skull. A clamoring in his blood. An ache in his heart. His hands shook as he splayed his fingers across her back. He smoothed his palms and sensitive fingertips over the warm silk that covered the warmer female body underneath, holding her even closer, as if he could merge his body with hers through their clothing.

Dear, God...

A fine trembling ran over Adrienne in jittery surges. He had been right up there in the belvedere. She did understand his desire, because the same dark craving hovered inside her. Her heart was trying to jump out of her chest, her mind whirled with disoriented giddiness. Her skin prickled with the need to be caressed, while her lips felt swollen and supersensitive. A word, a touch, and she would melt, becoming warm wax for his molding. That he could guess it left her achingly vulnerable, yet unbearably affected.

He would not hurt her physically, of that she was certain. If she had not been convinced, she would have fought harder, longer. She was also sure, almost, that she could break away from him. Yet the feel of his strength as he held her aroused some deep need she hardly recognized.

She didn't want to be released. She couldn't bear to end the turbulent intimacy that stretched between them there in the dark. The thought of pulling free and walking back out into the bright, sterile frenzy of the ball made her feel chilled and desolate.

Quiet strained between them. She could feel the heat and power of him. His heartbeat throbbed against her breast, covering, repeating her own. Her quick breathing slowed, caught in her chest.

Then, bending his head to rest his chin against

her hair, he whispered, "Don't go. Don't leave me."

It was a simple request, yet one made profound by the deep, rich timbre of his voice. Behind it, like a distant cry, she heard the plea of a small boy deserted once too often, unloved far too long. It was the latter that held her.

By degrees, as if giving her time to resist, he lowered his head and took her lips. Hot, possessive, they molded her own to their sensual curves before he pressed deeper in swift, liquid invasion. She moaned, a soft sound of completion. Easing on tiptoe, she slid her arms around his neck. Her senses swam. Her heart expanded with the sudden rush of blood in her veins. Then desire flooded through her like the bursting of a dam. It felt so right, so real. Nothing mattered, not time or place, doubt or fear. There was nothing except the singing pleasure of bodies perfectly attuned, exactly matched.

They were two halves coming together like opposite poles of a magnet in natural attraction. If she had lured him to her, then he had also beguiled her. The force they created between them welded them together in a fury of need.

He probed the sweet depths of her mouth even as he swept his hands over her tender curves. She clutched the taut muscles of his neck and shoulder, closed her fingers in the thick waves of his hair.

Still, it was not enough. Murmuring, holding, they stepped to the bed and sank down upon the mattress. He muttered a soft curse as her hoop belled upward, but there was an amused quirk to his mouth all the same.

She helped him lower the zipper of the white dress, ease the bodice down her arms. He was fascinated by the effect of the corset on her breasts and waist, and took his time tasting her nipples, which were thrust so high and firm for his mouth. He laved them, suckled them until they were hard and moist. Afterward, he found her navel through the nylon and boning and wet it with his tongue, delving into the indentation. As he traveled lower, pushing away layers of petticoats, she drew a hissing breath and arched against him. Through the lacy scrap of panties she wore, his breath and tongue were hot against the small, ultrasensitive peak of her femininity.

Pleasure raced along her veins like a drug. Awash in sensation, she felt the rise of gratitude and something so like love that she could accept it as nothing else.

In the need to share the response, she reached out to him. He eased higher again, dragging her skirts away, freeing her from them even as she tugged at his cravat.

Jacket, shirt, panties, shoes. There were so many clothes, too many. They stripped them away with shaking fingers and growing frenzy. The pieces collected around them, snaked over the bed, slipped from the mattress to lie like refuse on the floor.

Naked at last, they pressed close in shivering urgency, desperate for the abrasion of skin on skin, the fitting of curves and firm planes, soft to rough, hard to tender. He brushed his lips across the delicate golden freckles on the bridge of her nose. Then he took her mouth, at the same time parting her fine, silky curls, separating the delicate folds before easing his long finger into her. The muscles of her abdomen jerked and fluttered with the onslaught of wild desire. She turned against him, pressing closer as she twined her leg with his and reached for the silk and iron of his maleness.

He inhaled in abrupt need. Then he rolled above her in a single lunge. Parting her thighs, he guided himself to the moist heat of her and pressed inside.

She welcomed him, clenching her hands on the taut muscles of his sides and rubbing feverishly as he eased deeper into the tight constriction of her. The spreading wonder of it was such bright glory that she squeezed her eyes shut, turning her head from side to side. Then she felt the stinging discomfort as he reached the delicate internal barrier.

He hesitated; she felt it, heard his winded gasp. But she dug her fingers into the muscles of his back, holding him with her legs as she drew him deep with sudden, splintering force. And the stinging vanished, dissolving into beatitude as he plunged into her warm, resilient depths, coming up against the firm wall of deepest penetration.

For a long instant, he was still. Then a shiver of tested control shook him. Voice husky with strain and something more, he said, "What is your name?"

She shook her head, unable to think, unwilling to spare the effort.

"Tell me," he insisted, easing out, then pressing deep again even as he shivered with the effort of doing no more.

"A-Adrienne," she whispered on a sigh like a gentle surrender.

"Adrienne." He tested the syllables, then added, "I'm sorry. I didn't—know."

"It doesn't matter," she whispered, smoothing her palms along his arms as if it were he who needed comfort.

"It matters," he corrected in gruff regret, "only—"

"Only it's too late." Her breath caught as she urged him closer, deeper. "Please, could you—"

"The pleasure is mine," he answered on the ghost of a laugh. "And yours, if possible. Hold on to me, Adrienne, love. We'll take this as easy as we can."

As the words died away, he began to move. It was a slow glide, in and then out, again and yet again, a deliberate yet careful sounding. He tried to hold back; she could feel the effort in his ridged muscles. But after a moment the strokes came faster, with more force behind each one. She caught the cadence, matched it with a swift-drawn breath and trembling effort.

Together, they moved, force against force. He lifted her into his firm strokes. She opened to them. Gasping for air, grasping for purchase, seeking with body and mind to blend into oneness, they reveled in the fierce joining.

Magic. Physical nirvana more transcendent than

any mental delight. It swept over them like a wild wind, sending them rushing, spinning upward into that most vivid of earthly joys. He gave a final, hard lunge, pinning her beneath him, holding her safe and close in the whirlwind. She clung in passionate strength, fiercely protective.

And the seconds ticked down like the clock toward midnight while their hearts beat with dull interior chimes. Until at last they subsided, drew apart, lay staring, frowning, into the dark. Wondering if they should dress and leave before they were discovered. Afraid to turn on the light and face each other in their new and tender nakedness.

Nine

Adrienne was blinded by yards of white silk, fighting to get her arms into the sleeves of her dress, which Hunter had flung over her head, when she heard the first door open then bang shut again almost at once. It was followed by another, and another. The sharp, slamming sounds were in sequence. They had begun at the far end of the hall, but were coming closer.

Beside her, Hunter cursed in soft virulence and began to tug the dress down around her shoulders.

"Wait, let me—!" she said in breathless haste as she settled the bodice in place. She didn't have to be told what the doors opening and closing could mean. "Now!"

Hunter jerked the back edges of the dress together, reached for the zipper. It was at that moment that the bedroom door was flung wide. The bright white glare of the overhead light flashed on.

B.B. hovered in the doorway for a shocked instant, his gaze fixed on his daughter where she stood, half dressed and disheveled, with Hunter knee-deep in the froth of her crinoline and petticoats and wearing nothing more than his pants. Then the older man sent the heavy door crashing against the wall so hard that it cracked the plaster. With murder in his face, he lunged toward Hunter.

"No!" Adrienne cried, stumbling over her skirts as she tried to dart between the two men.

Her father barely glanced at her. Nor did Hunter pay any attention. They sidestepped her, then came together, one hard muscled body slamming into the other.

B.B. flung a quick punch at the younger man's jaw. Hunter blocked it, then came from beneath with a hard right toward B.B.'s belly. Adrienne's father grunted and twisted away from the full force of the punch. The two men grappled, pushing and shoving.

"Stop!" Adrienne shouted. "Stop it, Hunter! He's my dad!"

Hunter threw her a stunned look. In that moment, the older man connected with a right to his chin. Hunter's head snapped back and he spun away. Dropping his fists, he balled them at his sides, making no other move to defend himself. Regardless, it was clear he was more staggered by what Adrienne had said than by the hit he had taken.

The big, older man moved in for another round, but Adrienne caught his jacket sleeve and hung on. "Don't, B.B., it isn't Hunter's fault."

Her father hesitated, but murder still hovered in his eyes. "It has to be, Adrienne, *acushla*. You wouldn't be here any other way."

"Oh, yes." she said quietly, her face pale but

her gaze steady on the older man. "I'm—sorry, but that's the way it is."

Another voice, firm but shadowed with regret, came from the doorway. "I'm afraid I may share the blame."

It was Charles Duchaise. He paused a moment as he spoke, then stepped farther into the room, reaching for the door as if he meant to close it.

Adrienne's father turned on the new arrival with belligerence in his face. "What are you saying, Duchaise?"

"I had no idea it would come to this. I hope you'll believe that."

"Don't," Adrienne said. She put out a hand in an attempt to stop what was about to happen.

It was too late, Duchaise was already speaking. "If I had realized it would end this way, I would never have asked her to lure Sutherland away from my wife." He turned to Adrienne. "You're all right, my dear? You're not hurt?"

Hunter was silent, overwhelmed by the implications sinking into his mind. It was too much. Nothing was as he had thought. Nothing. He cursed, a soft, distinct phrase directed at himself.

His hand hurt. He looked down at it. There was a smear of red across his knuckles. He dried it on his pants leg. Mustn't get blood on anything, such as a white silk dress. He reached for Adrienne's zipper once more, sent it sliding upward with a vicious whine, a loud sound in the quiet.

Adrienne swung to put her chilled fingers on the

corded muscle of his forearm. "It wasn't like it sounds," she said in quiet entreaty. "Believe me."

His low laugh had a dull edge. "I thought you and Duchaise had a thing going. Guess not, unless it's a mighty strange arrangement."

Her brows drew together above her eyes. "I told you there was nothing between us."

"So you did. I should have listened. I don't suppose you and your dad the butler have any designs on the Sans Souci silver, either."

She drew back as if stung. It was B.B. who answered in tones rough with contempt. "I'm no butler, I'm a cop—or I was a cop. Now I'm head of my own security business. And the guy I'm investigating as a risk is you."

"With your daughter's help, no doubt," Hunter said, savagely polite.

"Bet your boots," came the immediate answer. "She found out you're the guy sniffing around Duchaise's wife."

Hunter stared at him with a startled look in his dark eyes. Adrienne put her hands to her face as a moan sounded in her throat. At the same time, a sharp exclamation came from the doorway.

Hard on the sound, Millie Duchaise pushed into the room. She snatched the door from the hands of her husband, who still held it, and slammed it behind her. Her figure was drawn up straight and her eyes flashed as she stepped up to him. In a voice that trembled with rage, she cried, "You dared— you actually dared—have someone investigate me?"

Duchaise stood his ground, though a white line appeared around his mouth. "It seemed the natural thing to do. You were having an affair. I wanted to know the name of the man."

"What in God's name ever made you think such a thing?" His wife's face flamed as if she had been slapped. Hunter eased to her side in a mute gesture of support.

Duchaise, watching her closely, answered, "I saw you."

"You—but you can't have!" Her confusion and outrage were plain.

"I did," her husband said with grim certainty. "Someone told me you'd been seen going into a French Quarter hotel one afternoon. You never mentioned it until I asked, then you gave some weak tale about meeting a woman friend. A day or two later, you left the house without explanation. I followed you, saw you meet a younger man at a restaurant, but I was too far away to recognize him. Why shouldn't I hire somebody to find out his name."

"And did you?" she asked with shrill precision and only a single brief glance in Hunter's direction.

Duchaise's nod was quick. "I did, this evening. It was Sutherland. He was seen entering this house by the back way. It wasn't me he came to see."

She wilted. Hunter found it painful to watch as her shoulders slumped, her face turned haggard, and her gaze flickered and fell. She gave an unsteady shake of her head. "Oh, Charles…"

He paled, swallowing with difficulty. "You admit it, then?"

"No, oh, no! You don't understand."

"Then make me," he said, ignoring the others, who watched as he reached for her hands. "If Sutherland isn't—if there's no one else, then why were you seeing him? Tell me what in the name of heaven is going on."

She pressed her lips tightly together and squeezed her eyes shut, then took a deep breath. As she let it out, she said in a tearful rush, "Oh, Charles, I'm so sorry."

"For what?" he pleaded, rubbing her hand as she stopped short. "Tell me, darling."

She searched his face, her gaze stark with hope and terror. "Hunter is—he's my son."

Charles Duchaise opened his mouth, but nothing came out.

Adrienne listened intently, though her gaze was on Hunter. It was no news to him, that much was plain. There was not a flicker of expression in the bleak darkness of his eyes.

Duchaise looked at him, his gaze measuring. Hunter returned it. Whatever passed between them, whatever resemblance Duchaise found, seemed to satisfy him, for he returned his attention to his wife. Drawing her closer, he held her captured hands against his chest as he said, "Why didn't you tell me?"

"I didn't know!" she cried with tears shimmering in her eyes. "At least, I didn't know where he

was, what had become of him, what name he had
been given. I had no way of knowing he was still
alive until he came to me a month ago, searching
for his birth mother.''

So that was it.

Adrienne, remembering the things Hunter had
said, felt a slow understanding creep in upon her.
Hunter's need for family, for connectedness, had
pushed him to contact the woman who gave him
life. With his resources, it would have been no
great problem to find her.

"But I never knew... You never said a word.''
There was pain in Charles Duchaise's voice, the
pain of betrayal, of being left out of an important
part of his wife's life.

A rasping sob caught in Millie's throat. "I meant
to tell you. I tried a thousand times in the beginning. But you thought I was perfect, you said so
over and over. How could I tell you I wasn't, never
had been, that I was a silly, reckless teenager who
paid for a few minutes in the back seat of Pontiac
Firebird with a married man by getting pregnant?''

Duchaise shook his head. "I only meant you
were perfect for me. I never expected you to be
without flaw. Why should you be when I'm not
myself?''

His wife's tears overflowed, running unchecked
down her face. "Oh, but you were so kind and
gentle and took such care of me. You were so different from my daddy. He said I had shamed him
when he found out I was pregnant. He wanted me
out of town, out of his sight. He drove me here

from Dallas in the dead of night, put me in a home for unwed mothers. The nuns who ran it were kind, but I never even saw my baby when he was born. Daddy told them I would give him up for adoption. I wasn't so sure, but how could I keep a baby when I couldn't keep myself? But afterward, I didn't go back to Texas. I stayed here, found a job." Her voice softened. "Then I met you, Charles."

"Oh, my dear, I am so sorry," Duchaise said, as a spasm of pain crossed his face. He rubbed her back in compulsive, soothing circles. "But—I thought our marriage was stronger than that. It must be my fault if you were afraid to let me know about it when Hunter finally came to you."

Tears stained with mascara collected in the hollows under her eyes as she gazed at him. "I wanted to, intended to as soon as I found the right time." She glanced toward Adrienne with wariness in her watery gaze before she turned back to him. "But then I found the bill for a woman's costume, a ball gown. It wasn't my size or my style, wasn't for me. It had to be for your—"

"It was for Adrienne, so she could mingle tonight. She was to help O'Banyon look out for the man you were seeing."

"Then... You aren't interested in her?" Beneath the hope in her eyes was both dread and guilt.

"No, not in the way you mean." Duchaise's smile was wry. "Though I'm flattered you think she might be interested in a graybeard like me."

Charles Duchaise looked beyond his wife to meet Hunter's gaze once more. His own was steady and determined as he stepped to offer the tall, dark-haired man his hand. Hunter took it in a careful grasp. The two stared at each other for long seconds, then a slow smile curved Hunter's mouth.

Millie watched them with tears of pride and love running down her face. Then her hazel gaze moved to Adrienne. Her lips quivered and she closed her eyes. "Oh, no," she said on a tightly drawn breath. "Oh, dear God."

"What is it?" Duchaise turned back to her at once.

She shook her head, unable to speak.

"Millie, please—!"

She lifted her head, flinging a quick, almost frightened glance at Adrienne where she stood next to her father. As she licked her dry lips, Adrienne was touched once more by dread.

"Oh, Charles, I was so jealous, so angry." The words were faint, gasping. "I know it's no excuse, but I never dreamed, at least, I didn't really expect…"

"What is it," he asked again more urgently.

Millie glanced at her son. He crossed his arms over his bare chest and looked away, his face pale. Swallowing hard, she compressed her trembling lips. When she spoke, her voice was almost inaudible. "I asked Hunter to—to see if he couldn't take Adrienne away from you. He agreed to seduce her, but only for my sake, because I begged him."

Adrienne heard the words through a roaring in her ears.

Seduce. It was a very high-toned word for what Hunter had done.

He had seduced her, all right. He had made love to her in cold blood, for no other reason than his mother had asked him to do it. Adrienne wanted to scream. She wanted to sink into the floor. She wanted to hide while she cried. Instead, she stood like an ice statue, trying not to think.

"You're disappointed, I know," Millie Duchaise went on, her voice thick with misery as she searched her husband's eyes. "I've always tried so hard to be the kind of wife you needed. I just don't fit the image. I—was never classy enough, never good enough."

"Oh, my love," Charles Duchaise said in sincerity as he gathered her close against him. "You've always been everything I ever needed or wanted. Nothing can change that. Nothing ever will."

Millie gave a low sob as she sagged against him and buried her face in his shoulder. Adrienne turned away. It was too painful to watch, too much to bear when there was no love, no absolution or relieving explanations for her.

Her chest hurt and her eyes burned. She had to leave. Now. She had to get away before the tears came.

Her shoes were here somewhere. She looked around wildly, found them, stepped into them. She was no Cinderella to leave things behind her. No, not even her heart.

"Adrienne, I can explain," Hunter said, the

words tentative, as if he was trying out the sound of it.

She barely glanced at him. Her hair was coming down, falling around her face. She snatched pins from the slipping mass and raked it back behind her shoulders. "Please, don't," she said in compressed tones as she worked feverishly to spread her crumpled skirts, make herself presentable. "Just—don't. I understand perfectly. I went after you for my father's sake. You came after me because your mother asked it. I guess that makes us even."

"No, it doesn't, not by a long shot," he answered, his eyes hot as he curled his fingers into a fist.

"Well, don't let it bother you. It really doesn't make any difference."

"I happen to think it does," he said, stepping toward her with swift grace.

B.B. moved to intercept him. His voice crackled in hard command as he said, "You heard my daughter, lad. She isn't interested."

Hunter paid him no attention. "Adrienne, we have to talk. There's so much you have to hear."

She shook her head, not quite trusting her voice. "It's all been said, everything that matters. Let it go. Just—let it go."

"I can't, damn it!"

"Sutherland," B.B. said, putting a hand on the younger man's shoulder as he tried to push past him. "Leave it."

Hunter rounded on the older man with ridged

muscles plain in his chest and arms and a savage look on his face.

Millie Duchaise lifted her head, her features taut with alarm as she watched B.B. and her son. Quickly, she said, "Hunter, maybe he's right. I think we've all imposed on Adrienne enough."

Hunter paused, looking at his mother. Adrienne took advantage of that second of hesitation to slip behind him and head for the only way out of the room. He plunged after her but was brought up short as B.B. tackled him. Millie screamed. Adrienne looked back as she snatched open the door. She was in time to see Hunter break her father's hold and swing around to follow her.

"Hunter, you can't go out there," Millie cried. "You're half-naked!"

He came on.

Adrienne could not stop to jerk the door shut since her skirts would only get in the way. Picking them up, she whirled and ran. Behind her she could hear the pounding of Hunter's feet on the Oriental rugs spaced down the hall.

B.B. shouted something she didn't quite catch. Charles Duchaise had apparently sprinted after them into the hall, for his voice was clearer as he rapped out, "Think of Adrienne, son," he called. "What will people think if they see you running after her, half-naked?"

She heard the footsteps jar to a reluctant halt. She redoubled her speed. The staircase was ahead of her, winding away down to safety. She didn't hesitate, but hit it at a run, feet flying on the treads, as she skimmed downward in a billow of silk skirts.

She didn't look back.

Ten

"What is this?" Adrienne looked up from the letter in her hand with suspicion on her face.

She and her father were sitting in the office he had rented for himself down near the docks, just past an area of warehouses that had been renovated a few years back for use as upscale art galleries. It was small and cluttered, but picturesque in its way. The best thing about it, however, was that it was in the middle of where things were happening. That was what mattered to B.B.

He shrugged, avoiding her eyes as he answered. "I guess it's exactly what it looks like, love. I've been invited to submit a bid for providing extra security for the city museum during the upcoming Imperial Jewelry Exhibition. Some of the pieces belonged to Catherine the Great. They're priceless, on top of which, they've never been out of Russia before."

"Yes, but why you? Why now?"

"I'm good," he said with a grin, leaning back in his chair and knitting his fingers behind his head. "I'm getting a rep."

"Influence," she said succinctly. "You're getting the benefit of influence."

He frowned. "I'd rather think it was because I'm the best at what I do."

Adrienne sighed. "I know you would, and you are. But that's not the point here. We both know who's behind this."

"Duchaise, I guess."

"Wrong."

"I don't know why you're so certain," B.B. complained. "Duchaise did promise to throw business my way. And it's not as if it's a handout, either. I have to make the low bid or I don't get the job."

"It isn't Duchaise," Adrienne said. "Hunter Sutherland is on the museum board."

"Know that for a fact, do you?"

"I've made it my business to find out," she said evenly, refusing to be flustered by the sardonic look in her father's eyes.

"Maybe so, but that doesn't mean—"

"Yes, it does. It means he's trying to get to me through you."

Her father studied her with a shrewd light in the blue of his eyes. "So," he said, "why don't you let him?"

"You know why!"

"Because you're embarrassed," he said with brutal frankness.

She flung the letter back onto the cluttered top of his desk. "Embarrassed, humiliated and madder than hell."

"Hurt, too," B.B. added, his gaze somber.

"All right, I was hurt," she said through her teeth. "Why not?"

"The only way anybody can hurt you," he said softly, "is if you care what they think."

"It isn't what he thinks that bothers me, it's what he did!"

"Be reasonable, *acushla*. You said yourself that the two of you were even."

"I lied."

"All right, I wasn't there, so I don't know exactly what happened. But, honey, I'm a male-type, too, and it looks to me like you weren't the only one who got in over your head."

"Are you trying to tell me Hunter was carried away by passion? Don't be ridiculous. He only put a move on me because his mother asked him."

"And a more stupid, harebrained scheme I've never heard. But I can tell you this much, Adrienne, my heart. Hunter Sutherland isn't the kind of man to mind his mama. If he did what she told him to, it was because it suited him down to the ground."

"Oh, fine," Adrienne said, her gaze level. "Great. He seduced me because he thought it would make pushing his way into his mother's life easier. That makes me feel so much better."

"What I'm trying to say," her father said with strained patience, "is that the man wanted you pretty desperately, considering how things turned out. Is that so hard to take?"

"Maybe not, if it were true. But the fact is, he had an agenda and I happened to be at the top of it."

B.B. laughed. "Men don't make love to women they don't want, *acushla*. It just doesn't work. It's one of the major differences between the sexes."

"Yes, well, here's another one for you," she said with hot color riding her cheekbones. "Any man can want just about any woman at least once."

"Some, maybe," he said in reluctant agreement, then added, "but not all. Is that the problem, then? You wanted more?"

She tried to smile, but couldn't. Tried to speak, but wasn't able. Looking away, she shook her head, but it was more to indicate that she didn't know than to disagree.

The night of the Mardi Gras ball was still an open sore in her mind. She had gone over every word, every action and gesture, accusation and answer, a thousand times.

She cringed when she thought of how bowled over she had been, how easy she had made it for Hunter. She winced, growing hot all over when she remembered the things she had said and done. She couldn't bear to consider what he must think of her.

She'd thought she was attractive to him, that he had danced with her, lain in wait for her on the terrace, followed her up to the belvedere at Sans Souci, because of the interest she aroused in him. That hadn't been it at all.

Forget it! she told herself as she had a million times before. *Let it go.*

She wanted to do that—would be glad to—if only Hunter would let her. He wouldn't, hadn't since that night. Instead, he called and left messages on her answering machine. He came and banged on her door until the neighbors called the police. He sent her white camellias. He sent her champagne. He sent her snowflakes made of gold—to match her freckles—in every shape and form, from trivets to earrings. And now this.

"Anyway," she said, "you'll have to ignore this bid request. It isn't legitimate. It can't be."

"It could be still be Duchaise's doing," B.B. insisted.

She gave him a jaundiced stare. He held it for long moments before he shrugged his massive shoulders. "Even if it isn't, I don't see the problem with at least making my bid."

"It's a payoff. You wouldn't want to get the job for that reason, would you?"

The look in his eyes turned sardonic. "Maybe. I'm not proud."

"Meaning I am?" she said with a lift of her chin. "I don't consider it a sign of pride to resent being used."

He pursed his lips as he watched her, then shook his head. "You're a hard woman, *acushla*. But I think the person you're being hardest on is yourself."

Was her dad right? Was she being unreasonable? Was she punishing Hunter for her own fall from grace?

It was true that she didn't understand what had come over her that night. She was angry with herself for it, but also enraged with Hunter for pushing it when she'd tried to get away from him, for making it so impossible to refuse. It was his fault. It had to be.

Yes, and now he didn't have the decency to leave her alone to get over it. He had to keep on wearing away at her resistance, reminding her so that the whirlwind of feeling and belonging that had been stirred up inside her would not die down.

What did he want from her? Explanations? Absolution? What? She would like to know.

She would really like to know.

Well, all right, so maybe she would find out. She would go and see him and demand to be told what he thought he was doing. She would insist that he stop involving her father, stop getting B.B.'s hopes up for nothing, stop making him feel as if accepting favors was the only way he could build his business. That should call a halt to the harassment, once and for all.

Indignation. Outrage. These were the things that moved her. They were, truly. She wasn't looking for an excuse. She wasn't sorry she had run away. Her inclination to see Hunter had nothing whatever to do with the memory of strong, enclosing arms, soul-shattering need or a deep voice whispering, "Don't go. Don't leave me."

No, no, never. That wasn't it at all. Not even if her dreams were haunted by his touch, by the feel of his body against hers or the desolation in his eyes as she left him. Not even if she thought she might hear his soft entreaty over and over again in her head until the day she drew her last breath.

"Don't go. Don't leave me."

She was the one who had been hurt and betrayed. She was the one who should be angry.

Wasn't she?

She found Hunter at home. She had no difficulty locating him; the Sutherland mansion was nearly as much of a landmark as Sans Souci and everybody knew where it sat on St. Charles. She had only to drive up to the house on a Saturday afternoon and knock on the door.

It was the housekeeper who answered. She must have been interrupted in some task in the kitchen, for she was wiping her hands on her uniform apron. Her brows lifted a little as she saw Adrienne, but her greeting was cordial and she led the way without hesitation toward a flagstoned courtyard at the back.

Hunter was standing on the top rung of a ladder, sawing a dead limb from the big oak that shaded the right rear corner. For an instant, Adrienne felt fear shift inside her for his precarious position. That was before she recognized how stupid her concern was, and how useless.

The housekeeper called out to Hunter from the lower gallery. Hunter stopped sawing and looked down through the branches of the oak. For the space of a long breath, he was still, then he gave his housekeeper a low-voiced request for coffee and cake to be served in the courtyard.

"This isn't a social visit," Adrienne said stiffly.

"We'll have coffee, anyway," Hunter said, avoiding her gaze as he dismissed the housekeeper with a nod. The woman gave Adrienne an instant of closer interest before she turned and went back into the house.

Hunter removed his saw from the half-severed limb, then backed down the ladder a step or two before leaping to the ground. He parked his saw against the tree trunk, then wrenched off his gloves and tossed them beside it before moving toward her.

He was dressed in a T-shirt and faded jeans and looked as if pruning a tree was as natural to him as signing a multimillion dollar contract. Flakes of tree bark dusted one cheekbone, and he had saw-dust in the dark waves of his hair. He brushed at it as he walked. The urge to help him by flicking away the bits that clung to his wide shoulders was so powerful that Adrienne tensed her muscles to force herself to remain still.

He had been a stunning man in evening clothes. In his jeans, with the scents of fresh oak and warm male surrounding him, he was so right, so natural and virile, that she felt light-headed with it. She should never have come, should not have ventured within a thousand miles of him. It was bad for her health, worse for her sanity.

"You're the last person I expected," he said, his gaze watchful as he halted a few feet away.

"I doubt that. You've been trying to get to me for days. You just finally figured out the best way to go about it."

His jaw set, but his eyes held hers. "Smart of me, wasn't it?"

"You admit it!"

"Actually, I don't, but I won't argue with anything that gets you here. Why don't we sit down in the shade and talk about it?" He nodded toward a set of small, sidewalk-café-type table and chairs positioned under the oak.

"I won't be here that long," she said in clipped tones. "What did you mean by setting it up so B.B. can bid on security for this jewelry exhibit? What are you trying to do?"

"Nothing," he said, his gaze watchful as he thrust his hands into the back pockets of his jeans.

"Nothing?" she said in disbelief. "I'm sure! If you think I'm going to be so grateful I'll fall into bed with you again, you're badly mistaken." In her agitation, she paced around him in a circle.

He turned to keep her in view. The sun gilded his skin with a bronze gleam and made an iridescent blue sheen in his hair. She did her best to avoid noticing, but was so distracted by the sight she didn't quite catch his answer.

"What?"

"I said," he repeated evenly, "what makes you think I'd go to the trouble of a repeat performance?"

She came to a halt with a gasp. "Of all the low things to say! Just because I wasn't experienced enough to live up to your exalted expectations—"

"Why weren't you?" His question cut across her diatribe as if he meant to take advantage of the opening she had given him before it closed again.

She stared at him for a disconcerted instant, then her chin came up. "That's none of your business."

"I think it is, since you decided to honor me with being the first man to make love to you."

"Decided?" she demanded, incensed. "I decided? It was you! You came on so strong that I..."

"What, Adrienne? I came on so strong you couldn't resist? Wrong. You could and you did, until you decided not to anymore. So why me? Why that night, instead of while you were in college or else down in the jungle with that professor you were going to marry?"

"I've been too busy, if you must know," she said in grim answer, since it looked as if he wasn't going to let the subject rest. "I worked two jobs to put myself through college and graduate school. There was hardly time to sleep, period, much less sleep around. That was even if I had found somebody who—"

"Turned you on?" he supplied as she paused again.

She distrusted the look in his eyes as much as the phrase he had used. Afraid of what else he might add, she hurried on. "As for my profes—the man I was engaged to, we were in a remote area and expected to be there for months. It would have been stupid to risk having to cancel everything because of pregnancy, all for the sake of a few minutes of pleasure."

"A few minutes," he echoed, then gave a harsh laugh. "It would have been more than a few minutes if I had been there."

"Well, you weren't." Her face was so hot that

she wished she had taken him up on his offer to sit in the shade.

"No, but I was at Sans Souci. I was there and so were you, Adrienne. And some time between nine and midnight, you decided that being in my arms was worth risking everything."

She drew in another whistling gasp. "That is so arrogant and pretentious it is beyond belief!"

"And so true?" he suggested, his gaze steady and infinitely penetrating.

He was right. She had held on to her virginity for so many long years, through so many clumsy passes and snide remarks. Refusing had never been particularly troublesome; her head had always ruled her heart. Until the Mardi Gras ball.

That she had let herself fall into Hunter's arms so easily that night was astonishing. Or just possibly it wasn't. Perhaps he was absolutely, perfectly correct.

"Oh, all right," she snapped in weary defeat. "The chemistry was right between us, okay? I had too much wine and music and romance, and I let it all go to my head. I'm sorry I didn't live up to your lofty requirements for a bed partner. But then why did you arrange the museum exhibit?"

"You didn't live up to them, no," he said in quiet tones. "You surpassed them by far. You were perfection, in fact. We were matchless together, and I'm glad you had sense enough to realize it then, even if you can hardly bring yourself to admit it now."

She stared at him in bewilderment. "But you

said—I thought you meant—'' She stopped, began again. "What was that about not being good enough for a repeat performance?"

"I wanted to hear what you would say," he answered simply. "But I'll tell you now, my lovely Adrienne, that if it had been any better, I wouldn't be here to talk about it. Though at the time, dying—or being caught in an embarrassing state in the middle of the most exclusive ball of the year— seemed a small price to pay for having you in my arms."

"Don't," she said sharply, turning away from him.

"Why?" he asked, moving after her with a single long stride. "Does it bother you to talk about it, to think about it?" He came up behind her, settling his hands on her shoulders, closing them on the bones with slow care. "I have a hard time thinking about anything else. The memory of you in that white dress won't go away. I think it will be with me when I'm an old man gibbering into my soup, talking to myself about Mardi Gras balls and white silk, stained glass windows and freckles like gold snowflakes."

"Oh, don't—please." Her voice broke in the middle and a shiver beaded her skin with goose bumps.

"I have to," he said, sliding his hands down her arms to her hands, holding them in a light clasp as he stepped closer to wrap his arms around her waist from behind. "I have to do it for the same reason I wanted desperately to get close to you at the ball.

I had to unmask you, undress you, find out everything about you. You were the most important thing to ever come into my life. I wanted no barriers between us, nothing to keep us from knowing exactly who and what we were. If I had to seduce you to discover that, then I was ready. More than ready."

"Your mother..."

"Millie Duchaise is a lovely lady, and I'm glad I found her, regardless of the trouble I caused her. But she is my past, while you are my future. Or you will be, if I can only persuade you to chance it. I want that family we talked about. I want to go to sleep beside you at night and wake up beside you in the morning. I want to find out what you like for breakfast and whether you sleep on your back or your side. I want you with me always. I want never, ever to be forced to stand and watch you walk away from—" He stopped, swallowing hard as he rested his cheek against her hair.

She moved against his hold, releasing herself with firm insistence. When she turned to face him, she reached out to touch the strong line of his jaw with her fingers. Her voice not quite under control, she said, "I'm not perfect, any more than your mother was."

His smile was crooked. "You're close enough for me."

"I don't want you to try single-handedly to make my father's business a success."

"That was Duchaise, I think. He may have guessed it would bring you here. He's a romantic at heart, you know, and he's been blaming himself for what went wrong.''

"Thank him for me, then." Her smile was brief before she sobered. "I'm still an archaeologist."

"I'll finance your expeditions and be there to watch out for snakes for you, snakes of all kinds. Though I'm keeping in mind that pregnancy and jungles don't go together."

She closed her eyes. "You are a manipulating, conniving, scheming bastard."

"I know," he said without a shred of contrition. "Are you going to marry me, anyway?"

"I may as well," she agreed on an unsteady laugh.

His smile was dazzling. "Because you're thinking of allowing yourself to be seduced again?"

"Something like that."

Her reward was a kiss that threatened to destroy her soul. When he lifted his head, he said, "Will your wedding dress be white silk with a hoop skirt?"

She gave him a darkling glance. "Most definitely not!"

"I guess that means no corset, either?"

"I don't think so."

"Come on, just for me?" Lowering his mouth to her ear, he whispered several advantages.

Laughing and flushed, Adrienne drew back to smile into his eyes. "Oh, all right! A hooped petticoat and a corset."

"You won't be sorry," he said in tones of low

and fervid promise.

"I'd better not be," she said, her voice husky. She wasn't.

THE TAMING OF KATHARINA
by Janet Dailey and Sonja Massie

One

"Ya did good, kid," Katharina Burnell whispered to herself as she looked with satisfaction at the magnificent ballroom, resplendent in its newly reclaimed glory. The restoration was, indeed, a job well done.

Expert at the art of renovating antebellum mansions to their original splendor, Burnell Construction had proven its mettle once again. The company was the best in the business. If anyone doubted it, all they had to do was look around this house, Sans Souci, one of the most exquisite estates in the Garden District of New Orleans.

From the glistening, refinished cypress floor, to the repaired plaster cherubs, roses and ribbons that swirled across the ceiling, the transformation was breathtaking. The tall burled walnut doorways had been reclaimed from beneath years of accumulated paint, and the French doors now opened without creaky protest onto the terrace and fanciful gardens. Everywhere she looked, the Burnell mark of excellence shone.

And Katharina Burnell *was* Burnell Construction. Whether anyone else acknowledged that fact or not, it was true. Standing here in the middle of her shining accomplishment, Kate felt pride swell inside her until she thought she would burst out of the silly costume she had been required to wear to this masquerade ball. She had been told it was the gown of a sixteenth-century noblewoman.

"Yeah, whatever..." had been her response when her younger sister, Natalie, had insisted that it was the best choice for the ball. Kate had taken her word for it. Parties, gowns and all that stuff was Natalie's department, not hers.

Though she hated to admit it, Kate felt wonderfully feminine tonight. The dark blue velvet fabric of the dress did bring out the auburn highlights of her hair and the cobalt blue of her eyes. The tightly laced bodice enhanced her figure in ways she had never thought possible.

But then, her physical appearance wasn't something that consumed a lot of Kate's time or energy. On her list of priorities it rated low, if at all.

Kate was happiest when she was working and didn't really know what to do with herself when she wasn't. Looking around her, she was sure she had her list of values in order. Only focused dedication could have brought this miracle to life.

At the sound of hurried steps behind her, she turned and saw the mistress of Sans Souci, Millicent Duchaise, scurrying toward her. As a rule, when Millie made an appearance, a room brightened several degrees by means of her sparkling personality. But in the time Kate had known her, she had watched that light dim a little and she wasn't sure why. Sometimes she wondered if all was well between the lady of the house and its lord, Charles Duchaise.

Tonight, the middle-aged, blond and petite Millie was dressed as Josephine, and Kate had seen Charles strutting around earlier as Napoléon.

"Oh, isn't everything beautiful!" Millie exclaimed as she crossed the polished floor, high heels clicking, her red-and-gold dress reflected in the wood's shining depths. She clapped her hands together like a delighted child. "It all turned out even better than I had hoped. And just in time for our twenty-fifth Mardi Gras ball! I can't believe you finished."

Kate thought back over the past six months—the sleepless nights, the obstacles overcome, the myriad problems solved. If anything *could* have gone wrong, it had. She couldn't quite believe they had met their deadline, either.

"We *had* to finish in time," she said. "I'm certainly not going to be the one to interfere with a tradition as sacred as the Sans Souci Masquerade Ball."

Kate had uttered the words half sarcastically, but when she saw the glow of pride in Millie's eyes, she wished she had been more sincere. These balls meant a lot to other people, even if they were a bunch of silly nonsense to her. Attending the never-ending stream of parties, wearing designer gowns and heirloom jewelry, entertaining and being entertained while climbing the social ladder—all these things meant nothing to Katharina Burnell.

While her family had compiled as much wealth,

if not more, than most of the prominent New Orleans families, the Burnells still worked for a living. They worked because they wanted to, because it gave them pleasure and satisfaction.

At least, Kate worked.

Lately, with her father becoming more adolescent with every passing year, and her sister being her predictable, lazy self, the greatest part of the responsibilities for the company had fallen on Kate's shoulders. But her shoulders and spirit were strong, and she didn't mind.

Most of the time.

Besides, she had found it was usually easier to just do the work herself and, thereby, make certain it was done right the first time.

"Oh, I do hope everyone likes it," Millie said. "This restoration has been the talk of the town. I'd be crushed if anyone was disappointed."

Kate studied her hostess curiously, wondering at the insecurity underlying this lady's exuberant facade. The house was beautiful, and Millie and Charles seemed well pleased. Why should anyone else's opinion matter so much?

Perhaps it was because Millie had married into New Orleans' high society, and its purebred members had never allowed her to forget that fact.

"If they don't like it, tough!" Kate said. "Tell 'em to go..." Kate saw Millie's eyebrow lift a notch and decided to amend her original thought. Millie Duchaise was a lady who, unlike Kate, didn't work with construction crews all day. "To go...um, hire their own restoration company."

In spite of Kate's self-restraint, Millie still appeared shocked. "Why, no, dear. I could never say something like that to one of my guests. That would be rude," Millie said with a slightly chiding tone that irritated Kate. Her hostess was warning her, in a not-so-subtle way, to watch her temper and her tongue tonight. Heaven forbid she should not play the part of the perfect lady.

Although she tried not to think about it, Kate knew her reputation preceded her. She was known as a woman who spoke her mind too often, who used terms that weren't always socially acceptable, and who needed some lessons in proper, south-of-the-Mason-Dixon-line etiquette.

All right...everyone thought she was a bitch.

It was no secret. Kate had heard the whispers. The gossip had made the circuit and found its way back to her, as gossip always did, sooner or later. Some people were actually afraid of her, and others simply disliked her.

They were wimps and fools.

That was Kate's explanation, and she was sticking to it.

Why couldn't a woman speak her mind plainly and honestly? If a man did, he was considered strong and forthright. Why should she act weak and insincere, just because she was female?

"What a lovely gown," Millie was saying, admiring the dark blue velvet with satin welting and ivory lace trim on Kate's dress. "Who are you this evening?"

"I don't know," Kate said with a shrug that

deepened her already exposed cleavage. "Some Italian noblewoman, Natalie told me. She chose our dresses. Hers is the same, only pink with more lace—of course."

"Of course. Natalie is such a lovely, feminine young lady."

Kate gritted her teeth, trying not to notice the subtext in her hostess's words: *Natalie is a respectable, southern gentlewoman, so why aren't you?*

Reminding herself that Millie was a kind soul who wouldn't deliberately hurt her for anything, Kate steeled herself for the rest of the speech.

"I saw her just a moment ago—" Millie pointed to a window "—out there on the terrace. Her costume is a bit mysterious, too. I asked her who she was, and she said she was Bianca. I don't have the foggiest notion who that might be."

Slowly, Kate's blood pressure began to rise, until her face flushed three shades of red as she realized what Natalie had done to her this evening. *She wouldn't. She couldn't.*

But she had.

At first, Kate couldn't believe it. But why shouldn't she? Natalie never missed an opportunity to hurt her. But she usually did it in subtle, passive-aggressive, "Oh, my, my, I would *never* do a thing like that" ways.

This was anything but subtle. It was an open declaration of war!

"Bianca. Such a pretty, dainty name," Millie mused. "Now, who do you suppose that is?"

Kate could feel her fury rising, like a red tide,

sweeping reason aside. Southern gentility and etiquette be damned. "I know who it is," she said. "Bianca is the sweet, beautiful, younger sister in Shakespeare's *The Taming of the Shrew*. So, guess who that makes *me!*"

Comprehension dawned on Millie's face. "Oh, dear me."

Hiking her heavy skirts several inches, Kate strode across the cypress floor and headed for the first door that led to the terrace.

"Now, Katharina," Millie called, scrambling after her, "please, you aren't going to make a scene at my ball, are you?"

"A scene?" Kate laughed, but there wasn't an ounce of humor in the sound. "Hell, yes, I'm going to make a scene. By the time I'm finished with my little sister, there'll be paramedics, homicide detectives and yellow police tape strung around the 'scene.'"

"You conniving little..." Kate muttered under her breath as she stomped across the perfectly manicured, dandelion-less lawn toward the gazebo, where she saw her sister having a serious discussion with her latest beau. *Bim-beau*, Kate had thought the first time she had laid eyes on the guy. Just like all the others Natalie chose. And so far, the *bim-beau du jour* hadn't given Kate any reason to change her initial opinion of him.

Jimmy Joe—or whatever his name was, she could never remember—looked slightly indignant and mildly forlorn as Natalie chattered on, appar-

ently scolding him about something. Kate had
never seen the young man display any passion that
could be described as more than "slight" or
"mild." She was certain this was his crowning vir-
tue in Natalie's eyes: a man she could completely
bully without even ruffling her demure maiden facade.

Of all people, Natalie had some nerve casting
anyone else in the role of shrew. Behind that lacy,
saccharine persona was a truly mean spirit.

"When I get my hands on you, I swear, I'll—"

At that moment, Natalie happened to glance
Kate's way and saw her older sister elbowing a
path through the already-thickening crowd of
guests. The simpering smile slid off Natalie's face,
and she quickly donned her mask, as though she
could hide behind its feeble covering.

"Natalie Burnell, I want to have a word with
you," Kate bellowed, mindless of the merrymakers
who had ceased their conversation to stare at her.

Behind Kate scurried a frantic Millie. Her hissed
whisper, "Katharina, please, don't..." reached
Kate, but she didn't slow her pace as she hurried
up the slight, grassy incline to the white wrought-
iron gazebo.

Kate knew the look on Natalie's face all too
well, even if it was half hidden behind the feathered
and rhinestone-studded mask. After more than
twenty years of living with her younger sister, Kate
could accurately read every expression. And this
one said, "Huh, oh...I'm in bi-i-ig trouble now."

And Natalie was absolutely right. This was a

down-and-dirty trick, even for her. And when Kate was hurt, Kate got even.

The gazebo had two entrances, and Natalie would have made her escape out the opposite doorway if her cumbersome skirt hadn't snagged on a honeysuckle vine. She muttered some expletives—under her breath, of course, because Natalie was always a lady. At least in public.

"Gotcha," Kate said as she grabbed her by the forearm and squeezed it far too tightly to be misconstrued as a gesture of affection. "Natalie, you are a devious, cruel little witch. I can't believe you would go to this much trouble to humiliate me."

Natalie glanced around, but even Jimmy Joe and Millie were several paces away, out of earshot. Lowering her voice, she gave Kate a nasty smirk and said, "It wasn't that much trouble, big sister. In fact, the character of the Shrew sprang to mind immediately when I thought of you."

Kate's palm itched to slap the snide expression off her sister's face and those hateful words out of her mouth. But several years ago, she had decided that physical violence—although tempting at times—wasn't an option now that they were both adults, supposedly.

"I don't know where you get off being so indignant," Natalie rattled on. "Everybody knows the part fits you perfectly. If you didn't treat people so rudely, they wouldn't call you a bit—"

Kate's hand contacted her sister's left cheek with a resounding "thwack," cutting off the end of the word.

A second later, Kate couldn't believe it had happened. If it hadn't been for the red mark on Natalie's face and the tingling in her palm, she never would have thought it possible. So much for making honorable decisions and behaving like an adult.

Remorse flowed over her, hotter than her anger had been only seconds before. Reaching for her younger sister, she said, "Oh, Nat...I'm sorry, honey. I didn't mean to—"

"No! Don't hit me again!" Natalie's emerald eyes were round with horror as she held trembling hands up to shield her face. "Please, don't hit me again!"

"What? I said I was sorry. I'm not going to..."

Turning, Kate saw that Natalie was playing to a full house. Around the gazebo stood a bevy of curious guests, wearing looks of shock and morbid fascination beneath their masks.

To Kate's deep humiliation, Natalie burst into hysterical sobs as she stumbled, practically falling over herself to get away.

The kid was trying for a daytime soap opera Emmy, Kate thought as she considered where she would like to shove the statuette if given the opportunity.

"Oh, God, did you see that?" Natalie asked her captivated audience. "She struck me. My sister *struck* me."

Backing out of the gazebo, Natalie continued to cry, wave her arms and gesticulate wildly. If Natalie was good at anything, Kate reminded herself, it was throwing a hissy fit. An underrated talent, she thought wryly, seeing the sympathy on the faces of the onlookers, as well as the hostile glances thrown her way.

"Natalie," she said, using her most patient, grit-your-teeth smile, "I didn't *strike* you. I smacked your jaws for you. Just an old-fashioned jaw-smacking was all it was, and you know you deserved it. So stop that bawling."

With a whirl of pink-and-lace skirts and a shriek of fear—or did it sound more like plain old anger?—Natalie spun around and fled across the lawn toward the garden pool, where she disappeared behind some camellias.

Kate couldn't decide whether to go after her and try to resolve the argument or turn around and make some sort of shameful retreat through the crowd of gawkers. Neither prospect appealed to her.

At that moment, she heard another shriek—this one sounding genuine—coming from the direction in which Natalie had just disappeared. The cry was closely followed by laughter—the deep, husky laughter of a male.

This time, Natalie really was hurt, and someone thought it was funny. Immediately, Kate's anger shifted gears as she ran to the spot behind the bushes where her sister had gone. Family came first. And nobody laughed at someone she loved who was in pain.

As she stormed through the camellias, raining bloodred petals onto the perfect green lawn, she saw Natalie. The pompous Bianca looked anything but arrogant. At the foot of a marble statue of Diana the Huntress, Natalie sat in a crumpled heap of velvet skirts. She was holding her right eye with both hands, rocking back and forth, sobbing.

"Nat! What is it?" Kate hurried toward her, expecting the worst but unable to imagine what it might be. What could have happened so quickly?

"O-o-o-ow," Natalie moaned, and continued to rock.

As Kate leaned over her sister, she pulled Natalie's hands away from her face and saw a dark swelling beginning to form around her eye.

"Wow, you've really hurt yourself," she said. "What happened?" But Natalie only amplified her hysterics and gave Kate a push.

Thus dismissed, Kate turned away from her screeching sister and looked at the man who stood a few yards away.

Dressed in clothing from the same era as theirs, he cut a dashing picture in forest green hose, a velvet tunic and a broad-rimmed hat with sweeping plumes. His black mask concealed his identity, but Kate didn't care who he was. He was making a feeble attempt not to laugh at her sister, and that was enough to pepper her gumbo.

She marched over to him. "Can't you see she's hurt?"

He only shook his head. "But...but you didn't see her."

A sudden, horrible thought crossed her mind. She took a step closer to him. "Did you do it? Did you hit my sister?"

"No, of course not. She came stomping through here," he said, "and she ran smack into that statue. Got her right in the eye with its fist."

He was starting to laugh again, and Kate turned to see what he meant. Diana the Huntress stood in an archer's pose, legs apart, braced to loose her arrow from its bow. With her left arm extended, her bow taut, her clenched fist was right at eye level.

Natalie's eye level.

Several of the gawkers from the gazebo had followed her and were gathered around Natalie, offering pats and words of comfort. Natalie seemed to be recovering rapidly in the center of the attention.

"Don't worry," the man said. "She isn't hurt all that badly. I checked her. She's got a bit of a shiner, and if you ask me, she deserves it."

Something about the man jogged Kate's memory. A certain husky rasp to his voice. The strong line of his chin with its slight dimple. The mischievous grin his mask couldn't hide.

"Max?" she said as the pieces of the mental puzzle began to fall into place. It was Max Colbert, the freelance architect whom Kate's father, Harry, had hired for the Sans Souci refurbishment. At first, Kate had been livid that Harry had hired anyone without even consulting her. But in the end, Kate had been forced to admit that Max had brought a great deal to the project.

But he was forever flirting with her, teasing her, pursuing her and essentially being a pain in the

backside. It was behavior she was all too familiar
with, having seen her father pursue females since
she could remember. Rumor had it that was why
her mother had left all those years ago.

Thanks to Harry's philandering and her mother's
abandonment, Kate was pretty much convinced that
both genders were worthless. When it came down
to it, the only thing you could trust people to do
was let you down. That was Kate's motto, and she
lived by it. Cynical though it might be, she found
it saved her a lot of grief.

True, Max Colbert had far more than his share
of charm, and sometimes she had to remind herself
about her motto. If she were honest, she hadn't
minded his teasing that much, but she still didn't
trust him. All that flattery couldn't be genuine.
Since when did men pay attention to her? That was
Natalie's department.

Besides, he was far too brash and boisterous for
her taste. Worse yet, he reminded her of Harry. All
flash and no substance. Men like that might be
charming, but you couldn't count on them. And
heaven help you if you loved one of them.

When she and Max had first met, Kate had convinced herself she would never love him. But she
couldn't help liking him, even now.

Lifting his mask for just a moment, Max gave
her a rakish wink. His wicked dark eyes made her
heart beat faster, in spite of her resolutions.

When he replaced the mask, doffed his hat and
bowed in courtly, Musketeer fashion, he looked

like a hero in one of those romance novels she often bought but never admitted to reading.

"At your service, milady," he said. "Though, sadly, I'm afraid I've been duped into playing the part of your Petruchio this evening. Believe me, I had no idea or I wouldn't have gone along with it."

He swept his hat in Natalie's direction. "Like I said, personally, I think she deserves that black eye."

"Petruchio, huh?" Kate considered the implications of having a sexy knave like Max play the part of her hero, the only man capable of taming the shrew Katharina. "Good casting," she muttered under her breath.

But he heard it. "I thought so, too," he added with a grin. Taking a step toward her, he caught her around the waist before she knew what he was intending. Pulling her tightly against him, he gave her a long, rough and ardently enthusiastic kiss that left her weak and unable to breathe in her tight corset.

Just like a man, she thought, pushing against him and fighting the urge to kiss him back. More specifically, just like Harry. All personality and no character.

"By the way," he said when he released her, "that's a great dress. Those...I mean, you look fantastic all cinched up like that."

"Oh!" She shoved him hard, sending him reeling backward, and marched away. She could hear him laughing and saw that several of the onlookers had noticed their exchange. Millie was staring at her with raised eyebrows and a look that clearly said she was sorry to have invited her.

First she had initiated a brawl with her sister. Now she was practically making love like a brazen hussy, right here in front of God and everyone. That sort of behavior might be common during Mardi Gras on Bourbon Street, but certainly not on the verdant, formal lawns of Sans Souci.

It was unsettling how quickly a man like Max Colbert could ruin a woman's reputation. Worse yet, while he was doing it, he could make her like it.

Deciding to redeem herself, Kate walked over to Natalie, intending to give her condolences to her sister for her black eye. As always, Natalie was the center of the social hub. A curious, sympathetic crowd had gathered around her. Jimmy Joe—whom Kate had just remembered was named Roger something—had dutifully fetched a plastic bag of frozen peas from the kitchen and was holding it over her eye.

Unfortunately, her other eye was still working perfectly, and when Natalie saw Kate coming through the crowd, she screeched again. "Oh, no...she's back," she told the nearest interested party. Instantly, everyone was interested. "My sister! She's going to hit me again."

Kate froze, speared by a dozen or more hostile looks. "What? What are you talking about?"

"Look what you did!" She ripped the bag away from Roger's hand, tearing it and spilling peas into

bout Kate by watching. Also, he loved to
lie. She was such an easy mark, and she
of the few people he had ever known
e considered ornery enough to deserve the
could dish out.

, Lady Bianca, you're getting a nasty black
o that eye of yours," he said as he watched
st guest leave her side and return to the house
e festivities. Only Roger the Faithful and Deed remained, whispering sweet consolations
holding the torn bag of peas in place.

Well, sir," she said in a syrupy southern drawl,
you were a gentleman, you would pretend not
notice."

"And if you were half the grand lady you pre-
nd to be, you wouldn't spread lies about your
ster."

Natalie's mouth popped open. She turned to
Roger, as though expecting him to come to her defense. Tough luck. His loyalty began with the frozen vegetables and ended with a larger, more intim-
idating opponent.

Max had at least five inches and fifty pounds on
him.

"Lies?" she said after giving Roger a scathing
look. "Whatever are you talking about? She
slapped me right there in the gazebo. Hard, too.
Everyone saw."

"I didn't. But I did see you run into that statue
and knock yourself flat on your rear. I have to tell
you, you looked ridiculous. One minute you're
prissing along, and the next, you're on your butt."

her lap. "You actually gave me a black eye! I
should call the police and have you arrested for
domestic violence."

Natalie turned to her sympathetic audience,
which was reveling in the performance. "It *is* domestic violence, isn't it? I mean, we're in the same
family, so it should be the same thing. I'm pretty
sure the cops have to arrest someone for that, if
there's physical evidence and all."

Heads nodded vigorously. More hostile looks
were sent in Kate's direction.

"But I only slapped you," she said, realizing
how incriminating the words sounded the moment
they left her mouth. "I smacked you on your left
cheek. That's your right eye."

Her words were lost in a new volley of shrieks
from Natalie. "See there, abusers never take responsibility for what they do," she sobbed. "They
think they can just hurt the people they love and
get away with it. I'm telling you, I've suffered so
much at the hands of my sister that I just can't bear
it any longer. Why, one time she..."

Kate's temper was about to boil over, and she
didn't trust herself to be in her sister's presence
another moment. Turning, she ran blindly in the
opposite direction, needing to put as much distance
between herself and this scene as possible.

She was only vaguely aware of bumping into
Max, of feeling his arms around her for a second,
before she shook him off and continued to race
back to the house. She thought she heard him call
her name. But she ignored him and kept running.

Kate had to get away. From her sister. From the humiliation of having everyone she knew think of her as a shrew. From the pain in her family that seemed to deepen with every passing year.

But mostly, Kate ran from her greatest enemy—her own rage.

Two

Max Colbert watched with a mi[x]tion and disgust as the remaining gu[] wounded Natalie their deepest cond[] a blatant manipulator, he thought as s[] about the horrors she had suffered at [] her wicked older sister.

After working with the family and spe[] siderable time in both sisters' presence, [] developed a distinct preference for the ol[] posedly plainer, of the two.

Natalie might have the beauty—at least b[] azine cover-girl standards. However, Max w[] his late thirties, and he had decided about fi[] years ago that blond hair, green eyes and an h[] glass figure were nice, but eventually, the wrappi[] came off the present, and it was better to find [] worthwhile gift inside.

He didn't need extrasensory perception to figure out what was beneath Natalie's tissue-thin wrapping. Under that pretty, spangled party paper was a spoiled, self-centered brat.

Ordinarily, he would have ignored a woman of her ilk, but he found the exchanges between her and Kate fascinating—mainly because of what he

He began to laugh again as the color welled in her cheeks. "It's a sight I'll never forget."

"Mr. Colbert, you are being very rude to me." She sprang to her feet and tossed the bag of peas at him. "My father was nice enough to give you a job, and you reward him by calling his daughter a liar and a bumbling fool."

He picked up the bag, took a few frozen peas from inside and stepped closer to her. "That's because you're both. And your daddy and his generosity have nothing to do with this."

"Oh, what a mean, terrible thing to say. Why are you being so unkind to me?" Tears filled her green eyes and spilled down her cheeks. Apparently, she thought that if temper couldn't persuade him, maybe the weeping maiden act would.

"Because," he said, "I resent the fact that you persuaded me to dress in this particular costume, without telling me who I was supposed to be. By doing that, you involved me in your scheme to hurt your sister, and Katharina is a friend of mine. She deserves better, and I'm going to see that she gets it. If at all possible, at your expense."

"Are you saying, sir, that you mean to do me harm?" The cold look in her one good eye was anything but genteel or feminine.

"I won't have to," he replied. "Fate has a way of taking care of people who hurt others. It's called sowing bad karma."

"What are you talking about?"

"You'll see." He dropped the frozen peas in her hand. "You'll see."

* * *

When Kate charged into the ballroom, her skirts hiked, her chest heaving, she fully intended to leave the ball that very minute. For her, the party was ruined beyond any hope of redemption. The sooner she put this miserable experience behind her, the better.

But one look at her father and she knew she was there for the remainder of the evening. He had begun drinking and was already so soused that she would have to stick around to make certain that he made his way home safely and without incident. Harry never left a party until the party was over.

The last social event they had attended, she had gone home ahead of him—and learned her lesson the hard way. At four in the morning a taxi had arrived, transporting a barely conscious Harry with a demeaning and hastily scribbled note pinned to the front of his shirt. Written by a frustrated host, the paper had said, "My name is Harry Burnell. I'm drunk. Take me to Apartment B, 172 Saint Michel Court."

With every passing day, Kate thought of her father less as an adult and more like an oversize kindergartner. It was a toss-up which would destroy his brain first, alcohol or senility. Then, there was the fact that he could be just plain cussed when he had a mind to be.

As she walked across the ballroom toward him, she saw he was wearing the costume that Natalie had selected for him. Although he looked a bit like some paintings she had seen of Henry VIII, she knew he was the Italian nobleman, Baptista Minola. Baptista was the father of the beautiful Bianca, and, of course, the shrew. Natalie had thought of everything.

Harry was talking to their construction foreman, Arnaud St. John. Arnaud and his young wife, Gertrude, had been thrilled to receive the invitation to this high-society ball. And Kate had been careful not to let Arnaud know that she was responsible for them receiving it.

Although Arnaud didn't seem to like her much, Kate harbored a deep fondness for the sensitive Creole, who worked very hard and tolerated a great deal from Harry without complaint.

Kate had another reason for liking him. Although she had stopped believing in true love long ago, she had to admit that Arnaud and Gertrude had the closest thing to it she had ever observed. And while she had given up on the idea of finding such a relationship herself, she was secretly glad that someone, somewhere, had one.

Gertrude stood near the men, shyly talking to a circle of other women. She was wearing the costume of a decidedly plump English peasant woman, with a tray of sweets and cream-filled pastries hung around her neck. Mrs. Jack Sprat.

Over six feet tall and painfully thin, Arnaud made a perfect Jack. He, too, was in peasant garb, but carried a basket of fruit and vegetables under his arm, supposedly to satisfy his "eat no fat" appetite.

He and Harry were engaged in a secretive conversation, but Kate overheard some of it as she approached them. "Feast your eyeballs on that, Arnaud," Harry was saying as he gave a nod toward one of the maids walking by, bearing glasses of champagne on a silver tray. "I always did like those little black-and-white French outfits. There's some fantasy material, eh?"

The maid had heard enough of Harry's comment to blush beneath her snow-white cap. Kate squirmed with embarrassment. Harry could be such a jerk sometimes.

Even Arnaud looked a bit uncomfortable. "My eyes and my fantasies," he said with his soft Creole accent, "are only for my Gertrude. She grows more beautiful every day as she waits to be a mother. No woman could be so lovely as she. Don't you think?"

It was Harry's turn to be embarrassed, having been so gently reproved.

Too gently, as far as Kate was concerned.

"Yeah, Harry," she told him as she joined them and slipped her arm through his. "You should lower that mask a bit—your snout is showing. Oink, oink."

With her hand on his forearm, she gave a squeeze that was intended to get his attention.

"Ouch." He pulled away from her with a wounded look. "So, what are you going to do now? Beat up the old man, too?"

"Oh, no. Not you, too." She took a deep breath of resignation. "I don't know what you heard, but I didn't give Natalie that black eye."

"Black eye? Who said anything about that? I just heard that you slapped her stupid in the gazebo."

"I slapped her on the cheek, not her gazebo...and she was already stupid."

"So, what about the black eye?"

Kate could tell she wasn't going to win this one. When it came to Natalie, she always lost with Harry.

"Never mind," she said. "I'm sure you'll hear all the gory details later."

She looked at Arnaud and saw an expression of fear and distrust on his face. "Really, Arnaud," she said, "I didn't actually hurt anyone. It was a misunderstanding, that's all."

"I'm sure it was, Mademoiselle Katharina." He nodded vigorously. "I'm certain you speak the truth."

He wasn't certain; he was just kissing up to her. She could see it all over his dark, sensitive face. This young man, whom she liked and respected very much, was actually afraid of her. Deserved or not, her reputation seemed to taint every relationship she had.

"I think I had better see to Gertrude. *Au revoir.*" Arnaud hurried away to his wife's side, where they talked in hushed tones. Gertrude sent Kate a quick, apprehensive glance before the two of them exited the room.

"What's the matter with him?" Kate asked as she watched them go. "It's not like I'm going to rip his head off and stick it in that basket he's carrying."

"It's not like you're above it," Harry muttered.

"What?" Several people turned to look, and Kate realized she had raised her voice several notches.

"You're always bossing him around on the job," Harry elaborated.

Kate stared at him, confused. "What's your point? He's the foreman, and I'm an owner. I *am* his boss."

"Well, that isn't easy for a man to swallow. It's one thing for you to hang around and contribute here and there about decorating and woman-stuff, but you don't need to be givin' orders like you do."

"Don't need to..."

Kate's blood pressure soared as she thought of all the difficult decisions she had made over the past six months when Harry had been too deeply "in his cups" to be of any use. She thought of all the orders she had executed that had been absolutely necessary under the circumstances, the responsibilities she had shouldered, the problems she'd solved. And this was the thanks she received?

How typical of Harry.

How typical of men in general, as far as she was concerned.

"Now that I think of it," she said, looking pointedly at the seat of his pants. "It isn't just your snout that's showing."

"What?" He twisted his head around, trying to see his rear. "What are you talking about?"

As she turned and walked away, Kate mumbled, "Apparently, Natalie isn't the only member of this family who doesn't have to be slapped to be stupid."

"My goodness, what is that dreadful noise?" asked Calamity Jane, who stood with Buffalo Bill beside one of the French doors leading onto the downstairs gallery.

Kate thought she had found her refuge here in the music room, with its gentle, quiet ambience— but that had just been shattered by some of the worst singing she had ever heard. Or at least, she thought it was singing. Either that, or someone was slaughtering hogs on the upstairs balcony.

Calamity and Buffalo hurried outside, along with several other famous and infamous couples, to investigate. Kate decided to remain behind and ignore the commotion. But seconds later, an excited Cleopatra stuck her head into the room and said, "Are you Katharina, the fair of face and sweet of spirit?"

"No. I'm Katharina of the premenstrual syndrome."

"Oh, sorry."

Cleopatra disappeared, but moments later, Peter Pan and Wendy decided to visit. "There's a guy up there on the roof," Peter told her.

"And he's asking for you," Wendy added cheerfully.

Max. The thought sent a rush of irritation through her, and something else she didn't want to consider right now.

"Tell him I'm not coming, to go ahead and jump."

Peter and Wendy ducked their heads and disappeared as efficiently as Cleo. But the wailing continued and so did the discordant guitar playing. Kate could see a crowd gathering outside the French doors. With a little effort, she could vaguely recognize the lyrics to "Beautiful Dreamer," one of her favorite old folk songs. And he was murdering it.

"Oh, for Pete's sake," she said as she threw open the doors and stomped out onto the gallery.

Leaning out from the rail, she looked up and saw Max on the balcony above. He was grinning broadly, strumming an old guitar with all his might, and singing in at least five different keys.

"What the hell do you think you're doing?" she shouted up at him.

"Ah...serenading you?"

"Embarrassing me is more like it." She heard the titters rippling through their audience. "Are you drunk?"

"Only with love for you, milady."

He strummed another discord across the strings and broke one. The end of it whipped up and hit him on the side of the face. "Bea-uuu-tiful—ooow! Damn, that hurt!"

"Max, has anyone ever told you that you can't

play the guitar worth a darn and you sing like a coyote sitting in a patch of prickly pear cactus?''

"Well, actually...yes. I have been told that on occasion. But I figured it was the thought that counted."

"Besides," she observed, "aren't *I* supposed to be on the balcony, and you on the ground beneath?"

"Oh, yeah. That's what it was. I knew something was backward."

Once again, he strummed his now-five-stringed guitar with an enthusiasm that would have been admirable, had there been any harmony to the sound. Still leaning over the railing and looking up at him, Kate suddenly felt something strike her between the eyes.

"Hey, what—" There at her feet lay a tiny plastic triangle.

"My pick! Hey, Kate, I think I dropped my pick. Could you look around down there and see if you can find it? Kate? Kate? Hey, Ka-a-a-te!"

Three

On the landing of the main staircase, Kate found the perfect hiding spot: a Victorian love seat, hidden by a copse of luxuriant potted palms. With the plants in place, hardly anyone could see her sitting there, and those who could hopefully wouldn't recognize her behind the mask she wore.

From this cozy alcove, she could sit, watch the guests glide up and down the curving stairway, listen to the band playing in the ballroom below and wait for this infernal evening to end.

It was a good plan and a good hiding place. Until, fifteen minutes later, Max found her.

"Hey, what a great idea," he said as he deftly slipped behind the palms and onto the seat beside her. Leaning over, he tugged one of the pots a foot or so to one side, creating an even more private screen. "There." He cocked his head and surveyed his results. "Now we have the perfect make-out spot."

"Make-out? Wh-what are you—"

Before Kate realized what he was doing, he had one arm around her shoulders, the other around her waist, and he'd yanked her into the middle of the love seat. Holding her tightly against him, he began to nuzzle her neck.

"For heaven's sake, stop that. I'm still mad at you for that ridiculous scene on the balcony." She tried to push him away, but the effort was as feeble as the conviction in her voice.

Delicious shivers traveled from the spot where his lips touched her and spread all over her body like the intoxication of a strong, sweet mint julep on a hot summer evening. For a moment she allowed herself to be caught up in the fantasy. Here she was, dressed in the gown of a noblewoman of long ago, being seduced by a lover wearing a black satin mask and full Musketeer regalia. It would be so easy to just enjoy the moment, to forget about her cold, colorless reality and lose herself in the illusion of a yesteryear romance.

But it *was* an illusion, after all, no matter how charming the illusionist. And the further she allowed herself to sink into the dream, the more acute her disappointment would be upon awakening.

Better now than later, she reminded herself.

"Max, I mean it," she mumbled halfheartedly. With one hand she pushed against his chest and tried not to be so aware of the hard definition of his muscles. She didn't really want to know that his heart was beating double time, like hers. "Stop doing that...um...right now. I mean it."

"Okay."

As quickly as he had begun the seduction, he ended it. With an abruptness that stunned her, he released her and faced forward with his arms crossed over his chest, wearing a mischievous smirk beneath his mask.

"You...you stopped." She heard the frustration in her own voice and cursed her transparency.

"Of course I did. I'm a gentleman. If a lady tells me to stop, I stop. That's it, that's all."

"Oh."

"Oh? Do I detect just a tad of disappointment? A smidgen of regret? A modicum of—"

"Oh, shut up. You're so blasted conceited. You think you're such a—"

"Good kisser? I am. A *damned* good kisser." He leaned closer, arms still crossed. "Wanna find out for yourself? That little peck in the garden this afternoon wasn't nearly enough to make a proper judgment."

"I'll just take your word for it."

"But I might be lying."

"You wouldn't be the first."

"Whoa. Do I detect a little bitterness in those words?" He placed one hand beneath her chin and forced her to look up at him. When she didn't reply, he said, "It sounds as though some of my predecessors were less than honest with you."

Kate hesitated. Her personal history wasn't a book she eagerly opened for anyone. But something in his dark eyes told her that his interest wasn't casual or nosy. He genuinely wanted to know.

She shrugged. "No big deal. Mr. Right Number One forgot to mention that there was a Mrs. Right and three little Right kiddies."

"Oooh, low blow."

"Yes, that's exactly what I gave him."

"Good."

"And then, Mr. Right Number Two courted me long enough to embezzle six figures from Burnell Construction, then *he* dumped *me*. Of course, that was before I found out about the money. Now he's serving a seven-to-ten-year sentence. Like I said, no big deal."

"Sounds like a big deal to me. If I were you, I'd be pretty peeved with men."

"Men? Why be so selective? We women are foolish enough to let you lie to us. We are co-conspirators in our own betrayals." She paused and drew a deep breath of resolve. "Nope, I believe in equal opportunities, Max. I'm peeved with everyone."

He studied her for a long time, as though deciding whether or not she was serious. Finally, he saw that she was. "That's hard work, being mad at the whole world. You'll wear yourself out, Kate."

For just a moment, his words rang like a clear note of truth through her tired spirit. Was that why she felt so empty, so drained?

Immediately, she dismissed the thought. No, she had just been working too hard. That had to be it.

"If I'm tired, it's because I do everyone else's job and get very little in return. Not even a thank-you or acknowledgment."

He nodded thoughtfully. "I noticed that. To hear Natalie tell it, she runs Burnell Construction single-handedly. But in the few months I worked with

Burnell, I didn't actually seen her lifting a single one of those hands to do anything useful.''

''Nor will you. Natalie has Harry convinced that she's a hothouse orchid who would positively wilt if given any responsibility. He buys the helpless female routine, because it falls in line with his own antiquated idea of women—beautiful but useless, unless they're in the kitchen, nursery or bedroom.''

''But I got the idea she's actually paid for her services.''

''She is. As much as I am. Harry holds fifty-two percent of the company. The remaining forty-eight is divided equally between Natalie and me. And we're both paid salaries for the work we do...or don't do, as is the case with her.''

''No wonder you're peeved. How do you sit still for that?''

Kate paused long enough to enjoy this rare moment of sharing. She had never discussed these matters with anyone and had never expected another person to understand and support her, even if she had confided in them. This was such a delightful surprise.

''I take it because I have to,'' she said. ''Don't think I haven't given Harry a piece of my mind about it. I have, but he doesn't listen. If I can't do anything about it, there's no point in continuing to bang my head against a stone wall.''

''I suppose. But it still isn't fair.''

''Besides...'' She felt a shy smile steal over her face and was grateful for the mask. If only she could wear it all the time. ''I don't do it for the money, anyway. I work because I enjoy it. Harry would let us both sit at home on our butts if we wanted. But then I would miss out on opportunities like this.'' She waved her hand, indicating the grand old house.

Catching her hand, he laced his fingers through hers. ''And you wouldn't have met me, heaven forbid.''

She snatched her hand away. ''Oh, yes…heaven forbid.''

''Admit it, Kate. I'm a nice guy,'' he said, grabbing her hand again and pressing her fingers, one by one, to his lips. ''I'm a nice guy.''

'' 'Nice guy' is an oxymoron.''

''Well, this guy's no moron…though I think I am a little crazy. About you, that is.''

He nibbled her pinkie, then sucked it into his mouth where he gave it a couple of provocative flicks with his tongue. Erotic thoughts danced through her mind, just enough to send a blush to her cheeks and the rest of her blood to other, more feminine areas of her body.

''How can you say that?'' she asked, trying not to sound breathless. ''You hardly even know me.''

''I'd like to get to know you better. Much better. You're the one preventing that.''

''You're teasing me.''

He began to trace sensual spirals with the tip of his tongue on the center of her palm, then inside her wrist. The sensation went through her—hot, liquid heat.

''Yes,'' he whispered as he worked his way up

the inside of her arm. "Just like you're teasing me by wearing that gorgeous gown. I mean...I thought you probably had a nice figure, but with that corset pushing everything up and...and out like that. Oh, man, it's all I can do not to just..."

Once again, he was nibbling at her neck. This time, inching his way downward toward her cleavage.

"Kate, my sweet Kate," he whispered, dipping lower and lower. "Promise me something."

"What?" She was both suspicious and tantalized by the gleam in his black eyes.

"Promise first, then I'll tell you what."

"No way. What is it?"

He smiled, then trailed the tip of his forefinger across the tops of her breasts. The touch was so light she hardly felt it, but it was enough to make her heart nearly stop. "Promise me," he said, his voice low and husky, "that you'll wear this corset the first time we go to bed together. Would you do that for me, sweet Kate?"

"Wha-what?"

"You heard me. It would make me the happiest man in the world if you would do that one little thing for me."

Before she knew it, his lips were moving, warm and moist, over her right breast, just above the lace edge of her bodice where he had touched. The contact felt better than anything on earth had a right to feel, but his words scared her to death.

"Why, no!" She tangled her fingers in his dark, curly hair and pulled him away. "I would not! I wouldn't wear this corset or anything else to bed with you, Max Colbert.''

For a moment he stared, speechless, into her blue eyes as they both fought to catch their breath and gather their composure. Then he threw back his head and laughed a deep, hearty laugh that washed over and through her. Grinning, he grabbed her by the upper arms and said, "Nothing at all! Oh, Kate, thank you, you little vixen! You *have* made me the happiest man in the world.''

Over his shoulder, she could see a couple of elderly ladies in antebellum finery peering at them through the palms. Their eyes were wide behind their masks, their mouths agape, positively scandalized!

"But that's not what I meant,'' Kate said, or rather tried to say. It was difficult to speak, because Max was kissing her, long...and deep...and hard....

And he had been absolutely right. Max Colbert was a damned good kisser!

Four

Sitting on the staircase landing love seat, hidden by the potted palms, Katharina Burnell reasoned that she was a person of at least average courage.

About five years ago, the warehouse where Burnell Construction stored their supplies had caught fire. Although Harry had panicked, forgetting even to call the fire department, and Natalie had run around screaming as though the seat of her britches had been aflame, Kate had kept her head. By the time the fire engines had arrived, the fire had been nearly put out, thanks to Kate's and Arnaud St. John's quick use of several fire extinguishers.

Then there had been the hurricane and the ensuing flood. Harry had paced the floor and worried. Natalie had taken off for an impromptu vacation to New York. And Kate had been the one teetering on a ladder, boarding up the windows of the family home, stocking the groceries and fresh water, which had been hers and Harry's mainstay for the better part of two weeks.

Yes, Kate figured she had at least average courage. But not enough to risk her heart to love a man like Max Colbert.

As soon as he released her from his kiss, she

sprang to her feet and made a desperate, and less than elegant, escape. Two minutes later, she felt like a fool, hiding in one of the upstairs bedrooms in the dark. With her back against the door, she was panting like an Australian sheepdog after a tough day of herding.

She heard him pass through the hallway a couple of times, calling her name, saying ridiculous things like, "Come out, sweet Kate...wherever you are. There's no point in running from it. Our fate has been sealed with a kiss. So, pucker up, buttercup."

Good grief, she thought, trying to breathe with the corset stays cutting into her ribs. What if someone hears him carrying on like that?

Her reputation, lousy though it might have been even before the ball, was in a shambles now, thanks to Natalie's temper tantrums. Did Max have to make things even worse with his ridiculous cater-wauling?

Everyone around her seemed to be going stark raving crazy tonight!

After waiting awhile to make sure Max was gone, she had decided to sneak out of the room, when she heard a sound behind her in the darkness. She jumped and nearly screamed. Geez, but her nerves were strung tightly after the evening's mis-events.

"Who's there?" she whispered to the darkness. "Who is it?" she repeated when no one answered.

Finally, she heard a sniffled reply. "It's me, Gertrude."

"Arnaud's Gertrude?"

The answer was more snuffling and wheezing.

Feeling along the wall beside the door, Kate located the light switch. She flipped it, and the room was bathed in a soft, rosy light—another of hers and Max's innovations: they had wired the old gas wall sconces for electricity.

Across the room, sitting on the edge of a four-posted bed, was Mrs. Jack Sprat. She held a handful of tissues from a box on the nightstand and was dabbing at her tear-reddened face. She had removed her mask and the blond wig with its springy curls and had tossed them onto the bed. Her own short, dark hair was plastered flat against her head.

Kate had seen her looking much better.

"Gertrude, what's wrong?" Kate was shocked at the complete change in the usually cheerful young woman's appearance and demeanor. Often, Gertrude showed up unexpectedly at their job sites with a gourmet lunch for Arnaud and would steal him away for an hour. He would return with an enormous grin on his face that suggested she might have furnished "dessert," as well. In the two years Arnaud had worked for them, Kate had never seen Gertrude down or depressed, let alone crying like this.

"It's nothing," Gertrude replied, rolling her tissues into a tight ball. "I'm just a little tired, I think."

"Tired? Since when do people cry like that just because they're tired?"

Kate walked over to her and sat beside her on the white crocheted bedspread. Although she couldn't be sure, Kate thought she saw Gertrude lean away from her—just a bit—as though she were uneasy to have Kate so near.

"Really, I'm all right," Gertrude said. "I was just feeling a little sorry for myself, but I'm over it now, Miss Burnell."

"Please, call me Kate. Everyone does. Unless, of course, they're calling me something much worse," Kate added with a wry laugh. She had intended the comment to be funny, but like everything else she said tonight, it had come out sounding bitter.

"Okay…Kate." Gertrude looked miserable, and Kate had the distinct impression that her presence was making the woman feel worse rather than better. Why did she always seem to have that effect on people?

"Gertrude, would you rather I leave?"

As soon as Kate had spoken the words, she wished she had thought of a more tactful way of asking. More than once she had been accused of being too blunt, abrupt, even rude. She didn't mean to be; she just didn't see any point in wasting time, beating around the bush.

But on the other hand, she didn't want to hurt or upset a gentle soul like Gertrude.

"What I meant to say—" she drew a deep breath, framing her words as carefully as she could "—is that if you would prefer to be alone, I'd be glad leave you to your solitude."

Gertrude twisted the tissues in her hand, and

Kate could have sworn that she actually looked afraid. Of what? Of her?

"Gertrude, are you afraid of me?" There, she had done it again. Just blurted the words out with no thought of finesse, diplomacy or tact. Oh, well, it was one way to get right to the heart of the matter.

"Well, I..."

Kate had seen a happier expression on the face of a deer caught in her headlights.

"If you are, just say so."

"Oh, dear. Miss Burn—I mean, Kate. I don't know what you want me to say. Arnaud needs his job so much, with the baby coming and all, and I—"

"For heaven's sake, Gertrude! I'm not going to fire Arnaud because you don't answer my question correctly. I just want you to tell me the truth. Are you afraid of me?"

Slowly, the young woman nodded, placing one hand protectively over her protruding tummy. Although Kate was certain the gesture was subconscious, it went straight to her heart.

"May I ask why?" she said as gently as she could.

Gertrude pulled a few more tissues from the box. "It's just...you know...things I've heard."

"Like what?"

"Like that you...ah...you raise your voice a lot to the men at work. And you tell them that if they don't do a good job, you'll fire them."

Kate thought that one over for a moment. "Yeah, so?"

"Arnaud says that some are lazy and don't work, or they mess up, and they need to be fired. But he says…"

"Go on."

"That some of them want very much to please you…but you still…you know…yell."

Kate's first impulse was to shout back an indignant response to defend herself, but she realized the folly of that approach and snapped her mouth shut just in time. Maybe there was a seed—a teeny, tiny grain—of truth in what Gertrude had said. There were times when she lost her patience and said things a bit more emphatically than she had intended.

Something Gertrude had said stuck in her mind, and she wanted to make certain she had heard correctly. "Arnaud said that some of them really do want to please me?"

"Sure they do. They're happy to work for such a fine company as Burnell Construction. They know you're the best in the business. They want you to be proud of them. They want you to think *they* are the best."

"But I do, or else I wouldn't have hired them. I wouldn't keep them on my payroll."

Gertrude shrugged her padded shoulders. "Then maybe you should tell them so…just once in a while."

"I thought I did. But now that you mention it, I

suppose I am more likely to tell them what isn't going right rather than to mention what is.''

The two women sat in silence for a few moments, as Kate assimilated her new information. Ordinarily, she might have been offended at this criticism, but coming from the gentle Gertrude, it hardly seemed judgmental at all. Just practical.

''Is there anything else you've heard?'' Kate asked. In for a penny, in for a pound of brass tacks. Even if they would be hard to swallow.

''Umm...just that maybe you may have sort of...last week you might have kinda...thrown your sister out of the office. And she might have fallen down a little, right there in the dirt, and might have skinned her knees. I may have heard a little something like that.''

''A little something, huh? Sounds like you heard all the gory details. And I suppose Arnaud told you about that, too?''

''No, it was someone else.''

''Well, did that someone else mention that the reason I was sending her home was because she showed up for work—as much as she ever does, that is—on a construction site, wearing short shorts and a skimpy halter top with a bare midriff?''

Gertrude's eyes widened, and Kate could tell she had scored a point. ''No, he didn't mention that.''

''And did he tell you that, while I may have given her a little, tiny push toward the door, she fell down the steps because she was wearing five-inch stiletto heels with her short shorts?''

''No way!''

"*Yes* way."

A fire of anger gleamed in Gertrude's soft eyes. "I'm glad you threw her out. I would have even thrown her down the stairs! She's got a lot of nerve wearing some getup like that in front of the men. In front of *my* man."

Without warning, Gertrude's face screwed up and tears began to roll again. "That's the problem. There are too many women like your sister in the world—a lot of them right here at this party. They're so pretty and sexy and...and just look at me!" She pointed to her swollen figure and began sobbing anew. "I love my Arnaud, but I can't even be pretty for him now. I look awful and I cry all the time over...over ev-ev-everything."

"Oh, Gertrude. I know your husband. He'd think you were beautiful and sexy if you were wearing a barrel—and shaped like one, too."

Instead of taking comfort from her words, Gertrude seemed to get even more upset, grabbing tissues and honking into them like a goose with a sinus blockage. Kate didn't know what to do; her knowledge of pregnant ladies and their idiosyncrasies was woefully inadequate for the occasion.

Just then she heard a movement toward the doorway and turned to see an angry Arnaud standing there, staring at them with a thunderous look on his face.

"What's going on here?" he demanded, striding into the room. "Gertie, what's wrong? Did she say something to you?"

Before waiting for Gertrude to reply, he turned

on Kate. "Why is my wife so upset? What did you
do to her?"

Kate was flabbergasted. Sure, he was feeling
overly protective under the circumstances, but to
accuse her?

"Nothing!" she snapped as she jumped to her
feet. "I didn't—"

Pushing her aside, he reached for Gertrude, who
was crying even harder now. "Gertie, *mon petit
chou.* Don't weep, my love. It is over now. Arnaud
is here."

He pulled her up from the bed and into his arms.
"Whatever Mademoiselle Burnell said or did, she
won't do it again, I promise you."

"I didn't *do* anything, except comfort her, you
jerk!" Kate had endured about all of this she could
stand. First she was a sister-beater and now an
abuser of expectant mothers. Where on earth had
this madness begun?

"She was...was...just talking to me," Gertrude
managed to say between hiccups. "I was feeling
fat and ugly, and Kate was trying to make me feel
better."

Arnaud's thin face blushed beneath its olive coloring. "*Mon Dieu, je regrette.* I am so sorry, Mademoiselle Burnell. I only thought—"

"I know what you thought," Kate replied more
angrily than she had intended. "You thought I had
insulted or hurt your wife. I suppose that tells me
what you think of me as a person."

She expected him to reply, but instead, he hung
his head and stared at the floor. His silence was,

somehow, more cutting than his previous accusations. Not knowing how to improve upon the miserable situation, Kate decided the best thing was to leave. But as she made her graceless exit, she had the uncomfortable realization that she was walking away from a lot of awkward situations lately.

Even worse, Kate felt as though she had been making graceless exits most of her life.

From the end of the hallway, Max Colbert watched Kate leave the bedroom and walk slowly down the staircase to the main floor. Her bowed head and dispirited posture told him that something had happened, again. Kate's problems seemed to follow her from room to room in this mansion as predictably as they did from one of her relationships to the next.

Her inability to get along with people fascinated him. He had never seen anyone so badly misunderstood. Between her sister and the other gossipmongers, Kate's reputation not only preceded her, but paved the way for trouble long before she arrived. And, although Max was extremely fond of Kate, he had to admit that she often precipitated her own problems. He had never known anyone so gifted at keeping people at a distance. He suspected it was a talent she despised and would be glad to be rid of. If she only knew how.

Playing amateur psychologist, Max theorized that Kate Burnell had erected the steel bars around herself years ago for protection. The irony was she was being held prisoner by her own fortress, yet those bars did nothing to stop the arrows and darts that easily penetrated and stung so badly.

He would find a way to break through those steel bars and rescue the dainty damsel in distress, whether she wanted to be or not. He just had to make sure that, while he was saving this fragile female from herself, he didn't wind up with his giblets in a blender.

Five

Katharina was grateful for the mask that hid her tears as she hurried down the stairs, through the house and into the gardens. Finding a tiny, cloistered cove beneath some giant oaks, she ducked between the boxwood hedges and secreted herself there.

She couldn't recall an evening where she had run from one hiding place, only to seek out another so soon. Usually, she didn't try to escape like this. Usually, she stood toe-to-toe with whatever bothered her, did battle and resolved the issue forthwith.

For some reason, she didn't feel as inclined to fight tonight. Maybe it was the ultrafeminine dress, she told herself. Fighting was a bit difficult when hampered by a corset and petticoats. But as Kate found a seat on a white wrought-iron bench and sat there, gazing at her reflection in the tiny goldfish pond at her feet, she knew that her lack of combative inclination had nothing to do with her apparel.

More than almost any time she could remember, tonight's events had really stung her deeply. Natalie's betrayals had never been so blatant or public. And never had anyone Kate regarded as highly as

Arnaud been so suspicious of her, so convinced that she had hurt an innocent person. Natalie's insensitivity, she could almost put aside, or at least pretend to. But Arnaud was different. He was an intelligent, caring soul who apparently thought she was capable of cruelty.

What had she done to gain such a reputation? Was Natalie right? Did *everyone* think she was a cold, hard shrew?

One by one, memories filled her mind. At first they came in a trickle, then a stream, and finally a flood. Times when she had been unnecessarily harsh with those around her, but had rationalized her behavior as nothing more than upholding high standards. Times when she had been ungrateful, telling herself that others didn't need or want her praise. After all, she didn't receive any, so why should they? They got their paychecks every two weeks; that should be enough.

She recalled so many times when her father had warned her to watch her temper, act like a lady, speak more kindly and treat those around her with more consideration. She had responded by telling him that sweet-speaking ladies got nowhere fast. She had reminded him that he had told her for years how disappointed he'd been that she had been born female. If ladies were such a valued commodity, why had he grieved that he had no son?

Now, looking back, she recalled the pain in Harry's eyes. Although her accusation may have been true, she had accomplished nothing by speaking it, and in such a harsh tone.

Yes, maybe Natalie had been right all along. Maybe everyone *did* think she was a bitch.

And what disturbed Kate most was the nagging fear that maybe they were right. When all was said and done, maybe she thought so, too.

"Excuse me, Mr. Burnell. Have you seen Kate?" Max asked Harry, whose height and girth were unmistakable beneath his Italian gentleman's costume. So was his booming voice, which resounded through the library, drowning out most of the conversations that were being attempted by the other guests in the room.

Since accepting the assignment months ago with Burnell Construction, Max had tried to convince himself that he liked Harry Burnell. He was a jolly sort, though sometimes his joviality became excessive to the point of downright irritation. His generosity was endearing, though Max often thought that some of that charity would have been well spent on his oldest daughter.

Mostly, Harry struck Max as a big, bombastic blowhard with a good heart. But he did require a lot of patience.

"What did you say, sonny?" Harry asked, cupping a hand to one ear. The other arm was wrapped tightly around a young lady wearing a French can-can girl's dress. The woman looked uncomfortable with the intimate level of attention Harry was paying her, and she seemed relieved for the interruption.

"I asked if you had seen Kate lately," Max repeated.

"Last time I saw her, she was hightailing it out to the garden. Looked like the back of her dress was on fire, the amount of ground she was covering."

He stopped and laughed loudly in the dancer's ear. Max didn't think the joke was particularly humorous, and it seemed the woman didn't, either. She tried to pull away from Harry, but his arm tightened, drawing her closer.

"I was gonna go after her," Harry continued, "but she was movin' too fast for this old fellow."

"Oh, I don't know," the girl mumbled. "You move pretty fast for an old far—I mean, fellow."

Harry was too far into his cups to catch the insult.

Max decided to do his good deed for the day. Turning to the woman, he said, "By the way, ah..."

"Jonquil," she supplied.

"Ah, yes, Jonquil. I heard Millie asking for you. They need you in the kitchen. Some sort of an emergency, I believe."

"The kitchen?" Harry asked. "Why would they want her in the kitchen? You aren't one of the waitresses, are you, sweet thing?"

"Well, no, but..." The woman looked helplessly at Max.

"They want her to do a cancan when they bring out the cake," Max said. "I think it's a surprise that Millie arranged for old Charles."

"Surprise him?" Harry laughed. "He'll likely have a stroke. The higher you raise that skirt of yours, honey, the higher his blood pressure will go! You'd better watch it, sugar. I know I will!"

Offering the woman his arm, Max ushered her out of the library before Harry made an even bigger ass of himself. The more time Max spent around Harry Burnell, the more he appreciated what a handful of trouble Kate had taken upon herself, trying to keep the company afloat and the old man in line.

Max recalled that, one time, when he and Kate had been arguing over some minor issue to do with the redesigning of the Sans Souci kitchen, she had accused Max of being too much like Harry. A "flamboyant fool" with "more flash than substance." Those had been her exact words; he remembered them all too well.

As Max ushered Harry's happily released conquest from the library, he could hear Harry laughing raucously, making yet another inappropriate remark aimed at some unlucky female in the room.

Max vowed to do whatever was necessary to change Kate's opinion of him in that respect. The last thing he wanted was to remind her of Harry.

When Kate looked up from her reflection in the pond and saw Max standing there, a dark, masculine silhouette against the distant terrace lights, she felt a mixture of emotions, all potent and frightening.

She was happy not to be alone with her disturbing thoughts, happy to have anyone's company. Especially his. But she was suspicious of her own feelings of joy. Something that felt so good never lasted. Particularly if there was a man involved.

She felt grateful and flattered that he had sought her out, had come to her without her beckoning, as though he sensed her need. On the other hand, why was he here? For all her romantic notions, Kate felt she had to be practical. No man pursued a woman the way Max was chasing her unless he had an ulterior motive. Harry and her own life experiences had taught her that. As much as she wished Max had come here for altruistic reasons, she couldn't be naive enough to believe such a thing.

And of all her emotions, shame was foremost. When he had entered her private alcove, she had been sobbing her eyes out. He had heard her. And now, standing there, he could see her humiliation firsthand.

Katharina Burnell hardly ever cried. And she certainly didn't do it in front of another person. The embarrassment of being caught like this was almost more than she could bear.

She heard him clear his throat as he took a tentative step closer to the bench where she sat. "I've been looking everywhere for you, Kate," he said. "May I join you?"

His politeness surprised her so much that she stopped crying. This was quite a change from the man who had practically mauled her behind the palm trees.

Not that you minded being mauled all that much,

she reminded herself in a brief moment of self-honesty.

"Umm...yeah...I guess so."

Slowly, she moved to one end of the wrought-iron bench, making room for him. But the main reason she moved was to place herself deeper into the shadows. Even with her mask on, she didn't want him to see her tear-swollen face.

If he did, he would start asking her questions she wouldn't want to answer, not even to herself, let alone him.

"So, tell me, sweet Kate," he said, his voice soft and low in the semidarkness, "why are you crying?"

So much for avoiding unwanted questions, she thought with a sigh. Sometimes this man's openness was refreshing, but just as often it disarmed and nonplussed her. Didn't he know how to play society's subtle, face-saving games?

"Nothing's wrong," she replied, challenging him with the blatant lie. If he were going to pry into her psyche, she didn't have to make it easy for him.

"You aren't the kind of person who cries over nothing," he said. "Please, tell me about it."

The gentleness of his tone was her undoing. Instead of steeling herself further against the intimacy he offered, instead of playing the game cool and collected, she found herself blubbering worse than before.

A badly needed handkerchief suddenly appeared

in his hand. He shoved it into hers, and she gratefully blew on it.

"I've just been sitting here, thinking," she offered, hoping he would be satisfied with this tidbit, knowing he wouldn't be.

"About?"

"Myself, okay?"

"Mmm, yourself. That's one of my favorite subjects." He placed one arm around her shoulders and gave her a little sideways hug. "Let's talk about yourself, Katharina."

She shrugged his arm off. "Let's not. Right now, I'm not my favorite subject. Far from it."

"A little down on ourselves, are we?"

"Why not? Everyone else is." Even as she spoke the petulant words, she heard the self-pity underlying them. She winced and prepared herself for him to call her on that, too.

"I'm not down on you."

His words were simple and went straight to her heart. He actually sounded as though he meant them. But then, she had learned by childhood observations and adult experiences that people, especially men, seldom meant even half of what they said.

"Well, if you aren't," she said, far more flippantly than she felt, "it's just because you don't know me well enough."

"I know you better than you think I do. For instance, I know where all that anger of yours is coming from."

She didn't want to travel this road of conversation. It hurt far too much. But she couldn't seem to resist hearing his insights. "Okay, Dr. Sigmund Colbert," she said, "do tell. Reveal to me the true roots of my rage, the foundations of my fury. Let me have it with both barrels."

He said nothing for a long moment, just stared at her. "My, my, you are good at sarcasm," he said finally. "Far too good for your own good...if you know what I mean."

"Thank you."

"I didn't exactly mean it to be a compliment."

"So much for you not being down on me, now that you've seen a fatal flaw in my character."

"Not at all. Your sarcasm, your anger, your cynicism—they're all a smoke screen you throw up to keep us from seeing inside."

"How astute of you, sir. And what a generous interpretation. Most people just chalk it up to me being a sarcastic, ill-tempered bitch."

"Very few people think that, and maybe you should consider the fact that it's to their advantage to paint you that way."

"What do you mean?"

"I mean, when you lose your temper and play the part of the shrew, it places you in the perfect position to be their scapegoat."

A cool, damp breeze blew through the oaks overhead, stirring their leaves with a soft, whispering rustle. Draped from the gnarled limbs, the Spanish moss swayed—delicate, black webbing that filtered the golden glow of the terrace gaslights. Kate shivered and crossed her arms over her chest.

"Cold?" he asked.

"No. More like chilled," she replied, thinking of Natalie, Harry and the occasional lazy worker she had fired. Being able to label her as a bitch had paid off handsomely for all of them. As long as she and her bad temper could be blamed, they didn't have to take responsibility for their own actions.

"I know why you do it, Kate," Max said. Once again, he placed his arm around her shoulder, and this time she didn't push him away. The gesture felt more companionable than sexual. It felt good— all the way to her heart.

"Why I do what?" she asked.

"Rage like you do."

She wanted to know, but she was afraid to ask. So she sat quietly, waiting for him to continue.

"You react with anger because you're hurt."

"Hurt! I'm not hurt!" She jumped up from her seat and backed away from him until she was against the hedges. "Natalie is the one who's always hurt, whining and blubbering all over the place like an idiot. I'm not like that."

"No, you aren't. Natalie isn't hurt—she just pretends to be to get her way. You, on the other hand, are the one who's really bleeding inside, because she and Harry—"

"Shut up! You're wrong. Those fools can't hurt me. I'm just plain mad!"

"They *can* hurt you and they do, all the time. They have the power to hurt you because you love them."

"That isn't true! Nothing they say hurts me. I

just get tired of their stupidity and..." She couldn't finish the rest of her tirade, because, to her deep humiliation, she was sobbing too hard.

Max rose from the bench and walked over to her. He handed her the handkerchief she had dropped on the ground. Slowly, he removed her mask, then wiped one of her tears away with his thumb. "If you can't be hurt, sweet Kate, why are you crying?"

Unable to think of anything intelligent to say, she said the first thing that came to her mind. "It's your fault...for being nice to me. Stop it! Right now." She grabbed her mask, then tried to slap his hand away, but he caught her wrist and held it tightly.

"No," he said. "I'm not going to stop it. It's high time somebody was nice to you, and it might as well be me."

With his other hand, he reached behind her and pulled her into his arms. As though comforting a hurt child, he began to kiss the top of her hair, her forehead, her tear-wet cheeks.

"Poor Kate," he whispered. "You've always had to be so strong. But you don't have to be strong with me, Katharina. Just be with me. Just be."

Just be. The words flowed through her as he held her close against his chest. *Just be.*

To be a part of the rain-moist night wind. To be part of the comforting darkness. For a single, precious moment in time, to be part of another human being, to feel him against her, warm and solid, lending his silent support. Someone else who could be strong for a blissful change. Someone who understood her and, miraculously, seemed to accept all he saw.

Someone who cared enough to allow her the freedom to just be.

Kate dropped her mask, and all it represented, to the ground, then wrapped her arms around his neck. "Thank you," she whispered, brushing her lips against his. She kissed him deeply and passionately for several long moments, trying to satisfy the need that was building inside her. But the longer they kissed, the more her sense of urgency rose.

"Please," she said breathlessly as she allowed her hands to travel over his chest, his shoulders, his back, enjoying every masculine contour. "Please..."

He didn't need to be asked again. Seconds later, he had lowered her to the soft, damp grass and was leaning over her, his hands working at the tight lacings on the front of her gown.

Suddenly, she could breathe again, and she needed to, because his warm fingers were gliding over the softness of her bare breasts, stroking the silken tips until she ached with pleasure.

"Is this what you wanted, Kate?" he asked, the familiar, teasing tone back in his voice. "Is this what you had in mind?"

He was baiting her, but she was far beyond caring.

"Yes," she gasped, coaxing his head to her breast.

He readily complied, replacing his fingers with

his tongue. The sensation was heavenly, but it created more longing than it satisfied.

For the first time she could recall, Kate allowed herself to fully enjoy touching a man, her hands exploring and appreciating the differences in their bodies. Voluminous skirts were pushed aside as he did some exploring of his own. Before long, the grass around them was littered with strange, antiquated articles of clothing, discarded in surrender to needs too long unfulfilled.

For the briefest moment, Kate considered how compromised they would be if any of Millie and Charles's guests were to discover them here, tumbling on the lawn like a couple of wantons. But her reputation was already in tatters, thanks to the evening's events. What was a bit more fuel on gossip's funeral pyre?

When all barriers had been thrown aside and they lay, warm skin against warm skin, he paused as though unsure and looked down into her dark blue eyes. "Is this what you want, Kate?" he asked, poised but waiting. "Are you sure?"

Kate answered by eagerly pulling him to her, into her.

She was sure, all right. She had never been so sure of anything in her life.

It was only later, when they lay apart, bodies and passions cooling, the first drops of cold rain falling on their bare skin, that Kate began to have doubts. Something this good couldn't last. There had to be a catch. There was always, always a catch.

Six

"What lamebrain decided to seat the five of *us* at the same table?" Natalie muttered as she licked a bit of garlic sauce from a prawn, then popped it into her mouth. Next she scooped an oyster from its half shell and tried it. "Umm...the *bienbille* is nice."

Upon the stroke of midnight, all the guests had unmasked—everyone except Natalie, who had refused because of her black eye. Her mood was as dark as her injury, and she didn't seem to be putting out any effort to mask her feelings.

Having helped themselves to the sumptuous buffet, the merrymakers had been ushered to their seats at intimate tables scattered along the gallery and dining room, and in sheltered areas on the terrace.

Kate had been pleased to find their table at the end of the gallery, not far from where she and Max had just enjoyed their rendezvous. Only one thing dampened the moment, and it wasn't the gentle rain falling just beyond the eaves.

It was Natalie's presence. As always, she promised to be a major source of irritation. Kate strapped on her emotional armor and decided to play defense for the rest of the evening. No offensive tactics.

"I believe it was our hostess who arranged the seating," Kate said as benignly as she could manage. "Millie was probably under the mistaken impression that we like each other, that silly woman."

Against her better judgment, Kate took her place across the table from Natalie. The purple cards with their gold lettering were clear enough: Millie had intended for all the Burnells and their assorted escorts to sit together.

Oh, joy.

After formally seating her, Max took the chair beside Kate's. On the opposite side of the small table sat Harry and Natalie's disgruntled date.

Kate wondered what her father and Natalie would say if they could have seen her only a few minutes ago, scrambling back into her clothes after making wild, passionate love on the lawn. She wondered if it showed, this newly found sense of freedom and vitality. Could anyone tell, just by looking, that she had somehow changed forever?

Quickly, she stole a sly, sideways look at Max, just in time to see him steal one her way. They both laughed. The sound was intimate and familiar, even to Kate, and wasn't lost on Miss All-Ears Natalie.

"Well, you two seem to be getting along all right," her sister said with a slightly perturbed tone.

"Yes, we do seem to be," Kate murmured as she chose a radish and celery stick from the iced relish dish in the center of the table. "And how are you and Lucentio enjoying your evening?"

"Who?" Natalie seemed confused.

"Lucentio," Roger replied as he tossed back a stiff belt of whiskey. "That's who I'm supposed to be tonight, remember? The suitor to the fair Bianca. That's you."

Natalie grinned. "Oh, yeah…I forgot."

"All these Italian names are hard to remember," Harry complained as he dug into his hearty helping of veal *grillades.* "Why was it, exactly, that we had to dress up like this?"

Kate cringed, but said nothing. This time she was determined to keep control of her temper, no matter what.

When Natalie didn't reply, Max spoke up. "I believe it was so that Natalie could embarrass and humiliate her sister."

"Humph," Natalie replied. "No one needs to embarrass Kate. She does that just fine all by herself."

Again, Kate reined in her anger. She was going to win this battle, one way or another. "It doesn't matter how we're dressed or why," she said as matter-of-factly as possible. "As long as we're here, we might as well enjoy ourselves—and each other, if that's possible."

"Well, it isn't easy to enjoy yourself when you're suffering the kind of pain I am," Natalie said, placing one hand dramatically to the right side of her mask. "Really, Kate, you shouldn't have struck me like that. It was a coarse, vulgar thing to do."

Kate shot a quick look at Max. To her surprise, he appeared more angry than she. Someone indignant on her behalf—now there was a pleasant change of events.

"That's enough, Natalie," he said, his voice low, but stern. "You and I both know what happened to your eye."

Natalie literally squirmed on her seat. Roger poured himself another drink from a leather flask inside his tunic, and Harry seemed to awaken momentarily from his alcohol-enhanced stupor.

"What are you talking about?" he asked Max.

"Don't worry, Mr. Burnell," Max replied. "Just a little something between me and Natalie."

Harry stared at Max quizzically. "What is it?"

"Oh, hush, Father," Natalie snapped. "Just never mind. It was Max's idea of a little joke, and not a very funny one at that. I think he's lost his sense of humor. He must have been hanging around Kate too long."

Kate felt anger rising in her, like a sour gorge. But she swallowed the temptation. No more. No more. She was going to act like a lady if it killed her. And, feeling her blood pressure soar, she determined that it just might.

"You know, Natalie," Roger said, rising shakily to his feet. "I wish..." He reached over and pounded the table for emphasis. Their dishes clattered, the glasses danced, and everyone within earshot turned to stare. "I wish you would just lay off your sister!'' He practically screamed the last words. Now everyone was staring, dumbstruck. The only sound was that of the soft patter of the rain.

''She hasn't done anything to you,'' he continued, his voice wavering, but shockingly loud. ''At least, not anything you didn't deserve. You outright *lied* about that black eye. You know damned well how you got it.''

Natalie reached up, grabbed his sleeve and tried to pull him down onto his seat. ''Roger, honey, I think you've had a little, bitty too much to drink,'' she said with the sweetness of a Victorian Christmas angel. ''Why don't you sit down now and—''

''I don't want to sit down. I want you to stop bossing me around, woman! I've had about enough from you!''

Harry rose from his chair and took a step toward his youngest daughter's unhappy suitor. ''Now, son, I don't think you should—''

''Leave me alone, Mr. Burnell. You're the cause of this, spoiling Natalie rotten, year after year, treating Kate like a second-class citizen. You ought to be ashamed of yourself.''

Like everyone else, Kate just sat there, stunned, not knowing what to say or do. On one hand, it felt wonderful to have this young man, whom she had considered gutless, coming to her defense. And in such a public way. On the other, Kate could feel Natalie's deep humiliation. Having recently experienced the same thing, she couldn't help feeling sorry for her sister.

But she didn't feel sorry enough to stop Roger as he continued his tirade.

"And there's something else I want to say." Roger drew himself up like a rooster about to crow in a new morning. "You don't know your Shakespeare very well, or you would realize how foolish you were to set this whole 'shrew' thing up in the first place. If you'd paid attention back in your high school English literature class you'd know— Shakespeare's Katharina wasn't really a shrew at all. She was just a nice woman who had been badly treated by her family. If there's a bitch in the story, it's the younger sister, Bianca. Good casting, Natalie!"

Kate could see Natalie's blush go an even deeper shade of scarlet. She didn't know whether to feel vindicated or miserable on her sister's behalf. She decided to be honest and wallow in the pleasure of sweet vindication.

Having said his piece, Roger pushed back his chair and marched away with a slightly unsteady but determined stride. Natalie looked around and saw everyone gawking at her. Bursting into hysterical sobs, she jumped up and ran after him.

Harry followed them both, muttering, "Oh, dear, oh, dear. Sweetie pie, wait for daddy."

"Don't worry," Max whispered in Kate's ear as they watched Natalie disappear in a flurry of pink skirts with Harry close behind. "She deserved it. Every word."

Kate rose, her dinner forgotten. "Maybe I should go to her. She seemed pretty upset."

Max stood and slipped an arm around her waist. "I have a much better idea, milady." He gave her a deep, courtly bow, then nodded toward in the direction of the ballroom. "Instead, let's dance."

"I shouldn't be having this much fun," Kate said as Max guided her in sweeping circles across the glistening cypress floor of the ballroom. "Not when my sister is somewhere upstairs, probably prostrate across one of the beds, crying her eyes out."

"Why not? She's only doing what she does best." Max laughed as he twirled her into his arms, gave her a peck on the cheek, then spun her out again to the rhythm of the lively polka.

"You're mean," she said, panting to keep his pace. "Natalie is my little sister. I can't help but worry that she might—"

"Well, she isn't my sister, little or otherwise, and I don't want to talk or even think about her. I'm dancing with the most beautiful woman at this party, and I want to enjoy myself—if you don't mind."

Mind? How could she mind, when he had just called her the most beautiful woman present? She had been accused of being many things in the past, but "beautiful" hadn't been on the list. Of course, he was just flattering her, but she wouldn't allow herself to think about that tonight. Not with the candelabra gleaming golden light down on them. Not with the magic of Mardi Gras in the air.

Kate giggled and wondered at how Max seemed

to reduce her to an adolescent, just by casting on her the twinkle of his eye. And she didn't even mind the regression. It was rather nice, really, not having to be so serious, so somber, so businesslike all the time. She loved the way the child in him seemed to persuade the little girl in her to come out and play.

How could she have ever thought him brash, shallow or frivolous? He wasn't like Harry at all. Later, when she wasn't so deliriously happy, she would apologize to Max for having compared him and Harry so unfavorably. It really wasn't fair. The two had so little in common. Thankfully.

The band finished the polka and began another, slower and more romantic waltz. Max pulled her so close that she could feel the heat of his chest against her breasts. Memories of their encounter swept over her, making her knees weak and the rest of her ache with longing. So recently satisfied, yet hungry again so soon. Kate had never thought of herself as a sexual or even sensual woman—until tonight.

Tonight, she could believe and hope for almost anything.

As they circled the ballroom, she felt as though she were spinning on a glittering carousel, giddy with a happiness she knew wouldn't last. But for once in her life, Kate was determined not to let her doubts and fears rob her of the joy of the moment.

Tomorrow, she might discover that it had all been an illusion. Later, she could find out that Max wasn't the man he seemed to be, this sensitive and gentle lover, the masculine counterpart she had always longed for to supply the male for the female in her.

There would be plenty of time to come down from the clouds tomorrow. For tonight, she just wanted to float a little while longer.

On the stroke of one, Harry Burnell climbed onto a chair—a risky business, to be sure—and announced to all that he had something of great importance to say.

From the other end of the ballroom, Kate cringed, hearing the level of intoxication in his voice. She turned to Max, who had just returned from the dining room with glasses of punch for them both.

"Why do I get the sinking feeling," she said, "that my family is about to embarrass itself at least once more before this night is over?"

Max watched Harry teeter on the chair and nodded. "It's a definite possibility," he said. "Let's go get him down from there before he falls and breaks something."

"Like his head?"

"Actually, I was more worried about those Ming vases there by the fireplace. They're irreplaceable."

"I see your point. Come on."

They hurried over to Harry, but he was already beginning his important announcement, to the amusement of all around him. The crowd seemed to be warming up to the antics of the Burnell bunch.

Except their hosts.

Millie shot Kate a warning look, as if to say, "The next time you or one of your crazy relatives makes a spectacle of themselves, you're all out of here."

"Ladies and gentlemen," Harry bellowed, his deep voice filling the ballroom. "I have something to say, so gather round."

"Harry, come down from there," Kate said, tugging at the hem of his tunic. "You're going to fall and hurt yourself."

"Get away, girl. You're interrupting my speech. As I was saying, I—"

"Mr. Burnell, please." Max grabbed him by the forearm and tried to force him down. But Harry was a strong old codger, and he wasn't easily relocated against his will.

"Oh, it's you, Max." Harry beamed. "I'm glad you're here. Listen up. This is important stuff."

Max turned to Kate and whispered, "Maybe you'd better let him make his speech and get down on his own. I think it's the simplest approach."

Kate nodded, feeling her face turn red, again. At this rate she could easily give up wearing rouge.

"As many of you may have noticed," Harry continued, "I'm not getting any younger. Neither are any of you, so wipe those stupid grins off your faces. You look like a bunch of goats eatin' briars." Harry listed to starboard so severely that Kate scrambled to catch him, but he corrected his course just in time.

"So, since I'm gettin' older, I thought it was about time I retired and left this business of mine to the younger set. They've got more energy than they know what to do with, so let them run it for a while."

Kate froze, her mouth open, her pulse thundering in her ears. She wasn't sure she had heard him right. Turning to Max, she whispered, "Did he say he's going to retire?"

Max nodded.

"As some of you know—and some of you don't, 'cause it ain't any of your business—I own the lion's share of this company, and my two daughters split the rest. But we did a good job on this here house, as you can all see, and I figure it's a nice, big hurrah for me to finish on."

Several people clapped, nodding their approval for the renovation. Kate felt the old pride welling up inside her. Tonight seemed to be magic in more ways than one.

"This last job wasn't easy, and I couldn't have done it by my lonesome," Harry continued. "There were a lot of problems we had to work out, a lot of new ideas used, a lot of old ideas rehashed. Nope, I never could have pulled it off alone. So, to show my gratitude for a job well done..." He threw his arms open in what was meant to be a magnanimous gesture and nearly tumbled off the chair.

Kate could feel her pulse pounding against her

eardrums. This was it. Finally, a public acknowledgment of her contributions. And for Harry to choose this forum to do it... She wanted to drag him off the chair and cover his ruddy, chubby face with kisses.

"To express my appreciation, I would like to announce that I am leaving my controlling interest to the person who has helped me make Burnell Construction what it is today—Maximillian Colbert."

At first there was nothing but silence in the ballroom. Then a few throats cleared, some skirts rustled, and there were some scattered murmurings. Kate couldn't move, couldn't breathe. She was certain her heart had stopped beating altogether.

"Max?" She mouthed the word, staring up at Harry, dumbstruck. "Max?"

Harry jumped down from the chair and landed on unsteady legs beside her. "Yeah, Max. I thought he was the perfect man for the job. It's a good thing you've been getting along so well. That'll make it nice and cozy, huh?"

He reached out his hand to Max, his face glowing with self-satisfaction. "Congratulations, young man," Harry said. "You just got yourself a free company, lock, stock and barrel. How does that feel?"

Kate stepped between them and grabbed her father's extended hand. "What are you saying?" she asked, her voice shaking with fury. "You're kidding, right?"

Harry seemed puzzled. "Huh?"

"You're going to leave your share of the company—control of the company—to a stranger?" Her voice was rising, word by word, along with her rage. "I work my butt off for you all these years, Harry, and you're going to leave it to someone who isn't even family? Someone who's only worked one job with us? One lousy job? Is that what you're saying?"

"Well, I couldn't leave it to you," Harry said. "You weren't expecting that, were you?"

"Why not? Why not me?"

"Because—" he reached over and patted her head as though she were a disgruntled cocker spaniel "—because if I left it to you, your sister Natalie would be all upset. And I can't leave it to her. She doesn't like doing the piddling little things she has to do now. Besides, you're both wom—"

"No!" She held up one hand, as though hoping to ward off the injury the word would cause. "Don't say it! I don't want to hear you say it. If I actually hear you say it, I'll never be able to forgive you for it."

"Oh, come on, Katie. You're taking this too hard."

"And you," she said, "are a selfish, thoughtless old fool. I've been mopping up after you for years, and you've never even known it, because I didn't want to injure that damned male ego of yours. Let's see if Max, here, will be so patient." Max. A horrible thought swept through her. A thought that had a sick ring of truth.

"You knew," she said, turning her anger on her

lover. "You knew all along. That's why you seduced me. Butter her up before the old man drops the bomb. Is that all it was?"

She didn't wait for Max's reply. When she turned to leave, she saw a ballroom full of curious eyes staring at her, shocked, as always, by her unladylike outburst. For once, Kate was too hurt to care.

"As far as I'm concerned, you can both go to hell in a handbasket," she said, delivering her final volley over her shoulder to her father and former lover. Then, to the rest of the room, she added, "In fact, you can *all* go dance with the devil in a red dress. Whatever the hell that means."

Seven

"Kate, you can't stand out here in the rain! It's thundering and lightning. Come inside this minute!"

Kate tried to ignore Max, but it wasn't easy because he had hold of her hand and was trying to drag her across the lawn toward the front steps of Sans Souci. Every step was the Battle Royale. She didn't intend to go.

"For Pete's sake, you're soaking wet," he said, tugging at her. She ground her heels into the lawn and refused to budge. "If you stay out here, you'll catch pneumonia and croak."

She stuck her face close to his—both had rainwater streaming off the ends of their noses—and shouted at him above the din of the storm, "So? What's it to you?"

"Whether you know it or not, I happen to have a very sensitive conscience," he yelled back. "And I'm not going to spend every Mardi Gras remembering how I let you die."

"Geez, you *are* sensitive."

"You're damned right. Now, are you going to move, or am I going to move you?"

"Just try it, buddy, and you'll wind up with testicles for tonsils."

"Kate, I'm losing my patience with you. Come inside, and we'll talk about this like rational adults."

"I'm waiting for the valet to bring my car. I'm going to go home and go to bed. You or my little sister can give Daddy Dearest a ride home—on the fender of your car, for all I care. The last thing I want right now is to talk to any of you so-called 'rational adults.' You're nutcases, all of you."

"Kate, I didn't know about your father's decision. Really, I didn't. And just for the record, I think it's stupid to put anyone other than you in charge of that company, and I intend to tell him so."

A crash of lightning flashed almost directly over their heads, illuminating the front lawns and wrought-iron gates with their decorative double *S*s. Kate felt herself melting, and it had nothing to do with the Wicked Witch Syndrome, or the fact that she was now soaked all the way through the heavy costume to her goose-pimpled flesh.

"When?" she shouted.

"When, what?"

"When are you going to tell him?"

"Right now. Are you coming with me?"

She stood there, debating. More than anything, she wanted to hear Max set Harry straight. But the thought of going back into that house, looking like a drowned sewer rat, was a definite turnoff.

"No, you go ahead. I just want to go home and get dry and warm."

"At least come stand under the porch while you wait for your car." He let go of her arm and held his hand out in a less demanding and more inviting gesture. "Please. I'm getting soaked myself, and I think this leather codpiece is shrinking."

She couldn't resist a quick look down and a chuckle. "All right, all right. I'll wait on the porch while you go inside. Heaven knows, we don't want you to risk a shriveled codfish."

"Cod*piece*."

"Whatever."

Max knew she wouldn't be able to resist; at least, he didn't think she could. As he strode along the rear gallery and through the back door into the crowded music room, he fervently hoped she was following him, but didn't dare turn around to look. He could hear Harry Burnell's booming bass echoing throughout the room. Ah, the fellow was in fine form tonight.

One didn't have to look far to see where Kate had inherited her fire and vitality. But, as with most personality traits, there were both positive and negative aspects to being high-spirited. Long ago, Max had realized, the very passion that made her such a captivating woman was the same characteristic that kept her in constant trouble and caused her such pain.

If ever a damsel had needed a champion, Katharina Burnell needed one now. But, if he really wanted to help her, he would have to play the part of villain, not shining knight. The fair, but tempestuous Katharina didn't need or want a man to fight her battles for her. Most of her dragons were internal, and only she could wage those wars.

What she really needed was someone to show her a mirror image of her own behavior. She wouldn't like it. And when all was said and done, she probably wouldn't like him, either. Let alone love him, as he had hoped she might someday. But it was a risk he had to take. Tonight, he was her Petruchio, whether she wanted one or not. Tonight might be his only chance to tame the shrew.

To his immense relief, he saw her from the corner of his eye, slipping through the back door behind him. She looked so pathetic, so vulnerable, in her sodden finery as she stood there against the wall, trying to blend in with the other guests.

Pretending not to see her, Max walked directly to Harry and declared in a loud, clear voice for all to hear, "Mr. Burnell, I want to have a word with you. Right now."

Harry's smile vanished to be replaced with a scowl. Even in his chemically altered state of mind, neither he, nor anyone else present, had missed the combative tone of Max's voice. He released his grip on the two young women he had pinned to his sides. They made their hasty escapes in opposite directions.

Max spotted Natalie, perched on a chair nearby, looking none the worse for her previous embarrassment. But she was without an escort. Apparently, Roger had delivered his speech and fled. In a way, Max was glad the younger sister would be here to witness this. If it went down the way he hoped, maybe it would be a good lesson for her, too.

"Okay, son," Harry said. "I'm all ears...and so is everybody else. Let 'er rip."

"First of all, I have to tell you that I'm going to decline your offer of controlling interest in your company. I'm turning it down on principle."

"On principle? What principle?"

"The principle that it should go to the person who has invested the most over the years. And since I only came to work for you a few months ago, that shouldn't be me."

"Oh, I see." Harry nodded knowingly. "Kate's gotten to you. She must have scared the crap out of you to get you to turn down an offer like that, son." He shrugged and laughed. "Frankly, I'm surprised. I didn't have you pegged as the type to be henpecked."

A ripple of giggles went through the crowd, and Harry beamed, proud of having made a joke.

"Henpecked? Oh, I see." Max crossed his arms over his chest and assumed a thoughtful look. "Is that what you call any man who isn't a misogynistic jerk like yourself? Any man who considers a woman his equal, instead of something to chase, then use and throw away?"

"You'd better watch your mouth, boy. I don't use women. I love women."

"You don't *know* women. How can you possibly

love them?" Max glanced over at Kate, to see how she was receiving all this. But her expression seemed to be one of shock more than anything else. He would have to dig his grave even deeper.

"All these years," he continued, "your daughter has stood by your side, working with you, putting up with you—which is no easy task, I'm sure—and you turn around and stab her in the back. That's the way you love the women in your life, Harry Burnell. Is that the way you loved your wife? Is that why she left you all those years ago?"

Kate stood there, listening, observing, dying a little with every word Max spoke. Everything he was saying was true. She knew it, and from the look on Harry's face, everyone present knew it. But just because something was true didn't mean it should be spoken here, now, and in this way. A blade of truth had the capacity to cut sharply and deeply. And Harry was being disemboweled before almost everyone he knew.

She saw him shrinking beneath Max's onslaught, becoming far less than the bombastic giant he had always been, climbing inside himself to escape. She saw the crowd, horrified but fascinated by the process. An oh-so-polite bunch of ghouls, reveling in a terrible moment.

But, most of all, Kate saw the many times over the years when she had done the same thing to Harry, cutting him apart with no concern for who was around to witness his shame. In front of his closest friends, his business associates, even his employees, she had spoken the truth loudly and clearly, as Max was. And by doing so, she had made a fool of Harry and a shrew of herself.

So much for the value of honesty. Funny, after all these years, while speaking all that truth, she hadn't been sincere about her own feelings.

There was no time like the present.

"Max, please," Kate said as she pushed her way through the crowd to stand beside him. "I appreciate why you're doing this. But it's something I should do myself."

"Oh, great." Harry rolled his eyes. "So, now you're going to come in for the kill."

"No, Daddy, I'm not," she said. It had been years since she had used any term of address other than "Harry" with her father. The change wasn't lost on either of them. Kate thought she saw tears in Harry's eyes, but she couldn't see them clearly because of the moisture in her own. "Max is trying to tell you something that I've been meaning to say for years."

"That you're mad at me? Oh, no. I've heard that plenty times and plenty loud. I don't need to hear it again."

Kate reached inside herself and gathered her courage. Who would have ever thought it would take so much to be vulnerable with someone you loved? "No, Daddy. You don't need to hear that again. You've heard it often enough, and it's only half the story. Not even the important half, at that. The truth is, I *have* been mad, but mostly I've..." Kate paused, choking on her own words. She felt

Max's hand, warm and reassuring on her shoulder. "Mostly, I've been hurt because—"

To her surprise, Harry stepped toward her, a look of astonishment on his face, which quickly turned to concern. "Hurt? You mean, I hurt your feelings?"

"Yes, Dad. I do have feelings other than just mad and madder, you know."

"No, I guess I didn't know. How have I hurt your feelings, Katie?"

Kate felt a knot closing off her throat, and she didn't think she could get the words out. Not here, in front of everyone. Not now, in front of her sister, who was sitting nearby with a slight smile on her face, obviously enjoying the show. But this was the perfect time and place. If she could do it here and now, she would know she had won at least one battle in what had been a lifelong war with her own emotions.

She looked to Max for reassurance and saw it shining in his dark eyes. She saw something else there: pride. He was proud of her for taking this step, and she silently blessed him for it.

"How did I hurt your feelings?" Harry repeated. And he sounded as though he really wanted to know.

"By loving Natalie best," she said as hot, salty tears rolled down her face and into the corners of her mouth. A long, awkward silence stretched between them. No one in the room said anything or even moved, until Natalie hopped up from her seat and hurried over to them.

"Well, why wouldn't he love me best?" she said, hands on her hips, chin lifted several haughty degrees. "I've always been good to father, while you've been such a—"

"Oh, shut up, Natalie," Harry said, without taking his eyes off his oldest daughter.

"But—"

"I said shut up and sit down. This is between your sister and me."

"Yeah, Nat," Max muttered. "Butt out."

Natalie flounced out of the room, skirts and curls bouncing.

"I'm sorry, Katie," Harry said, taking her hands in his.

Kate had forgotten how comforting her dad's touch could be. His hands were so large as they folded around hers. He was so capable and strong...when he wanted to be. And now, thank heaven, he seemed to want to be strong for his daughter.

"I didn't love Natalie best," he said. "I just loved her differently. But you..." He brushed a wet curl out of her eyes and placed a kiss on her forehead. "You have always been precious to me."

"Then why didn't you tell me?"

Harry looked confused. "Didn't I?"

"No, not even once. You always told Natalie, but you never, ever told me."

"Oh, well, I'm always telling Natalie because she's always asking. She pesters me all the time, wanting to know if I love her, if I'll give her this, or do that for her. You know how she is. But you—you never asked.''

Kate held out her arms to her father. ''If I ask more, would you tell me more often?''

He folded her into a bear hug. ''Maybe I'll remember to tell you without you having to ask.''

Burying her face against his chest, Kate allowed herself the luxury of absorbing a love she had never known was hers, simply for the taking. ''That would be nice,'' she told him. ''That would be really nice.''

Eight

When Kate left the music room, she noticed how few people had remained to witness her reconciliation with her father. Sometime during the conversation, they had faded away into the newly refinished woodwork. Apparently they weren't as interested in cease-fires as in open warfare. She reminded herself that, sadly, most people wanted to think the worst of others. And she had given them far too many reasons over the years to think the worst of her.

Enough of that.

While she was on a roll, Kate decided to seek out her sister and set things right with her, too, if at all possible. As it was, she could hardly make things worse.

"Excuse me. Have you seen Natalie?" she asked Gertrude, who was standing with Arnaud at the foot of the staircase. Rather than answer her, Mr. and Mrs. Sprat gave each other telling looks that caused Kate a sinking sensation in the pit of her stomach.

Maybe things could be worse.

At that moment, Kate heard it, the shrieking wails coming from somewhere upstairs. The high pitch, the quavering treble tone were all too familiar. Lady Bianca was throwing one of her famous fits.

Oh, lightness and joy, Kate thought as she climbed the stairs. Here we go again.

"Let me in, Natalie. Please, I need to talk to you." Kate stood, knocking on the bathroom door, trying to sound patient. It wasn't easy, considering the volume of the caterwauling on the other side of the door.

She decided to change tactics—maybe a bit of humor? "Nat-a-lie, Nat-a-lie, let me in," she sang, "or I'll huff and I'll puff..." The door remained closed. She lowered her voice to a harsh, sinister whisper. "And I'll blow the friggin' door in. With any luck, you'll be standing behind it."

Silently, she chastised herself for her momentary lapse in charitable attitude. Over and over, she told herself she was on a mission of mercy, on a hunt for harmony, in the pursuit of peace. Ah, heck, she just wanted to find a way to get along with her stupid sister. Although, as she listened to the squalling inside, it was difficult to remember why.

A dozen schemes raced through her head, ways to persuade her sister to open the door. She ran over a list of Natalie's favorite things: men, food, the Bahamas, jewelry, clothes—

Ah-ha!

"Nat, don't be silly," she said through gritted teeth. "Open the door. Caroline Waterstreet is standing here with me, and she wants to see your gown. She heard it's beautiful, a much prettier version of mine.''

She waited, counting under her breath. ''Ten, nine, eight, seven…'' Yep. Vanity. It worked every time.

The door opened a crack. Kate wedged her foot inside and gave it a shove. A second later, she was in the bathroom with an indignant Natalie.

''You liar! Liar!'' her sister screamed, stamping her size five-and-a-half shoe.

''Yeah, yeah, pants on fire. So, sue me.'' Kate walked over to the toilet, dropped the lid into place and sat down with a tired sigh. ''Natalie, stop screaming and listen to me. I'm not here to fight with you.''

Watching her sister closely, Kate could have sworn Natalie actually deflated a bit. Maybe Max had been right. Maybe Natalie *did* have her own reasons for keeping this war going. Well, it took two to battle, and she was laying down her ax. That meant it was over.

''I've come to apologize, because I—''

''Well, it's about time! You—''

''As I was saying…'' Kate tried to keep her voice well modulated, her temper under control. It was easier than she had thought it would be. Even a little practice seemed to help. ''I want to apologize to you for slapping you earlier. It was an irresponsible, immature, foolish thing to do, and I'm asking you to forgive me.''

Yes, Kate thought, watching the conflict of emotions cross Natalie's face, *deflate* is the word. It was

as though the air had gone out of an overblown tire
as it flapped limply against the pavement.

"Well, I don't know." Natalie put her hand to
her eye. "You gave me a real shiner and—"

"I'm not going to play that game with you, Natalie. I gave you a slap on the cheek, and I'm asking
you to forgive me for that. Will you?"

"I don't think I can. That was a really rotten
thing to do."

"Okay, I accept your feelings on the matter. If
you ever do reach the point where you feel you can
forgive me, let me know. Will you do that?"

"Yeah, well, all right." Natalie walked over to
the mirror, opened her beaded bag and began to
refresh her makeup.

"I also want to say I'm sorry for all the mean
things I've done and said to you over the years.
I'm going to be more civil to you in the future,
even if it means that I'll have to spend less time
with you."

"Less time? What does that mean?" Natalie
paused, lipstick in hand, with only her upper lip
reddened.

"I mean that unless you begin to show me more
respect and kindness—as I intend to show you—
I'm not going to be around you as much as I have
been in the past."

"So, you're disowning me?"

"I'm not disowning you. You are, and always
will be, my sister. But I'm not going to spend my
time, my love and my energy on people who don't
treat me with affection and respect. You've treated

me badly, Natalie, and I've allowed you to do it. I'm not going to anymore. It's bad for you, for me and for our relationship.''

"You are! You're disowning me. My own sister is throwing me out like a pile of trash.'' Tears filled her green eyes and cascaded down her recently blushed cheeks, leaving white streaks.

Kate sighed, feeling more tired and empty than she could ever remember. But she had a quiet sense of peace that made it all worthwhile. Rising, she said, "If that's the way you want to see it, Natalie, I won't argue with you. Like I said, I'm finished with that. It saps too much of my energy, and I have important work to do.''

"Oh, yeah. Miss Fancy Pants has important work to do.'' Natalie followed Kate to the door, her face twisted in an unpleasant caricature of a bratty child. But the face looked ridiculous and somehow obscene on a woman's body. "Just what kind of important work do *you* have to do?'' Kate heard her shout after her as she walked down the hall.

"The work of just living,'' she said in a voice too quiet for Natalie to hear, "just being. It's highly underrated.''

But Kate knew that her own heart had heard— and for now, that was all that mattered.

Once again, Kate stood on the porch, waiting for the patient valet to bring her car around—a second time.

"I really *am* going home this time," she had told him.

"Yes, ma'am," he'd replied. The suspicious twinkle in his eye made her think he didn't quite believe her.

Just as he was pulling her Volvo station wagon up to the door, Kate felt a warm hand close around her elbow.

"Could I offer you a ride home, Kate?" She turned to see Max, smiling down at her, but looking almost as tired as she felt. It had been a long night for them both, but one she wouldn't have missed for the world.

"My car is here," she said. "But thanks, anyway."

"The valet will store it for you overnight. Let me drive you home. It would be my pleasure."

She took his hand and gave him a quick, friendly kiss on the cheek. "I appreciate what you said in there on my behalf. And I know what you were trying to do. It worked beautifully, by the way."

"Thank you. No applause necessary, just throw coins."

"I'll do better than that. I'll stuff a hundred dollar bill in your codpiece with my teeth. But not tonight, darling. I have a headache."

"I'll bet you do, so let me drive you home, Kate. Accept it as a small token of affection from a friend whose head probably doesn't hurt as much as yours."

Bending down, he kissed her lightly on the lips.

"Let somebody take care of *you* for a change. This somebody really wants to."

"Okay, okay," she said. "But you have to explain it to the valet."

"So, Lady Katharina, what's next?" Max cut the key of the Peugeot and leaned back in the leather seat. Turning to her, he slipped one hand beneath her hair and gently massaged her neck. "Do you need me to take you inside and tuck you in?"

His offer was tempting, but as Kate sat there in his car and stared at the old brownstone on St. Michel Court, she knew this wasn't the night for tucking in.

Rain pattered softly on the car's roof as condensation collected and rolled in silver tracks down the insides of the windows. A pale, gray dawn was signaling the end of the night's events. A new day. A day for changes long overdue.

"This isn't *my* house," Kate said, placing her hand on Max's knee and giving it an affectionate squeeze. "It's Harry's house. Natalie and I have lived here our entire lives. I've stayed because...well, I've told myself I had to keep an eye on my father. But Harry is going to do whatever he wants, whether I'm there or not."

"As he should. Every man has an inalienable right to make a jackass of himself if he wants."

"And far be it from me to deny him his God-given rights."

"Here, here."

"But, on the other hand, I don't have to live with

him and watch him exercise those privileges first-hand. I need a place of my own.'' She turned to look at him and saw the depth of intimacy she had always craved in his eyes. ''I need a place where you can...tuck me in.''

He grinned broadly. ''I'll help you find someplace today. I'll help you pack. I'll even help you move, if you feed me beer and pizza.''

She laughed, then looked back at the house in the court. ''I have to, Max. I don't have the patience or strength to cope with Harry or Natalie anymore.''

His hands stroked the nape of her neck, warm and comforting. ''I think you have enormous patience and strength, Kate. But I think it's time you used all that power to further your own life's work.''

''I intend to. There's something else I'm going to do today. As soon as Harry sleeps it off, I'm going to set things straight with him about the company. If he's retiring, I'll be the one in charge. No ifs, ands or buts about it.''

''And if he says no?''

''He won't. Harry may act foolish sometimes, but he's no dummy. He loves that business, and in his heart, he knows I'm the only one who can run it the way he wants. He'll gripe, but in the end, he'll cave. And I'm going to set my foot down about Natalie, too. No more of her prissing around in short shorts and causing scenes. Either she works, or she leaves. That'll be an easy decision for her. I'll never see her face around the office again."

Max nodded thoughtfully. "Those sound like very positive changes. I'm proud of you."

"Thanks, but it's high time. For years, we Burnells have worked together, lived together, fought together. I've enjoyed about all the family togetherness I can stand. It's time to grow up, for all of us."

Leaning over, he kissed the tip of her nose. "As long as you don't outgrow me."

"Not likely. I'm afraid you're a childish habit I intend to keep, like carousel rides and cotton candy."

"I'm so relieved."

She could tell he meant it by the way his lips took hers; they were greedy and grateful. And so were hers.

"It's stopped raining," he said when they were finally satisfied. "You'd better go inside, get dry and grab some sleep, if you're going to rearrange your entire life in the next twenty-four hours."

She agreed and reached for the door handle, but he grabbed her hand. "No way. At least for a few more minutes, you're the Lady Katharina. And you're in *my* carriage. What's the point in dressing like a gentleman of Verona if you don't let me act like one?"

"Oh, sorry, Petruchio." She laughed and rolled her eyes. "Whatever was I thinking?"

A moment later, he opened her door with all the flourish of a Renaissance coachman. Offering his hand, he helped her—and all her skirts and petti-coats—to alight. But as she was stepping out, her right high heel caught on some of the lace at her hem. The shoe fell to the sidewalk.

"Oops, what a klutz," she said, reaching for it.

"Not at all, milady. Allow me."

Dropping to one knee, he scooped up the shoe. She sat back down on the car seat and lifted her skirt daintily, exposing her bare foot.

"You do that very well," he said, running his forefinger above and below her arch. "Maybe next year, you should go to Millie's ball as Cinderella."

"Oh, please! How hokey!" She tried to pull her foot back, but he held it firmly. Instead of replacing her shoe, he began to slowly kiss the inside of her ankle.

"Max! What are you—"

"Petruchio," he corrected her, then proceeded upward to her calf.

"Okay, Petruchio. That's enough. What are you...?"

Pushing her skirt higher, he began to apply the same attention to the inside of her knee.

"Stop that!" She grabbed him by his hair and tried to pull him away. "We're in the middle of my father's court! The neighbors might be watch-ing."

"All right, I'll stop—for now." He lowered her skirt and gracefully replaced the high heel. "But I'll take a rain check."

They both looked up at the cloudy sky and laughed.

"This time, next year?" he said.

"Sure," she replied. "I'll be Cinderella, we'll let Natalie be Drizella, and you...you can be my Prince Charming."

"And to think that earlier this evening, I didn't even qualify as a nice guy." He reached down, grabbed her around the waist and lifted her out of the car and into his arms. "Pucker up, Lady Katharina, and give me a good-night kiss."

She did as he asked, kissing him as though it were the first time, but deeply happy to know it wouldn't be the last.

Finally, he released her and sighed his satisfaction. "You're a damned good kisser yourself, woman," he said. "Or in the more gracious words of the bard himself, 'You have witchcraft in your lips, Kate. There is more eloquence in a sugar touch of them than in the tongues of the French council.'"

She laughed. "What a load of poppycock! You're just trying to get into my pantaloons."

"Been there, done that." He lowered his voice and glanced around. "Not that I wouldn't welcome another opportunity as soon as possible."

"I think it can be arranged."

His smile disappeared for a moment, and she saw a hint of vulnerability just beneath the bold facade. Her Petruchio needed reassurance as badly as she did. How alike they were.

"I'll call you as soon as I wake up," she said. "And until then, may we have 'As many farewells as be stars in heaven.'''

His eyes thanked her. "And one more hello."

"Yes, my love. And one more hello."

TAPESTRY
by Elizabeth Gage

One

"Marc Belfort will be there. Did I mention that?"

From the moment Karen Madison heard those words on her friend Jeannie's lips, she felt herself in danger. The masked ball at Sans Souci, which she'd been thinking of as a charming vacation from reality, now seemed a flight into unnamed peril.

They got out of the cab together—Karen dressed in an all-purpose Italian Renaissance outfit intended to represent Juliet, Jeannie in a rather eccentric imitation of Isolde—and went in to meet the hosts. Charles Duchaise, dressed as Napoléon, introduced them to his wife, Millicent, whose Josephine costume did not hide her preoccupied look.

"Jeannie!" exclaimed Charles. "You're looking lovelier than ever tonight."

"Thanks," Jeannie said. "The mask helps."

"Nonsense, my dear." Charles's face sketched a movement that expressed reproach and pity in one stroke. Reproach at Jeannie's tendency to run herself down, and pity that it was necessary for her to do so. Jeannie was not a pretty girl. Her tight costume did little to hide her overweight figure, and there was, alas, truth in her claim that the mask helped to hide her unattractive face. Jeannie had been hiding behind her "life of the party" personality for so many years that her Isolde character was like a second mask added to the first.

"And this must be the famous friend from Connecticut of whom we've heard so much," said Charles, holding out a hand to Karen.

"I'm delighted to meet you," Karen said. "You have a lovely house."

"If you paid the taxes on it you might look at it in a different light," Charles said. "But, yes, I admit that it is a pretty place."

"It's like a doorway into the past," Karen said.

"Sometimes I feel as though it's a one-way door," Millie said. "It's easy to slip backward into all this overstuffed antebellum charm and not be able to find your way out again. That's a feeling we southerners are all too familiar with."

"I don't imagine that a Connecticut Yankee like yourself has to worry too much about the past," Charles said.

"Perhaps you're right," Karen said. "I'm not sure."

The fact was that at that particular moment Karen felt the lure of the past all too strongly. The news that Marc Belfort was to be here tonight was like a violent hand turning over the hourglass of her life and thrusting her into a set of feelings she had not confronted in many years. The Old World look of the Duchaise mansion only accentuated a revolution that was going on in her mind and her senses.

"Come on," Jeannie said a trifle too briskly, as

though intuiting what her friend was thinking. "I'll introduce you to some people."

"Oh, let me do that, dear," protested Charles.

"No, you stay here and greet the late arrivals," Jeannie said. "I know everybody, anyway. I'll keep Karen away from the bores, and make sure she gets the right impression of Crescent City society."

Gesturing agreeably with his hand, Charles let her do as she wished. The two young women took their leave as Millie waved irritably at the cigar smoke she obviously detested.

Jeannie did indeed seem to know everyone. Astonishingly, people's masks did not slow her down for a minute as she introduced Karen to an interesting collection of guests from all the best families of New Orleans. A mellifluous assortment of French names, all pronounced in a delicate southern drawl, added to the charm of the evening.

Unfortunately, Karen lacked Jeannie's familiarity with those present, so their real identities quickly receded behind their dark masks and elaborate costumes as they slipped away from her, forming an exotic panorama against the panelled walls of the old mansion. Already there was something unreal about this evening. And that unreality was dangerously exciting.

Karen clung to Jeannie as to a precious ballast that might prevent her from floating away on a tide of champagne and memory. Jeannie was the only friend from New Orleans that Karen had stayed in touch with over the years. The two had struck up a tenuous friendship when Karen had been a lonely sixteen-year-old student here for only a year, and Jeannie, an ugly duckling never to blossom into a beauty, was a tongue-tied teenager.

Their friendship had known its ups and downs. Conceived at school, it had persisted for a year afterward as a pen-pal relationship. Then it had waned as they'd both become preoccupied with their respective futures, Jeannie remaining in New Orleans and Karen preparing for college at Barnard. Jeannie spent a year in Paris as part of her French major, and, as luck would have it, Karen went there for a semester herself to study mathematics and sociology at the Sorbonne. Karen was a confident collegian at this point, and Jeannie had assumed her permanent role as "life of the party." They enjoyed many long walks around the Latin Quarter, and by the time Karen returned home, the friendship had cemented permanently. Regular letters and occasional phone calls had kept them in close touch over the years.

Karen enjoyed Jeannie's great energy and ease with other people. But she could not help wondering whether the real reason for her continuing the relationship was the past to which Jeannie was a living link. Jeannie was the only person in Karen's present-day life who had known her when the emotional crucible of her adolescence had made its mark on her. Of course, even Jeannie did not know the whole truth about that shrouded time. No one did, except Karen—and Marc Belfort.

Karen found herself at once shrinking from the strangers around her and on the lookout for a composite figure, at once familiar and strange. She had not seen Marc for a dozen years. If he had changed as much as she had, he would be unrecognizable in the flesh, not to mention behind his mask—whatever that mask might be.

She caught a glimpse of herself in the drawing room mirror. She looked striking in the low-cut brocade, with her dark hair coiffed in the Renaissance style. She had lost weight this past year, and her face looked attractively wan and thoughtful. The gown's tight bodice showed off her slim figure. She had to smile at the illusion. She was a twentieth-century woman, made thin by overwork and worry, trying to ape a sixteenth-century girl whose slimness was virginal and allegorical.

The music played; the guests conversed. Karen waited to be introduced to the man she did not want to see. Meanwhile she rehearsed a conversation in which he would not remember her, in which she would pretend not to remember him.

Just before ten, Millie brought a masked figure dressed as Don Juan into the room where Karen was chatting with some people.

"Juliet, I want you to meet Don Juan," Millie said. "Have you ever thought how different history would have been had you two met? The ending might have been happier."

For an instant Karen blushed, wondering whether Marc Belfort might be hiding behind Don Juan's mask. But the man before her seemed too stockily built for Marc.

When she heard his voice she knew he was someone else.

"Chris Carpenter," he said. "I'm down from Chicago on business. Jeannie told me about you."

"How do you do?" Karen said. "How do you know Jeannie?"

He lifted his mask long enough for her to see a friendly face with clear gray eyes and tanned skin.

"I used to work with her ex-boyfriend," he said. "That was a long time ago. But Jeannie doesn't let friends slip away. I guess you know that."

"Yes, I do."

"I hear you're a computer consultant. I could use you in my business."

"What business is that?"

"I'm with a firm of architects. We do a lot of the planning for public buildings around the city. Our boss is pretty old-fashioned—we're still in the Stone Age as far as records and accounting are concerned."

"I know how that goes." Karen smiled.

Chris looked around at the Duchaise mansion. "This is all new to me," he said. "I've never been to New Orleans before."

"How do you like it?" Karen asked.

"It's fantastic. Like stepping into a time machine," he said. "I'm not used to so much charm. Chicago is not a city that dwells much on the past. Even if we wanted to, the Chicago fire eliminated most of the old landmarks."

"Yes, it is charming," Karen said. Her smile faded for an instant as an unbidden memory brought her back to this strange and beautiful place. New Orleans had made more of a mark on her than she had ever planned. "Why don't you stay awhile?"

"I'd like to. But I have to get back the day after tomorrow. Duty calls."

"Well, perhaps some day you'll return," Karen said. "I did."

He was smiling at her calmly, expectantly. In that moment she guessed he was unattached. Perhaps because he had not mentioned a wife or family back in Chicago. Perhaps because of the way he looked at her.

Millie Duchaise reappeared and spirited him away. Karen left the room. She saw Jeannie waving at her from a doorway with two new people, but Karen slipped out of sight, not wishing to meet anyone else.

At eleven-thirty she found herself alone in the upstairs library, with its balcony supported by the massive Greek columns that made the house's front so famous. There were portraits on the walls, one of which showed a handsome young man in riding boots, with brooding dark eyes that looked remarkably alive, though the picture was at least a hundred years old. They seemed to bore into her, his gaze asking a wordless but urgent question.

She went out onto the balcony. Her thoughts turned to Brett. He had been almost relieved when she told him Jeannie had invited her for this week. But his relief was full of depression. Things had been getting worse between them this last year. They both worked long hours and seemed to see each other less and less. Their careers, once a source of satisfaction, were now a wedge driven between them. Connecticut, once their dream home, now seemed crowded and harried, with expressways breathing down the neck of every country road.

The passion of their marriage seemed gone, as exhausted as their store of optimism. The most passionate moment they had had together this year had been that brief flare-up of jealousy on Brett's part when Karen seemed to pay too much attention to Ron Haverling at the Martins' party. Their argument seemed to have a life all its own, further inflamed by their efforts to be mature and reasonable.

In the end Karen had had to admit to herself that she had brought it on. She was jealous of Brett, deeply and irrationally so. In his work he dealt with sleek and aggressive female lawyers, women who shared his ideals about civil liberties and constitutional law. Karen, a computer consultant whose work tended toward the mundane, felt insecure about herself. She had flirted with Ron Haverling deliberately.

During that endless quarrel neither Karen nor Brett mentioned children. But children were very much on Karen's mind. She was painfully aware that her mother had been just her age—twenty-eight—when Karen herself was born. As for Brett, he was thirty, and much more eager to have children than he let on.

It was hard—hard to have a child in today's world. Hard to feel secure enough to take the plunge, when you knew that cutbacks, layoffs and downsizing might destroy your earning power overnight.

But the financial insecurity was only a mask for something deeper. As you worked harder and harder, longer and longer hours, in search of a security that receded each day, you gradually found that your will to be happy, your courage to be optimistic, was being sapped along with your energy. Perhaps even your sense of yourself, of your marriage. So that the struggle to maintain that dream turned out to be precisely the acid that ate away at it.

Brett had taken the words out her mouth when he'd said, sadly, "Go ahead, then. We can probably use a vacation from each other." Those words had hurt.

Karen had rarely felt more alone. Downstairs Jeannie was laughing and joking with people who would have welcomed Karen had she not felt so exiled. And perhaps, also, Marc was down there somewhere. She realized the real reason she was up here alone was so that she would not have to meet him.

It had never occurred to her that he might be here. Her one year spent in New Orleans, as an unhappy teenager, seemed as remote as another life. For a long time she had not allowed herself even to think of Marc—particularly after she met and married Brett. Marc was a footnote to her own development, a moment as fragile as the spring night that had brought him to her. It had all amounted to nothing, though the memory of it was marked, much to her chagrin, on her own body. All the more reason to forget.

Yet now it seemed perfectly logical that her ill-advised return to New Orleans should bring her into Marc's orbit. This was his place of birth, his family's city. She had not been south of the Mason-Dixon line since that very year, her seventeenth. Jeannie had been her only link with the South. Did that very fact not suggest that in accepting Jeannie's invitation she had been reaching out to the past and betraying Brett in the process?

She had opened a window and was looking out at the stately homes with their thickly wooded lawns. Magnolia, live oak and night-blooming jasmine scented the air. It was like looking into the past, her gaze leaping over the decades into a different world.

"You can't bring back the past," said the voice of reason. But wasn't this city, and indeed the whole South, testimony to the past's ability to live on, to color and taint the present? For good, or for ill?

She leaned over the rampart, feeling pulled by the night, her will sapped by the years.

A voice sounded low behind her.

"Karen."

She thought for a moment that it was her imagination. She rested her face on her hands, still looking down at the street.

"Karen." Again the voice rang out. It sounded familiar. Turning from the window, Karen saw that the lights inside the room were now out. A man was standing in the shadows looking at her.

"See how she leans her cheek upon her hand.
O that I were a glove upon that hand
That I might touch that cheek."

"Who is there?" she asked.

There was no answer. The silence seemed to smile at her, the darkness.

"Who is it?" Her voice trembled.

"Your voice hasn't changed," he said. "But your

body has. You grew taller, Karen. And I know you've grown prettier. All evening I've been waiting to see what's under that mask.''

Karen blushed. Her knees felt weak. His voice had not changed, either. It was deep, smooth, knowing.

"You didn't forget me, did you?'' he asked.

She willed herself not to answer.

"Did you?'' he pursued, his voice caressing her. "Did you take your revenge by forgetting? I wouldn't blame you if you had.''

She shrank from him against the balustrade. She felt him approach. She was afraid of him, and of herself. She should never have come here.

"Thou know'st the mask of night is on my face." A hand touched her shoulder, pulling her forward. She saw his mask in the shadows, coming off his face. Moonlight danced on the aquiline nose, the strong jaw. The eyes still hid under the shadow of his dark brow.

"You must remember this." He kissed her slowly, parting her lips with a tongue that seemed to know all of her in that instant. She tried feebly to push him away. A great moan surged inside her. His arm curled under her waist, pulling her closer.

Two

Jeannie Cooperman had such a good time at the Duchaises' midnight supper that she did not miss Karen until after one. Somewhat the gayer for the champagne she had drunk, she strolled through the mansion at a leisurely pace, greeting old friends in every room.

She began to worry about Karen when her first tour of the place was complete. She sought out Charles Duchaise and had him accompany her on a more thorough search. There was no sign of Karen.

Charles Duchaise asked the servants whether they had seen Karen leave. No one knew what she looked like out of her costume, so he had to refer to her as Juliet. This made the task more difficult, for at least half a dozen female guests had dressed as Juliet for the ball.

Finally a bartender, hired for the evening, remembered seeing a Juliet disappearing down a hallway toward the back of the house not long after midnight.

"She wasn't alone," he told Charles Duchaise. "She had Romeo with her."

Jeannie Cooperman listened in silence, her face growing pensive.

* * *

Karen lay naked on a canopied bed in a room she had never seen before.

The walls bore paintings of Belfort ancestors from before the Civil War. The women were delicate, with porcelain skin and quiet poses. The men were tall and lean, like Marc, with dark, intense eyes and something dashing in their manner. The family resemblance was striking, so much so that it was almost too easy to imagine Marc, in flesh and blood, leaping from one of those paintings. Or, for that matter, disappearing into one of them.

Karen closed her eyes, savoring the silence of the room. The thick windows completely blocked out whatever late-night sounds might emanate from the street outside. The night seemed bewitched. Her body throbbed from Marc's caresses. Her will seemed paralyzed. It was all she could do to reopen her eyes and contemplate the shadows around her.

She heard steps on the stairs. Marc entered the room, bearing champagne in an ice bucket and fluted glasses. He was naked, too. The body that had just made love to her was in motion, hard and smooth. She had to suppress a sigh at the sight of him.

"You didn't go to sleep?" he asked.

She smiled lazily. "No, I didn't."

"You're interested, then." He set the ice bucket down on the table and poured two glasses.

She said nothing as he handed her a glass. He looked down at her admiringly.

"You've changed," he said. "I noticed that right away."

"When did you see me?" she asked.

"The moment you and Jeannie arrived."

"Oh." This surprised Karen. "I didn't see you," she admitted.

"Were you looking for me?" He smiled.

Karen nodded. "I wanted to avoid you. I knew you might be behind one of those masks. I didn't know which one. I didn't want to meet you again."

"Why not?" He seemed hurt.

"Because I was afraid of this. Of us. I didn't trust myself."

He kissed her breast. "Afraid of this?" he mused. "What has the world done to you, Karen?"

There was a silence. She lay on her back, feeling the moist touch of his lips on her nipple. It was hard to accept this. She had spent her whole adult life trying to forget Marc Belfort. Now the clock had been turned back. It had happened so quickly. One kiss was all he had needed. She had not fought it hard enough.

But something in her savored this very defeat. The power of what had happened amazed her. And if the clock had turned back, time had also rolled forward. Because this was not the same Marc she had known when she was a girl. This was not an adolescent boy, but a subtle, mature man. His newfound polish had increased his charm a hundredfold.

"How did it make you feel?" she asked. "When you saw that I had changed?"

He thought for a moment. "At first, it intrigued me. You were a mystery. I wondered what thoughts had been put in that bright mind of yours by twelve years of living. It gave me a feeling of adventure.

"But then," he said, "it was more. It thrilled me.

Delighted me. It was one thing to be crazy about you when you were a sixteen-year-old girl. It was something else to want you now that you are a woman. It was as though you had changed from a short story into a novel. I wanted to know you. I still want to know you.''

There was a silence. They sipped their champagne. Her hand reached out to stroke the tuft of hair between his pectoral muscles. She looked at her fingers. They seemed almost foreign, sensual creatures with a will of their own, eager to caress him all over.

"Tell me about your husband," he said.

"Why?" Karen blushed.

"I want to know everything," he said. "I'm not jealous of him, you know. If he knew you, loved you, that makes him part of you. And every part of you is dear to me." He smiled, kissing her hair. "Don't you remember the end of *Madame Bovary?* When Charles Bovary met Emma's lover at the cemetery where she was buried, he felt only affection for him. The idea that she had loved him—that was a bond between them.''

"You're very well-read," Karen said.

"No, I'm not." Marc shook his head. "It's just that I have a few favorite authors. I've read their books so often that I remember a lot. Flaubert, Shakespeare, Dostoyevsky."

"Passionate authors," Karen observed.

"What's the point of writing about life if you don't write about passion?" Marc asked. "It's the only real subject of literature. At least the literature I read."

Karen looked up at him, her face clouded now. His

mention of Charles Bovary, the cuckolded husband, had struck a nerve.

"I'm sorry," he said. "Have I upset you?"

"No." Karen shook her head.

"Tell me, then. About your husband. About your marriage."

He drank his champagne, watching her. This time it was his hand that reached out, reflexively, to touch between her breasts and down her stomach.

She grasped the hand in her own. "We met at a party my last year of college," she said. "Brett was a law student. He was very idealistic, very caring about people. I needed that. I felt at the time that my life was going nowhere. Brett was passionate about the law. He's never lost that," she added, as though to defend her husband. "He's a civil liberties lawyer. He only cares about helping people. He doesn't make much money." She laughed. "We've had arguments about money. Lots of them. But I respect him for his vocation. He's a fine lawyer."

"Sounds like it," Marc said. "What about your marriage? Have you been happy?"

She lay back. She could feel him drinking in her nudity, studying her body. It sent an involuntary thrill of pleasure through her senses.

"Happy..." She tested the word on her lips. "For a while I thought we were the definition of happy. We lived in an apartment, then a little house. We went grocery shopping together. We watched TV, we shopped for things like microwaves, lawn furniture, our first set of real dishes. I thought it was heaven. Then, somehow, something was wrong. For a while

I thought I was the only one who felt that way. But then Brett told me he was worried, too. We started talking about it, trying to understand it. But we never succeeded.''

"No children?" Marc asked.

She shook her head. Again she felt his eyes on her naked body. He already knew it well enough to know that there was no evidence of childbirth.

"We keep saying we're going to have a baby," she said. "But the more time passes, the more it seems something is standing in the way. I mean, something more than just money troubles, or work, or wondering if this is the right moment. Something deeper that we *haven't* talked about."

Marc's hand had come to rest over the center of her. His fingers warmed her naked thigh. It occurred to her that life had not really changed her body since Marc had first known her. When Marc first made love to her, she had been a virgin. And now, as he made love to her, she was still a woman who had not had children. Both times, he knew her when she was incomplete, when her body had not yet fulfilled its feminine destiny. In a way this deepened his claim on her.

"What are you thinking?" she asked.

He smiled. "I'm embarrassed to admit it."

"Tell me." She touched the hand on her pelvis.

"I was thinking that the children you have with me will be your first children," he said. "And I'm happy it's that way. I know how selfish that sounds. But I admit it. I'm glad your marriage didn't touch you in that way. Glad you saved that for me."

So he had read her thoughts.

He sat up and pulled her to him. He cradled her face against his chest. She smelled their lovemaking on him, and the pungent fresh scent of his manhood. She felt something forbidden go through her. She kissed his nipple, as he had kissed hers. Instantly he stiffened in response. Her hand found its way to him. A groan sounded in his throat.

Their lovemaking was quicker this time, hotter. She guided him inside her hungrily and held him close with both hands, pulling him deeper and deeper until she lost control of her body completely.

The intimacy of him was almost painful to her. She reflected that this sudden hunger was a further betrayal of Brett. For Brett's name had been on her lips and on Marc's as they discussed him. The things she had confided about Brett were like an offering to Marc, another way to let him possess her. And, despite herself, she had been thrilled by Marc's allusion to the children she might bear him.

When it was over they lay in silence for a long time. Karen felt as though she were surrounded by ghosts. The room was filled with images from the past.

She turned on her side and kissed his stomach.

"And what about you?" she asked. "Tell me about yourself."

"What do you want to know?"

"Everything." The word sounded strange on her lips. She decided it had a sexual ring to it. Hearing everything, knowing everything, was another way of *doing* everything—with this man, in this bed, on this strange and scary night.

Marc frowned. "There's not that much to tell," he said. "Nothing good, anyway."

"Nonsense," she protested. "You're the one with the exciting life. My life has been mundane compared to yours."

He raised an eyebrow. "Do you really think that?" Karen nodded.

"Well, you don't know much about old southern families," Marc said, lighting a small, dark cigar. "The Belforts might have been exciting a hundred and twenty years ago, but they're not exciting now. Take my word for it."

"I don't believe you." She kissed his stomach and felt his hand curl in her hair, pulling her closer.

"New Orleans fell to Admiral Farragut's navy in April 1862," Marc said. "We lived under Reconstruction until 1877. Fifteen years. Longer than any other city in the Confederacy. Take my word for it, that has an effect. It got so bad that there was nothing to live for except the memory of how things had been. We gave up on the present. We lived only in the past."

Karen was touched by his use of the word *we*. He remained deeply rooted to his ancestors. In spirit he felt their longings and their disillusionments.

"Of course," he said, "we learned to survive after the war. New Orleans was the biggest city in the South—did you know that? There was a lot of building, a lot of investment. And, of course, a lot of graft and corruption. But those were Yankee things. That's what you have to understand. There was always the sense that the world was no longer a beautiful place. Do you remember in *The Great Gatsby*, when the narrator says that after Daisy betrayed him Gatsby saw the world as being material without being real? That's what it was like. Reality was something you could touch, but not something you could believe in. Not anymore. A dance of ghosts.''

Karen was hanging on his every word. He was so eloquent, even in his bitterness. ''At least you had something to believe in,'' she said, unwittingly identifying him with his ancestors.

''Maybe,'' he said. ''But you can't live in the past forever.''

He looked at her with sudden intensity.

''You see,'' he said, ''that's why it matters so much that I met you. A girl from outside this society. A girl who has her own life, her own ideas. You're something real. You're what I've been waiting for all these years.''

This speech struck Karen oddly. He seemed to sense it.

''Every young man in the South seems to reenact the same old drama,'' he said. ''You wake up in a world that seems ugly and hopeless, and you try to find a way through that world to something you can believe in. But your family and friends believe in only one thing—the past. It embitters you, it confuses you.

''They say I'm wild,'' he continued. ''A gambler, a prodigal son. My father doesn't care about me, but only about what I can do for him. My brother doesn't care about anything but himself. They don't understand. They're part of the problem. They don't really believe in anything. They reproach me for being rootless, but they're the rootless ones, the empty ones." He laughed. "Try to tell them that, though."

Karen felt a glimmer of understanding. Her own world might seem empty sometimes, and cruel, but she had been brought up by two caring parents to believe that her task in life should be to find a meaning for her own life. No one tried to impose that meaning on her by holding up shibboleths like money or success or fame—or the gentility of days gone by. She understood why things were more difficult for a southerner like Marc. His search for personal values was contaminated by his family's blind belief in the past.

"You've had a lot of women," she said.

He nodded. "They were my way of searching for something real," he said.

"But none of them lasted," Karen said. "Or did they?"

"No. Not one of them." He sighed. "The pursuit of women is a way of denying loneliness. Not really different from gambling, I think. A way of throwing yourself away." He looked at Karen. "But that's all behind me now."

He touched her breasts slowly, his fingertips caressing the nipples. "You're what I was waiting for," he said. "And the odd thing is, I think I knew it all along. You were never out of my mind, not for a moment. Your face was floating behind all those other faces."

"A lot of faces," Karen said, watching the fingers grazing her breasts.

He smiled. "There were a lot of lady-killers in my family. We're a passionate race, the Belforts. And my mother's family, the Courvoisiers, even more so. A lot of duels were fought over women in the family. There was a great-great-great uncle who killed himself over a woman. He looks a lot like me, or so the relatives say."

These words had shifted the balance of their intimacy somehow. He reached for his champagne glass and took a sip.

"Penny for your thoughts," he said.

She shook her head, as though to push away the question.

"You're full of secrets," he said. "Your mind is your own. I can see that." He raised himself to contemplate her. "I'd like to know all those secrets."

"What secrets?"

And as she lay gazing up at him, he drizzled some of the champagne from his glass between her breasts. The liquid tingled down her stomach, and he began to lick it off her.

"Silly," she said.

"Every secret." His lips were moving lower. Her skin came alive as he licked away the champagne with a long tongue. She arched her back and buried her fingers in his hair to pull him closer. His tongue found parts of her that were still throbbing with the memory of what he had done to her earlier.

"Every part of you is a secret," he said, crouching over her. "This one, and this one..." He kissed at forbidden corners, setting them aflame. "I want to know everything. I want to feel everything."

She couldn't stand any more. She pulled him into her with eager fingers and wrapped her legs around him.

"Marc," she said. "Marc."

He took pity on her. He moved inside her quickly, knowing once again the private place he had known before. And she couldn't escape the feeling that this entire bewitched night was a repetition of something that had already happened, a burrowing into the past.

She tried to clarify this thought, but it was too late. Pleasure overwhelmed her, and she gave him her moans and sighs like so many oaths of surrender. She felt him smile against her breast; then he lost his own control and came to her harder and harder until it was over.

They lay together for a long time, too drained even to finish their champagne. Karen felt the past surround her like the web of a spider. She had come to this city to tempt fate and had lost herself in something she should have put behind her a long time ago. If she was smart she would get out now, while there was still time.

After a while, a soft gray glow at the windows told her dawn was near.

She looked at Marc. "I have to go."

He shook his head, smiling. "No."

She looked at his naked body. It was so long, so lean and tight.

"What do you mean?" she asked.

"You're going someplace," he said. "But you're going with me."

She pondered these words. Her hand reached out for him again, as though pulled by a magnet.

"At least let me go back to Jeannie's and get my clothes," she said.

"You won't need them." He sat up and pulled her to him. "Now do you understand?"

His lips sought hers. His hands were on her shoulders. She felt her fingers explore him and heard her own sigh.

"Yes. I understand."

Three

As a girl of sixteen Karen Madison—then Karen Embry—spent ten months in New Orleans.

Her father, a structural engineer, had been hired to design the reconstruction of several historic buildings in the central business district. He brought Karen and her mother with him. The family stayed in a small rented house near Kenner. Karen's high grades brought her admission to the snobbish and exclusive St. Charles Academy, a private school located in an old plantation house ten miles upriver from New Orleans.

She was to regret later that her parents didn't simply enroll her in public school. The Academy had a very small student body, made up almost entirely of children of old New Orleans families. Karen quickly found herself ostracized, not only as an outsider but as a Yankee. Her schoolmates hid their contempt behind an armor of southern gentility. But as her ears became attuned to their speech, she learned to hear the mockery behind their mellifluous words.

By October she was completely miserable and begged her father to let her return alone to Boston, where she could stay with relatives while she finished tenth grade. Both parents refused, insisting that Karen had had too much of Boston life already and needed exposure to another atmosphere.

When Karen saw that further pleading was pointless, she retreated inside herself and resolved to endure her isolation until June. Participating as little as possible in her classes, she volunteered even less of herself to those around her. By Christmas she was thought of as a nonentity, a colorless northerner who would be forgotten as soon as she departed.

She met Jeannie Cooperman at a debate club meeting, which was Karen's only extracurricular activity at school. Jeannie seemed as isolated as Karen, and the two shared their misery over a lot of sodas and cheeseburgers at the local café, where they could only ogle from afar the more popular kids. In another life, Karen could have truly enjoyed Jeannie for her humor, her endurance and her high intelligence. But as things stood, a gray cloud of unhappiness colored their relationship, and they spent few happy moments together.

Then came Mardi Gras.

A special celebration was held at school, including costumes, a barbecue and a dance. Participation was mandatory, and so Karen found herself dressed in a wildly colorful Cajun costume, standing against the wall of the school's Big Hall while she watched her classmates dance to traditional music.

A tall, slim boy whose face was hidden by his pirate's mask appeared from nowhere and asked her to dance. She agreed. He twirled her around the hall to a tune that made her dizzy and left her without a word.

Later, to her surprise, he reappeared and asked her to take a walk with him. Once outside in the moonlight, he took off his mask. She recognized Marc Belfort. He was, even at his tender age, a great ladies' man. She had heard murmurs in the girls' bathroom about his scandalous reputation and his prowess as a lover.

There was nothing of the irresponsible Lothario in Marc as he took her for a long walk in the woods surrounding the school. On the contrary, he seemed serious and somewhat driven. He felt stifled by his southern family, he said. The inbred society of New Orleans disgusted him. His favorite writers were New Englanders, Transcendentalists, or Europeans like Nietzsche, Proust, Thomas Mann.

"We live in the past here," he said. "We've barely entered the nineteenth century, not to mention the twentieth. I'm counting the days until I can get out."

"Where will you go?" Karen asked.

He smiled, taking her hand. "Europe," he said. "Or maybe South America. Or China. Anywhere!"

They went deeper and deeper into the woods, until Karen knew she could not find her way back alone. He led her to a clearing where the moon turned the grass silver. They sat down together. He told her of fantasies that had devoured him since he was a boy, riotous dreams that made him feel permanently exiled from his peers. His whole life was a search for fresh air, he said. He had never yet breathed it, and he was literally dying of suffocation.

Karen found his intensity exciting. As the night went on, he drew from her breathless admissions of her own yearnings, the ideal ones she sometimes wrote about in her diary and the forbidden ones she had never revealed to a soul.

She had never met anyone like him. His exile from his southern roots was articulated in a sweet antebellum accent that had something almost Shakespearean about it. His hunger for other places, other times, was incarnated in a body that looked as though it came from one of the paintings in the Academy's gallery of portraits, the body of a plantation scion destined for proud service in the Civil War. He was a composite figure, with one foot in the present and one in a glorious past. He was too beautiful to be entirely real.

His arms were around her now, his lips on hers as he shared the almost intolerable passion driving him. To Karen, his embrace seemed a way out of her own thwarted life, an open door to something exalted and pure.

In the end, carried away by his longing and by the response it kindled inside her, Karen gave him what was most secret, in the pale moonlight of a night stolen from the world. She did so with an awe appropriate to the occasion. Later they returned in silence to the dance, arriving when nearly everyone was gone. He stopped her at the edge of the woods, held her to him for one last kiss and released her.

"Remember me," he said.

Memory was all she was to have, for he never spoke to her again or acknowledged her existence. She endured a hundred more days at the Academy, lonelier than ever. She saw Marc surrounded by his friends, the admiring girls as well as the laughing, shouting boys. And as she waited for the end of the school year to come, she realized that she had been only a conquest to him, and that all his beautiful words, his poetry and his yearning were merely the trappings of his seduction of her.

She resolved to forget all about Marc Belfort. What remained of him would serve as a warning to her. She must respect herself, stand on her own two feet, and never again allow herself to be the victim of her own fantasies. Her one night as a southern belle, the creature of a man's graces and of his dalliance, was over forever.

Ironically, her plan worked. The memory of Marc Belfort remained on her flesh and in her senses, but years went by without her devoting a moment's thought to him. She lived for the present and for the future. Marc was a relic of her past. And the past, Karen felt, was only a thing to be overcome.

She finished high school in Boston and went on to college in New York. She became interested in computers and chose programming as a career. She savored the exactitude of computer language. She enjoyed the feeling of control and power as she set up systems for people who admired her expertise and followed her instructions to the letter. When glitches occurred, it was Karen who came to the rescue, patiently explaining what had gone wrong and how to correct it.

Karen had become the woman she wanted to be. Crisp, bright, responsible, a woman on whom people of both sexes depended for knowledge and judgment.

She married a man who was himself serious and responsible. She began a life that would surely bring her happiness, because it was conceived in love and in commitment. She never thought about the past, because the future was her element.

Then came Jeannie's invitation, and Karen's impulsive acceptance of it. And the handsome stranger on the balcony at the Duchaise mansion, with his verses from *Romeo and Juliet* and his masked face. In one stroke, the weakness underlying Karen's plan for her life fell away. Her struggle was brief, her surrender complete. The past had won. The future became something unknowable.

Four

The day after the ball at Sans Souci Karen flew to Europe with Marc Belfort.

Karen didn't have time to collect herself. Only a short time before, her life had been a familiar thing with clear boundaries. Now she had abandoned her job, her husband, her home, and she was on her way to Europe with a man she barely knew.

They landed in Paris and spent a glorious, sensual week in an apartment owned by Marc's family on the Quai des Grands Augustins. It was a charming place, slightly unreal, with paintings of Belfort ancestors who had made grand tours of Europe in the nineteenth century. It was almost more redolent of the Old South than of France. Yet Karen reflected that the Belforts came from France, and that their particular brand of southern gentility originated in the Paris of the eighteenth century.

That first week was spent behind closed doors, except at dinnertime. Marc took Karen to Le Cerf Volant, La Tour d'Argent, the Drouant and Lasserre. After dinner they took carriage rides in the Bois de Boulogne or long walks in the Latin Quarter. Karen was sinking deeper into the dream Marc spun around her. It was harder to concentrate on moment-to-

moment reality. She floated in a sea of images, each
more exotic than the last.

Then they drove to the Côte d'Azur. Marc seemed
to know the roads very well, and he was unafraid of
the French drivers, who thought nothing of driving at
a hundred and fifty kilometers per hour until a stop
sign or light made them slow down.

They spent four nights in Monte Carlo, where Marc
gambled with a skill no less impressive than his aban-
don. He kept Karen by his side at all times, "For
luck," he said. As the hour grew later he would notice
her fatigue and whisper in her ear that soon the game
would be over and he would take her to bed. She'd
blush, fearing that the others around the table sensed
her guilty anticipation.

Somehow the gambling made lovemaking more exciting. All of life seemed a risk, a desperate skating
on the surface of something supremely dangerous.
Throwing his winnings carelessly on the dresser,
Marc would watch her sit back on the bed. He'd remove his clothes, knowing that the sight of his emerg-
ing body was exciting her, himself thrilled by her desire. They made love again and again as the wee
hours passed, finally falling asleep exhausted in each
other's arms, waking up to breakfast on the terrace
just before noon.

She noticed during this time that his body had a
chameleonlike ability to reflect his mood. Sometimes
he seemed leaner, almost knifelike in his agility.
Sometimes she saw to her astonishment that his pec-
torals and thighs were actually much bigger than she
had thought. His eyes, black as night one day, seemed

a light tawny gold the next. His hands, so delicate and aristocratic, could seem cruelly strong when he lifted something heavy—or when he took her in his arms.

She also noticed that his naked body had no blemishes of any kind. No birthmark or mole touched the pale perfection of his limbs. The proportion of him was also perfect. She had never imagined that a male body could be so beautiful. Marc had no self-consciousness about his beauty. He bore himself with a careless grace that made him seem all the more human, all the more touchable.

After four days Marc said he was "bored" with Monte Carlo, so they went on to Deauville, then to Biarritz and Trouville. After that it was on to Baden-Baden, and to Spain, where the Casino Gran Madrid, according to Marc, brought out the best in him as a player.

Karen came to know the games and to admire Marc's betting strategies, which were invariably bold, even reckless. The croupiers would smile when he approached their table, for they knew he brought with him excitement and danger. One night in Biarritz he won so much that the casino's manager had to sign a note himself. Another night he lost so much that, had he not been well-known to the management, he would have been arrested.

"Why do you gamble, Marc?" she asked him one night.

"So I can feel real," he said simply.

"Don't you feel real with me?" she asked.

He raised an eyebrow. "I see what you mean," he

said. "You're right. I probably won't be gambling much longer. Let's consider this a last fling."

"Can you afford all this?" she asked.

His face darkened. "You're not asking me about money, are you?" he said. "Because that's the one thing I can't allow you to ask. Ever."

"I'm sorry," she said. "I couldn't help wondering. I've never seen so much money risked this way."

Marc relented. "I'm making up for six generations of Belforts who never risked a penny. They were too busy pinching them."

"Is your family very wealthy, then?"

"I ought to know. I manage the money."

"Really?"

He nodded, a wry smile on his face. "My brother can't be bothered. He handles the management end of two of the bigger corporations we hold stock in. He doesn't understand money. Never has and never will. My father almost begged me to major in business at Tulane. I took over the money management to please him. Or I should say, to please my mother— before her death. It was probably the dumbest thing I ever did."

"Why?" Karen asked.

"Because I bound myself to him, and to the family's fortunes. I didn't rebel until it was too late. Or I should say, I stopped rebelling when I should have rebelled even more. You see, I felt guilty about my wild youth. I wanted to help the family. I couldn't know at the time that it would become such a millstone around my neck."

"You don't like your family much, do you?" Karen asked.

"I liked my mother. Loved her a lot, in fact. She was gentle. A kind soul. When she went, there wasn't much left."

He smiled. "In any case, don't worry about my gambling. I'm not really risking anything. If we Belforts weren't scandalously ahead on our investments, I wouldn't gamble a penny. Investing money in an outright loss like gambling is the only way I can keep the IRS happy. So stop worrying."

Through his gambling Karen came to know almost as much about Marc as she knew from his lovemaking. Yet the two things were very different. As a gambler, Marc was desperate, almost insane in his desire to take risks. As a lover, he was tender, slow, only revealing his explosive power in the final moments.

The two sides of him joined to intoxicate Karen. As they traveled from town to town, casino to casino, she felt her connection to the real world diminishing. She became Marc's creature, his "good luck charm." Perversely, she relished her passive role, sitting in silence as he risked larger and larger sums, knowing that when the game was over they would go back to their room and he would possess her, just as he had possessed, in the rolling roulette ball or the falling cards, his own destiny.

She began to glow, and not only from the sunbathing she did on European beaches by her lover's side. There was a look of mystery and expectancy on her face that did not go unnoticed by those who crossed her path. Eyes would turn to her as she sat by Marc's side. Men and women alike would murmur to each other about her charms. She could feel their curiosity about the pleasures Marc gave her in private, and about the attraction she held for him.

She took on some of his own mystery, and she actually began to look more exotic. Her fair complexion was rosier now, her hair more lush. Her eyes seemed darker. She looked European, in an odd composite way that united the charms of French, Spanish and Italian girls whom she saw on the arms of wealthy men at the luxurious hotels she frequented.

Occasionally one of these men, bored with his own companion, would dare to speak to Karen, and would express his surprise on learning that she was an American girl from Boston.

"I thought I had seen everything," said a handsome Spanish businessman who spoke to her at the Gran Madrid. "I would have sworn you were French, if it were not for that something in your eyes that made me think of our Spanish girls. Tell me—how does a girl from Boston find her way to the Gran Madrid with Mr. Belfort?"

"Oh, you know Marc?" Karen asked, surprised.

"We all know Mr. Belfort." He smiled. "He has lost more money at the casino than my family lost in the war. On the other hand, he has won more than my family ever had to begin with. Yes, Mr. Belfort is well-known."

The man, who introduced himself as Señor Lopez-Muñoz, invited Karen and Marc for a drink at his home in the Calle Princesa. He talked about America with Karen, and about gambling with Marc. It turned out the two men had crossed paths at casinos not only in Europe but in the Caribbean, as well. Marc was affable and even expansive with Señor Lopez-Muñoz, but he looked at his watch after an hour and said it was time to say goodbye. "I've had a long day, and Karen needs her sleep," he explained.

For some reason Karen was more excited than usual to make love after that pleasant interval in the stranger's company. After a mere sip of the champagne Marc poured for her in the hotel room, she gave him an impish look and let her skirt fall to her ankles.

"What's got into you?" he asked.

"I don't know. Maybe it was the moonlight," she said, slowly removing her bra as he watched.

"Whatever it was, we'll do it again tomorrow," he said, pulling her to him and burying his face against her breast.

A strange impulse made her bold, and she pushed him down on his back and caressed him all over before mounting him and guiding him inside her. She arched her back like a sensual little rider, her hands encouraging him as his thrusts grew more urgent. As the end approached she looked down at him. He was staring at her through wide eyes that seemed obsessed. She recalled the way Señor Lopez-Muñoz had looked at her tonight. For the first time, she realized her power as a temptress. She gloried in the soft seductions of her own flesh as she surrounded her lover. She wanted to be sensual for him, to be irresistible. And as the last wave came, the tremors of his ecstasy firing her own loins, she knew she had succeeded.

She was surprised the next morning when she awoke to find Marc packing their bags.

"What's the matter?" she asked.

"Nothing's the matter," he said. "We're going home, that's all."

"Why?"

"It's time," he said. "No more dallying in all these watering spots. I want you all to myself now."

At the time Karen saw no particular significance in these words. She regretted leaving Europe, for she had been feeling more relaxed about the foreign landscape, more sure of herself. On the other hand, she relished the thought of going home with Marc. *Home.* The word excited her, because it meant that his home was to be hers also.

They boarded a Swedish liner at Cherbourg and sailed for New York harbor. Marc had correctly guessed that Karen had never been on an ocean liner before. They spent long hours in deck chairs watching the other passengers take their promenades. They swam in the pool, feeling the water shift with the rolling of the ship. At night they danced in the ballroom, watched the stars, and Marc gambled. And they made love. And always, at every moment, the sweet, smooth roll of the ship reminded Karen, not only of the great ocean heaving underneath them, but of the endless rhythm of their bodies and their intimacy, which was also an ocean of limitless depth and mystery.

Five

It was only when she got home that she realized something was wrong.

The Belfort mansion was empty save for a servant, Mrs. Crittendon. Karen had had the vague hope of meeting Marc's family. When she asked him where they were he told her his father was on an extended visit to some Belfort relatives in France.

"We probably passed him on the way over," he said. "That's fine with me. I don't need to get any closer to my father than that."

"What about your brother?" she asked.

"David has an apartment of his own in the suburbs," Marc said. "You'll be seeing him one of these days. Don't look forward to it, though. He's as dull as dishwater."

Something in this explanation seemed evasive to Karen, but she said nothing.

The ship had docked in New York very early that morning, and the flight to New Orleans had been delayed, so Karen was feeling tired and a little foggy as Marc led her through the darkened mansion to a lavish upstairs bedroom. It was decorated in thick brocades, with tapestries on the walls and heavy drapes hiding the tall windows.

"This isn't the room we were in before," Karen observed.

"I hope you like it," he said.

"It's beautiful." Karen admired the room. "It looks not quite real. I feel as though I've stepped into a time machine."

He smiled. "There isn't a thing in here that wasn't in my family a hundred years ago. Except, of course, the mattress."

She smiled, looking at the bed.

"Those tapestries used to hang in the library of our plantation upriver," Marc said. "The Union Army burned the place, but the Belfort slaves managed to save some things." He pointed to a dull gold toilet set on the vanity. "That belonged to my great-great-great-great-grandmother," he said. "She brought it with her from France when she married into the family. Those Yankee soldiers would have loved to get their hands on it. Look at the initials."

Karen picked up the brush. The gold handle bore the initials ACV.

"What do they stand for?" she asked.

"Amélie Courvoisier was her name," Marc said. "She came from one of the oldest families in France. They were peers of the realm since the Middle Ages."

A heavy bronze bust of a woman sat on the bedside table. It was quite beautiful, with magnificent details in the drapery. The woman's face was strikingly distinctive.

"Who is she?" Karen asked.

"No one knows for sure. If you look closely you

can see the Belfort characteristics in her face. But none of the family historians has ever succeeded in determining for sure who she was. The bronze dates from the early nineteenth century."

Marc seemed to change as he pointed out the treasures in the room. Pride sounded in his deep voice, along with a bitterness Karen had never heard before.

"Is something the matter, Marc?" she asked.

"Not anymore." He took her in his arms and kissed her.

"Are you sure?" she asked. "You seem so strange."

He sat her gently on the bed and stood looking down at her. "To think that a poison so destructive can be made of simple flesh and blood...." His voice had a faraway, musing tone.

Karen was alarmed by his words. "What do you mean?"

"Just something someone wrote," he said. "Never mind."

He sat down beside her and pushed her back onto the spread. He kissed her, long and deep, his arms covering her. His weight pressed her into the soft covers.

"Do you know," she said, "for the first time I feel like I'm home? Like this place could be home to me, after all."

He kissed her again. "It will."

"I want it to."

"When you truly understand," he said.

"Understand what?"

"That there can be no more Señor Lopez-Muñozes."

Karen looked at him in perplexity. "What do you mean?"

"No more admiring Spanish gentlemen," he said. "Or French gentlemen, or Swiss or Germans or Englishmen. No more men."

Karen was taken aback. "Marc, what are you talking about?"

He leaned back to look at her. "You're so beautiful," he said. "I just want to keep you that way. You see, the desire of other men tarnishes you."

This rather stilted phrase, along with the suspicious look on Marc's face, sufficed to unnerve Karen even more.

"Marc, you're so strange."

"I ask only one thing of you," he said. "Fidelity."

"Fidelity?" she asked.

"Ah, the sound of that word on a woman's lips," he observed. "The greatest contradiction known to language."

Karen was angry now. "What are you saying?" she asked.

"I saw the way other men looked at you when we were in Europe," he said. "The closer we got—the more I depended on you—the more I saw them looking. I feel sorry for you, Karen. You didn't even know."

"Didn't know what? That they were looking? Every woman knows when she's looked at, Marc."

He shook his head, as though amused by her obtuseness. "What you didn't know," he said, "was that it was you who was sending out the signals that attracted them. But I saw it. I saw how you glowed. How you smiled.''

He shook his head again. ''The female never knows. It's her nature. She doesn't have to say a word, or even appear at the window. Her scent will draw the males from miles around. You can hear them howl all night long.''

Karen sat up to look at his face.

''Marc, you're not making sense. I'm a person. Not an animal.''

''Is that why you flirted with Lopez-Muñoz?'' he asked.

''I didn't flirt with him. I chatted with him. So did you.''

Marc sat back, farther away from her than before. ''If that's what you call it, I rest my case,'' he said.

Karen was at a loss. Marc seemed almost unrecognizable. He had never spoken to her in this tone or looked at her in this way. The man whose lovemaking had become the center of her world these past weeks now seemed a million miles away, walled off from her by that suspicious look and—come to think of it—by this dark house.

He must have guessed what she was thinking, for he took her in his arms, roughly, and kissed her hard.

''Marc...''

''No. No more words.''

He made love to her without taking off her clothes. He pinioned her to the bed while he found his way to her secret places and caressed her. The power of him, combined with the unfamiliarity of the room, shocked her into a heat of desire that made her throb madly against him.

Her hands clawed at the rich bedclothes. Her eyes were closed. Her legs spread pearly white in the emptiness, wrapping themselves around his waist. When he was inside her she moaned her passion and a sort of entreaty, as though begging him to be what he had been for her from the first, what he must be.

There was something triumphant and almost cruel about his thrusts. Large hands cradled her loins, pulling her harder onto him. She thought she heard words on his lips, and she tried to make them out, but the storm in her senses took away her power to understand anything but ecstasy.

"Marc," she cried. "Marc!"

It was over. They lay panting, Karen holding him against her breast. She wanted desperately to believe that their physical intimacy had banished whatever misunderstanding had upset him before.

He came to himself slowly, caressing her and kissing her hair. He was the same Marc, she was sure. He smelled the same, tasted the same, possessed her in the same absolute way.

At length he stood up. "Don't move," he said. He stared down at her, a woman still fully dressed, her naked legs betraying what had happened between them. Her hair awry, her face distorted by pleasure.

"My thoughts and my discourse as madmen's are,
At random from the truth vainly expressed.
For I have sworn thee fair, and thought thee

bright,
Who art as black as Hell, as dark as night.''

Karen did not know the quotation that Marc re-
cited. But she recognized Shakespeare from the melancholy beauty of the words and because she knew
Marc adored Shakespeare.

"Marc, how can you say that?" she asked. "How
can you think that of me?"

Again she saw the peculiar, wan smile on his face,
a look of sadness and cynicism.

"You don't even see it," he said, studying her
body. "Because of the kind of woman you are. And
because of where you're from."

"What do you mean?"

He buttoned his shirt where her impassioned fingers had undone it. "You're going to understand,"
he said. "That will be my gift to you, Karen. To make
you understand."

He turned on his heel and melted into the shadows.
She heard the door open and close, then a muted
click.

She lay for a long moment pondering what had
happened tonight. Her mind still numbed from their
journey, she had difficulty being lucid. The conflict
that had arisen so unexpectedly between her and Marc
seemed unreal. Yet their lovemaking had never been
more intense. It almost seemed that the depth of the
chasm between her and Marc had increased the erotic
power of their physical contact.

After a while she got up to try the door. It was
locked.

She stood in the shadows, reflecting on what had happened, pondering this extraordinary return to a place that had seemed like home until it took on the strangeness of the ends of the earth.

Then she threw open the tall curtains.

There was no window behind them. Only a huge, empty wall bearing a satin wallpaper from a hundred years ago.

A second, smaller door was on the wall opposite the bed. She tried it. It opened to reveal a small bathroom, beautifully decorated, with a toilet, a tub and a sink—but no window.

There were no other doors or windows. Karen was trapped.

Six

Karen's imprisonment had several phases, interior and unrelated to the physical walls of the house that shut her in.

At first she was furious, rebellious. She was a woman of the twentieth century, a woman who had been standing on her own two feet all her adult life. Marc's obsession with her seemed quaint and passé, like something out of the dusty old paintings that covered the walls of the Belfort mansion. And his sequestration of her seemed even more absurd. It came from the eighteenth century, not the twentieth. No man could keep a woman prisoner in the modern world. It was unthinkable.

But late that first night, when Karen was still woozy from the long journey and dazed by what had happened upon her return, Marc came to her. He entered the room soundlessly when she was half-asleep and slipped into bed by her side.

All the violence in him was gone. He soothed her with delicate caresses until her flesh began to tingle with feminine hunger. His hands were slow. The fresh scent of his skin suffused her. She felt protected by his body, by his affection.

Finally, as though taking pity on her, he removed

her nightgown and covered her with kisses, each more intimate than the last. Her breath came short as his tongue found her nipples and teased them into hardness. She buried her hands in his hair and pulled him lower, so he could know more of her. In that instant she sensed a hesitation in him, as though her boldness shocked him.

He stood up to remove his clothes. The erect power of his body awed her. The deep chest, the broad, lean shoulders made him look daring and dangerous, like an intruder who knew all too well what his charms could do to a woman.

"Oh, Marc..." She held out her arms to him.

He came to cover her with himself. Her hands touched his shoulders. And then he did something she would never forget as long as she lived. Crouched atop her, he slowly moved his lean body upward as he kissed her stomach, her rib cage, her breasts and finally her face. And as he did so, he slipped himself inside her, all the way to the hilt and back out again, in one smooth motion. It was a mere caress, a hint of things to come; but it was so unexpected, so intimate, that Karen gasped her ecstasy aloud.

Their lovemaking was so slow, so warm and languorous that night, that Karen could not help feeling she was truly home at last. The communion of her flesh with that of Marc's seemed to break down all the walls of her life. She fell asleep in his arms, more at peace than she had felt in a long time.

But when she awoke she was alone. Mrs. Crittendon brought her a breakfast of rolls, fruit, juice and coffee, a fresh rose in a tiny vase sitting on the platter.

There were magazines and newspapers on the table, as well as writing paper. Karen spent her morning reading and thinking. Her mind was awake now, and she fought to assess her situation. She could not let things go on this way. It was insane, it was absurd. She must have it out with Marc.

In the afternoon Marc came to her again. He was wearing a business suit she had never seen before. He looked crisp, handsome and civilized.

"You're looking rested," he said. "How has your day been?"

"Marc," she began to remonstrate with him. But he silenced her with his lips.

"Don't say anything," he murmured. "Not yet."

He took her in his arms and began to caress her. Before she knew it the skirt and blouse she wore— both souvenirs of their European sojourn—were coming off under his moving hands. The suit he had arrived in came off, as well, and her arguments on behalf of the real world were soon drowned out by her senses, which spoke only of naked bodies and lovemaking.

He came back at the dinner hour and took her downstairs to the dining room, where they were served a traditional New Orleans meal by a cook she saw for the first time. Marc's conversation was almost too gentle and commonplace. He told Karen about his day at work, the news of the city. She could hardly believe that all this ordinary conversation could be a prelude to renewed imprisonment. She dared not even broach the subject.

After dinner, they had brandy together in the li-

brary upstairs, with its view of thick tree branches and
the street outside, a vision itself as lovely as an old
painting. Music was playing somewhere, Chopin, perhaps. Marc showed Karen some of the books on the
old shelves, including a Belfort family Bible with a
genealogy dating back to the sixteenth century. He
talked about some of them, relating stories that had
been handed down over the generations.

"We're an unusual family," he said. "We've got
a little bit of everything in our history. A few thieves,
some alcoholics, some nutcases. Quite a number of
'great men,' as great men go. Judges, philosophers,
statesmen, writers. But the Belfort blood is thicker
than water. You can see that in the paintings."

It was true. There was a particular Belfort look—
a sort of narrowing of the brows, a shrouded or
hooded expression—that touched the faces of all the
ancestors, making them look almost like brothers and
sisters. It was a determined look, inward and somehow obsessed. They seemed to embody the romance
of the world they had lived in.

Karen looked from the painting above the mantel
to the face of her lover. The Belfort look was in
Marc's eyes, too, dark and enigmatic. It gave a peculiar luster to the face of this twentieth-century man.
Through the eyes of her memory she saw it once
again on the face of the handsome boy who had swept
her off her feet the night of the Mardi Gras dance at
the St. Charles Academy. She realized it had bewitched her even then.

"How does it feel to be so connected to the past?"

she asked. "So much of a piece with your ancestors?"

He shrugged, swirling the brandy in his glass. "It's a limitation," he said. "Or at least it can feel like one. I don't want to be defined by things outside my own life. I want to make my own destiny. Sometimes I look upon the Belforts as a tiresome crowd of relatives with whom I'm stuck at an obligatory dinner party. I can hardly wait to get away."

He sipped his brandy and glanced once again at the paintings. "But sometimes they feel like home to me," he said. "They make me feel less alone in the world than I might feel otherwise. It's a trade-off. Like everything else in life."

He smiled at Karen. "What about you?" he asked. "Do you ever feel a bond with your ancestors?"

She shook her head. "They're just faces in a family album," she said. "And only a few generations of them at that. A great-grandmother who was a suffragette in Boston. We have a daguerreotype of her, very faded."

"Time isn't the same thing up north," Marc observed. "You're a hurried race of people, with an eye on the future. You're too busy to linger over the past."

Karen thought this remark over. "Do you mean that as a criticism?" she asked at length.

"Not at all. Did you ever read de Tocqueville? His trip through America?"

Karen shook her head.

"You should. You would learn a lot from it. One day de Tocqueville found himself at a place along the

Mississippi where one bank of the river was slave-owning plantation land, and the opposite bank was Yankee land. He said the difference was like night and day. The Yankee side was vibrant with activity. The southern side looked as though it had been asleep for a hundred years. Nothing was happening. Nothing at all.''

Karen saw his point. The past was a good thing if it equipped you to make your own future. But not if it paralyzed you.

In any case, she could not deny the truth of his observations, as they related to herself. The future had always seemed like a precious fabric that she must weave into the shape of her own destiny. She thought back on the way she had been brought up by her parents. They always spoke of her future and what she would make of it. Come to think of it, they rarely spoke about the past, except to reminisce with amused smiles about their own courtship.

Marc was right. Karen came from a culture that disdained the past, that idealized the future. A culture in which the initiative of the individual was all that counted, as opposed to the traditions handed down by those who had gone before.

He was looking at the portrait. ''There's a lot in my family to think about,'' he said. ''But there's one thing that can't be found in any of those portraits.''

''What is that?'' Karen asked.

''You.''

He came to her side, stood her up and took her back to her room to make love to her. She did not protest.

Dimly she realized what was happening. Marc was using his various attractions to paralyze her will. What his conversation failed to accomplish, his hands and lips could not fail to finish. As he spread her legs and prepared to enter her, she felt her mind rebel, then felt her rebellion die amid the ecstasy he was giving her. Her legs curled around him, her hands slipped beneath his waist. Flesh was more powerful than mind—for tonight, at least.

The next morning she awoke alone again.

The second phase of Karen's imprisonment had asserted itself. It was a phase of indecision. Karen knew she was a prisoner, but something about her prison was not entirely unattractive. The solitude and silence of her new life were oddly restful. The pleasures Marc gave her were so overpowering that they seemed an open door to another existence. She still wanted to return to the real world, but she found herself putting off her escape from day to day. She could not make up her mind to be free, to want freedom.

She found herself depending more on Marc, seeing and feeling through him. Her hours alone were a burden. She looked forward hungrily to his arrival. When she heard his key in the lock and saw him enter the room, she awaited his approach with bated breath. The touch of his hands on her shoulders released a paroxysm of pent-up wanting. She returned his kiss passionately and moved her slim body so as to make room for him, to invite him to her.

"So you missed me, did you?" he'd ask.

She'd respond by pulling his face to her breast, her desire so great that she could not speak.

Indeed, his physical power over her increased in proportion to her bondage. As her captor, Marc was necessarily strange, less familiar than he'd been at first. His will was a foreign thing that held her hostage. This made his lovemaking more exotic. The hands that explored her were full of their own secrets, unknowable. Thus their caresses felt more like a violation, a forbidden and excessive knowledge. When she guided them to her secret places, her surrender was all the hotter. Her sense of transgression was like a drug. In the early days, when they had traveled freely between European countries, her feelings for Marc sprung from her own initiative. Now she was truly his slave. It was a new experience for her, alien to everything she had ever been taught, everything she had ever believed about herself. Giving in to it was enthralling, like a sin committed far from the eyes that might judge her.

By now Marc knew all Karen's sexual secrets. During his visits he experimented on her senses with caresses, words, suggestions that left no corner of her imagination or fantasy unexplored. This made her feel even more his slave. If she ever did escape this place, she would never dare speak of what she had experienced here to a living soul, what forbidden pleasures she had enjoyed.

She suspected she could never belong entirely to another man, now that Marc had known her in these secret, forbidden ways. And perhaps this was his intention. To know her so utterly that no other man could ever begin to satisfy her.

If she did escape, could she ever live without those pleasures? She was not sure.

Marc revealed more about his personal history now that he had Karen all to himself. He told her of impressions from his earliest youth that had defined his character, memories that haunted him, conflicts that had left their mark on his adulthood. He showed her little corners of the mansion where he had played hide-and-seek with his brother, where he had experimented sexually with his girl cousins, the attic room he had been afraid of as a boy.

Marc showed Karen the chair his mother had liked to sit in when the afternoon light came in the windows. The writings of Marquise de Sévigné she used to read was on the shelf alongside the chair. In the drawer beneath it was a piece of the knitting she used to do.

"No one sits in that chair anymore," Marc said. "I don't think anyone has sat in it since the night she died."

A portrait of his mother hung on the opposite wall. She had been a fragile-looking woman despite her plump body. The look in her eyes was subtle. It combined obedient southern diffidence with something more knowing.

"She was the best of us," Marc said simply. "I didn't expect her to live forever. But I also didn't foresee how empty the place would be without her."

The more Karen learned about the house, the more it began to take on the mysterious character of Marc's past, and his personality became ever more embedded in the walls around her.

But even as Karen heard these things, each more intimate than the last, the more she realized that Marc could not possibly intend letting her go after giving over such secrets. The confidences were part and parcel of her enslavement. Now that she belonged to him absolutely, he could say whatever he wished to her. He knew she would never repeat it to another human soul.

Sometimes he let her wander the mansion at her leisure, provided she was accompanied by Mrs. Crittendon.

One day she stopped before a painting. It showed a handsome young man dressed in a nineteenth-century redingote and high polished boots. A man who looked strikingly like Marc.

"Who is that?" she asked.

Mrs. Crittendon smiled. "That's Marcel Auguste Belfort," she said. "A great-great-great uncle of Mr. Marc. He was the poet of the family. He had many volumes of poetry published here in New Orleans. Some of them are still to be found in anthologies of Confederate poetry. He was wounded at Gettysburg and finished out his life in this very house."

Karen vaguely remembered something Marc had told her about this ancestor. "Was he the man who killed himself over a woman?" Karen asked.

Mrs. Crittendon narrowed her eyes as she looked at Karen. "Did Mr. Marc tell you that?" she asked.

"No," Karen lied. "I heard it from someone at the Sans Souci ball."

"There was more to the story," said Mrs. Crittendon. "Marcel Belfort fell in love with a girl from a fine Catholic family in Maryland. But the Belforts were Protestants. Her family refused to consent to the match. Marcel seduced her and brought her here to New Orleans. He bought a house near the river and kept her there for years. He never let her out of his sight."

"Didn't she try to escape?" Karen asked.

"At first, yes," the older woman said. "But Marcel—so the story goes—kept her prisoner with his poetry. He wrote sonnets and lyric poems for her, every single day. He put them under her door and sometimes read them aloud to her. The power of his love was so great that his words kept her a slave when the walls of the house could not."

"Did any of those poems survive?" Karen asked.

The old woman smiled, shaking her head. "He destroyed them all. Burned them in the old library, right above where we are standing. Just before he killed himself."

"So he did kill himself for love," Karen observed.

"The young woman became with child," Mrs. Crittendon said. "She could not bear the shame, with her strict religious upbringing. She turned on the gas and killed herself and her unborn child. When Mr. Marcel found out about it, he shot himself in the heart. They found his body alongside hers."

So Marc lied, Karen thought. The story he had told of his famous ancestor was not completely true.

On the other hand, it was no wonder he had suppressed the part of it that was closest to his own heart. The sequestration of a woman by a lover who knew he could not survive without her.

"And Marc's other ancestors?" Karen asked. "Were there other—stories?"

"There are stories in every family." Mrs. Crittendon did not seem to want to say any more. But Karen sensed that the older woman was hiding something, out of her loyalty to Marc.

Karen felt Marc's increasing dependence. Often she held him in her arms like a mother, cradling him, stroking his hair, murmuring endearments as though to comfort him.

She felt a strange power over him in those moments, and she wondered if she might one day use it to make him see reason, to make him free her. But always he turned, always he escaped her caressing embrace and became her master again, accusing her, taunting her, driving her to extremities of passion with his lovemaking. He seemed to see the danger of his own dependency. He was on his guard. And, deep down, he did not trust her. This was the essence of his passion.

They were in the third phase of Karen's sequestration. She felt needed now, she felt important to Marc. She knew that his attachment to her went beyond his physical passion. He lived for her. There was a bond that tied her more firmly to him than ever.

The call of the outside world grew weaker. The siren song of her exile was too powerful to resist.

Marc's obsession, which initially took her as an object, had now found its way into her own veins. She felt as though she were slipping subtly into one of those beautiful old paintings on the walls, disappearing into a world of exalted passion and obsession, drawn there by Marc. Like stunned prey in a spider's web, she lacked the will to resist.

Marc seemed to know she had abrogated her free will, for now he took her out with him. They went to restaurants, nightclubs, even to social gatherings at the homes of people from his society. They greeted Karen with courtly respect, inquiring about her life. She went through the motions of these evenings, never once thinking of using her freedom to try to escape. The web extended to the whole city, the only caveat being that Marc took her out only at night. He seemed to sense that the bustle of the day would be too great a temptation for her. The world was less real at night, and that was how he wanted it.

They also traveled. Marc took her to the Caribbean to visit casinos in Aruba, Antigua, St. Martin and San Juan. They made weekend trips, leaving from New Orleans airport on Friday and returning late Sunday. The old life they had had together in Europe came back to Karen. She always sat beside Marc as his good luck charm, and once again she felt proud to belong to him, proud to have others see how important she was to him.

She would return from these trips, tired from their late nights but still excited by the risk of so much money, and make love to Marc for long hours before sleep took them both.

Now the threads of the web extended not only across the city, but across the ocean. Karen's prison was inside her own soul. She could travel to the ends of the earth with Marc Belfort and still not dream of trying to run away from him.

Slowly she was giving up on her own life, adjusting her imagination to the walls of her prison. She looked back dazedly on the world she had taken for granted for so many years. Then she looked forward to the future with Marc, a future that would lead her, like his beloved mother, to a place in one of those paintings in the Belfort mansion. And that destiny seemed gentle and sweet to her now. Why fight it?

She thought her battle was over. Marc had won, and she wanted it that way.

Seven

Time passed.

Karen did not know how much time, for she was too wrapped up in her own intoxication to pay much attention to the real world. But the seasons were changing. There was a crispness in the air. She was allowed to take walks around the neighborhood now. Mrs. Crittendon had a dog, a charming little corgi named Spenser, whom she occasionally brought to work with her. Karen enjoyed walking the dog around the Garden District.

Her walks were hardly a contrast to the life she lived inside the house. The neighborhood was filled with other mansions similar in size and age to the Belfort house. They all bespoke a world distant in time and spirit from the present day. Karen could walk six blocks in any direction without really feeling that she had escaped home.

Life was smooth and lyrical, without shocks of any kind. Karen had time for reflection, time for dreaming during her solitary hours. She padded around the house, letting herself be suffused by the artifacts of a time gone by. She savored her descent into the past. Occasionally she turned on the TV or the radio for a brief cacophonous foray into the present, but she quickly turned it off.

Always Marc returned, and always he made love to her. When daydreaming or thinking began to pale, she turned to anticipation. The clock promised her ecstasy, its hands indicating that only a few hours remained until Marc's return.

Then something happened.

One morning Karen was alone in the downstairs reading room and found a pile of Marc's mail. Several of the letters seemed to be from creditors. One was from a law firm. None were opened.

But there was an opened letter from Marc's brother. Karen had seen his face in a family portrait on the mantel. He was several years older than Marc, with none of Marc's handsomeness. He looked more like an uncle than a brother.

> I know what you think of my father, and of me. We may be bores, but we have something you don't have, Marc—a sense of reality. The Belfort family has always had money, but this is the twentieth century. We're not plantation owners anymore. It takes all the investing skill and hard work we can muster to keep the family's possessions together. Your gambling has become more than an embarrassment.
>
> But this latest trick will land you in jail. Embezzling your own family's money to pay off your gambling debts! I have talked the whole matter over with our attorneys, and they agree

that there is no option left but prosecution, unless
you voluntarily agree…

Karen read no further. She closed the letter and put
it back in the envelope.

So it had all been a lie, she realized. Marc's handsome business suits, his daily departure for "work,"
his life as a twentieth-century man. It had all been a
semblance of normality intended to impress her, to
seduce her into remaining his slave.

This realization did not restore Karen entirely to
reality, but it did inject a profound restlessness into
her. When Marc came home that night she begged
him to make love to her right away. She helped him
off with his clothes and pulled him into bed, covering
his body with kisses. He asked her if anything was
wrong. She shook her head. How could she admit to
him that she was savoring the contrast between his
lovemaking and his lies? She had always sensed that
she did not know Marc completely, that there were
silent rooms of his character that she had not been
allowed to penetrate. Now she was sure of it. This
made their intimacy more troubling and, in a way,
more exciting.

The next day Marc told her he had to leave town
for several days on business. "Baton Rouge, then Savannah, then Atlanta," he said. "I'll miss you."

"I'll be waiting when you come back," Karen said
in the soft voice that had come to symbolize her surrender.

Marc was gone when she awoke the next morning.
Her senses were still dulled from his caresses, but the
restlessness inside her remained. She paced the rooms

of the house. She knew Mrs. Crittendon was watching her, had been told by Marc to keep an eye on her in his absence.

But fate took a hand. Karen was reading in the library when she heard Mrs. Crittendon answer a phone call. The urgency of her responses left no doubt that something had happened. A few moments later Mrs. Crittendon appeared at the library door.

"My daughter is in the hospital," she said. "She had an accident this morning."

"Is it serious?" Karen asked.

"They wouldn't tell me. I have to go there now. Can you look after things while I'm gone, Miss?"

"Of course." Karen got up to touch the older woman's arm. "Call me when you know something. And don't worry. I'll take care of things here."

"Thank you, Miss."

A moment later Karen heard the front door open and close. She went to the window and saw Mrs. Crittendon hurrying off down the street.

Karen knew that Marc had stopped fearing that she would escape. He was confident in his power over her. He knew he could go away for a month and leave her to take care of the mansion, and she would have been there waiting for him when he returned.

But the discovery of the letter had changed her.

She went upstairs, dressed in a skirt and blouse, and let herself out of the house. She walked to St. Charles Avenue and took the streetcar downtown. She went to the central business district, wanting to avoid the antebellum charm of the Vieux Carré, and went shopping. She went to Canal Place and to Riverwalk, looking into one store after another. She shunned the quaint old New Orleans shops, preferring places like Saks, Lord & Taylor, Macy's. She wanted to bathe in present-day America, and to get as far away as possible from the antebellum dream in which she had been floating.

Toward noon she realized she had eaten nothing all day. She went into a crowded food court and had a baked potato with all the trimmings. She savored the smells of pizza and french fries and hamburgers, and the sight of children with their mothers at the tables. She filled her senses with the everyday feel of the place, even the irritation of the mothers and the occasional peevish cries of temperamental children. This was the real world. This was the world that had nourished Karen all her life.

But when she had finished her meal and was sipping distractedly at the diet soda before her, she felt her resolve begin to weaken. The lure of the Belfort mansion made itself felt once more. At first it was a mere image of darkness and silence—a silence that signified security and protection in a place where she was precious, coveted. Then the idea became a wave of feeling that started deep in her senses and radiated through every part of her body, singing of sensual delights unknown to all these people around her. Delights that can only be felt by the kind of woman who has known a Marc Belfort. The kind of woman, indeed, who has been kept prisoner by her lover in an ivory tower far from the world.

Now it was Marc's world that seemed real, and not the crowded, noisy mall around her. She was on the point of getting up to go back home when a familiar-sounding voice startled her from her reverie.

"Fancy meeting you here. And without your mask, too."

She looked up to see a friendly-looking man in his thirties smiling down at her. She was sure she had never seen his face before.

"Ah—you don't recognize me, do you?" He smiled. "No wonder. Without my Don Juan attire, who would? Chris Carpenter. We met at the Duchaises' masked ball."

A profound dislocation shook Karen. She had to pull herself back from an enormous distance to greet him. "Oh. Oh, yes, of course. How are you?"

"Not bad. Making ends meet, as usual. How about you?"

"Oh—fine. Just fine."

She caught herself staring at him like a child before she remembered her manners. "Would you like to sit down?" she asked.

"I'd love to. Frankly, I've been shopping my legs off. I'm not much for malls. Never have been."

"Few men are." She smiled.

He sat down. She was amazed at his physical presence, not only because she had not really gotten a good look at him at the Duchaises' ball, but because she hadn't noticed another man since she had returned from Europe with Marc. She had almost forgotten that such creatures existed. Normal, busy, harried men dressed in slacks and sport shirts, hair a bit awry from the rigors of shopping, eyes expressing the irritation and deliberate good humor of everyday living. Chris

Carpenter looked almost as exotic today as Marc had looked when she first met him.

"What brings you to New Orleans?" she asked. "I thought you lived in Chicago."

"I do. This is the first time I've been back. How about you?" he asked. "Didn't you say you lived in Connecticut?"

Karen flushed. "Yes, I did. I've been—away. Business. This is my first time back, too."

If he sensed the enormity of her lie, he didn't show it. "Well, it's nice to see you again. Though I didn't expect to. There was something about that ball at Sans Souci. It was sort of—unreal. It didn't feel like part of the real world. I never expected to see any of those people again." He grinned. "That makes it all the more fun."

He looked around at the crowded food court. "Have you been shopping?" he asked.

She held up her Lord & Taylor bag. "Yes."

"I promised my daughters I would bring them something from New Orleans," he said. "As you can see, so far I haven't succeeded."

"How old are they?" Karen asked.

"Seven and nine. They're getting old enough that my taste in presents falls way short of being adequate," he said. "My ex-wife and I have joint custody, so every time they come back to me they seem to think I'm dumber than the last time. It's hard for a single man to keep up with daughters."

"I don't suppose you have a picture of them," Karen volunteered.

"Sure. You're nice to ask." He removed his wallet

and produced three small photos. Two were candid snapshots of the little girls, and one was a studio portrait of them together.

"They're very pretty," Karen said. "They take after you."

"Actually, Josie takes after her mother," he observed. "See the shape of her nose? But Kate does look more like my side of the family. The funny thing is, temperamentally, it's the opposite. Josie is a hard worker, like I am, and Kate is the one with all the imagination. And a temper to match."

Karen had difficulty tearing herself away from the pictures. The little girls looked so vibrant, so connected to Chris by their smiles and by their physiognomy.

"How long have you been divorced?" she asked him.

"Four years." A wistful look came over his face. "They were so little back then, I thought of them as babies. Now I see how fast they're growing up."

Karen handed him back the pictures. "Does your ex-wife live in Chicago, too?"

"Oh, I don't live in the city myself," he said. "I just say Chicago for convenience. Actually, I live in Evanston, a town north of the city."

"I know Evanston," Karen said, recalling the quiet town with its massive square houses and large lawns. "I had a friend who went to Northwestern. I used to visit her there."

"Then you probably know Lake Forest," Chris said. "That's where my wife lives."

"You never remarried?"

He shrugged. "Haven't found the right girl, I guess." He seemed lost in thought as he looked at Karen. "It's taking care of the kids, you know. Worrying about them. It takes something out of you. The energy to go out to parties, to ask women out for dates, just isn't there." He laughed. "Not that the need isn't there."

"I understand." His words reminded Karen obscurely of her own predicament.

"Has it been a long time since you've been back to my neck of the woods?" he asked.

Karen nodded. "Seven or eight years. Connecticut is a long way from Chicago when you're busy working. It's hard to find the time."

"So your work keeps you busy," he offered.

"Pretty busy, yes."

She was afraid he was going to ask her about her marriage. She lacked the energy for the elaborate lies she would have to tell. But he simply sat looking at her.

"You know," he said, "you look different than you did at the ball."

"Different?"

"Softer." He seemed to ponder. "More—more ethereal. Almost like you stepped out of a painting."

Karen flushed. "That's an odd thing to say."

"I know." He furrowed his brow. "When I saw you at the ball you looked agile, energetic. Like a racehorse, if that isn't too unflattering a comparison. I had an impression of you striding briskly through life, sidestepping any obstacle that got in your path.

No-nonsense, if you know what I mean. Now you look softer, more settled.''

Karen thought his words over carefully. So the change in her was that visible. She had come that far from her old self, lost touch that profoundly with her past.

''Are your girls athletic?'' she asked suddenly.

''Josie is. She plays soccer at school. Kate can't be bothered,'' he said.

''Perhaps I can help you find something for them,'' Karen offered. ''I don't have little girls of my own, but I used to be one. I remember it pretty well.''

''Would you really?'' he asked. ''That's awfully kind of you. I was about to give up and get them stuffed animals.''

They spent an hour walking through the stores. Karen helped Chris pick out an outfit for Kate and a set of doll furniture for Josie. By the time they finished she felt she knew both girls. She also felt she knew Chris. He was a fairly typical modern man— hardworking, friendly, sincere. He was very intelligent, Karen realized. A thoughtful man perplexed by the misfortune that had come to him, and genuinely concerned that he give his daughters as carefree a childhood as he could.

They stopped for coffee at a little espresso shop before taking leave of each other.

''You've saved my life,'' Chris said, holding up his parcels. ''This will be the first time I've been able to give them things with any confidence. How can I repay you?''

"As long as they like them, that's all I need." Karen smiled.

"But how will you know?" he asked. "I'll be so far away from you."

Karen shrugged. "We'll meet again someday. Then you'll tell me."

He nodded. He seemed to understand that he must not get in touch with her. "Don't tell me," he said. "You would like to have children yourself, but you're too busy working to make ends meet."

Karen raised an eyebrow. "How did you figure that out?" she asked.

"I guessed." He turned his plastic coffee cup in a large freckled hand. "You look like excellent mother material to me. But you also seem like a career woman."

"You're right on both counts," Karen said. "Though we'll have to reserve judgment on the mother front until I find time to have babies."

A brief tremor went through her at her own words. She found herself thinking more and more about children nowadays. The children she had not had with Brett, and the children she might have with Marc. She was acutely aware of the fact that she had not become pregnant from her liaison with Marc. She wondered why this was. Could it be that the pervasive unreality she had with Marc precluded children? She did not like to reflect too much on this.

"Oh, you'll do well," Chris said. "I have no doubt of that."

Karen noticed that he looked as though he got a lot of sun. His hair was sandy-colored, and there was a slightly rosy tinge to his skin. This added to the robust, everyday reality that emanated from him.

"Are you a golfer?" she asked.

"What makes you ask that?"

"You seem tanned."

He looked at the back of his own hand. "I see what you mean. No, I'm not a golfer. I can't afford the greens fees. I never had any talent for the game, anyway. No, I'm a jogger."

"A jogger."

"Yes. I try to get in an hour every day. It's hard to find the time, but if I didn't keep at it I would gain weight." He grinned. "I have a weakness for pizzas. And potato chips, and corned beef sandwiches, and about a hundred other things that are bad for you. The body you see is the result of my latest diet. Six months of low-fat food and as much running as I could manage."

"You should be proud to have stayed at it so long," Karen said.

"I do try," he said. "The girls keep telling me to stay in shape so that when the right woman comes along I won't turn her off."

"You won't turn anybody off." Karen felt embarrassed by her own words. But she could not deny that in a sweet, down-to-earth way, Chris Carpenter was a very attractive man.

"I'll bet you don't have a problem with weight," he observed. "You look like you haven't been a pound overweight all your life."

"Do I really?" Karen asked.

"Sure." He was making an effort not to seem too interested, but his admiration of her body was evident.

"Well, I would gain if I didn't watch what I eat," she said. But she realized that since she had been with Marc she had lost even more weight than in the old days in Connecticut. She wasn't interested in food anymore. Passion and lovemaking had made food seem irrelevant to her. Sometimes her slenderness made her look more ethereal in the mirror, as though by losing weight she was attenuating even further her connection to the real world.

He seemed to have read her thoughts, for he said, "You look to me as though you were wrapped up in more important things than eating."

"Really?" she asked.

"Yes." He looked at the crowd of shoppers passing by the window of the coffee shop. "You don't look like the rest of the people here. I can't put my finger on it, but you seem separate."

"Really." Karen could not think of a response. It was as though he were obscurely aware of the truth of her situation.

"Something important is going on in your life," he said. "Not the kind of ordinary thing that is going on in everyone else's life. Something really significant. Something that is taking you away from the world."

"Oh, I don't know that anything significant has happened to me in a long time," Karen lied.

"Well, maybe it's just in the eye of the beholder." He seemed to retreat deliberately, not wishing to embarrass her. "You do have an exotic air about you, though."

"I guess I should take that as a compliment," she said, blushing slightly. "I never thought of myself as an exotic person."

"Oh, you're exotic, all right." Chris looked away, clearly abashed at his own forwardness.

There was a silence. Karen was aware of the interest she felt in this kindly, down-to-earth man, and was very aware that he admired her. His admiration gave her a warm feeling very different from the passion Marc Belfort inspired. It was a gentle, calming warmth rather than a hot, urgent passion. But it felt good, and she was loath to see it end. She knew the hands of her watch were showing it was time to get home, but she did not look at it.

"Listen," Chris said. "I'm leaving tomorrow morning early. If you're not too busy, would you like to have dinner tonight? It will be my way of thanking you."

Karen considered his invitation. Only an hour ago she had been on the point of returning to the Belfort mansion, surrendering to the drug that had taken her so far away from life. But Chris Carpenter spoke for the world in a more eloquent voice than the people at the shopping mall. His love for his daughters, his hunger for happiness, seemed to blow the clouds of fog from Karen's mind and to bring fresh air she hadn't breathed in a long time.

Of course, she knew she was taking a chance. More than that. There was no way she could absent herself for an evening without destroying the fragile entente she had with Marc. This one transgression might plunge her back into the days of being a prisoner, locked in her room. But she didn't care.

"I'd love to," she said.

"Great. Shall I pick you up?"

"No," she said a bit too hurriedly. "I have some things to do. Why don't I meet you?"

"I'm at the Royal Sonesta," he said. "Why don't we meet there for a drink? The Desire Oyster Bar is a nice, relaxed place. Then we can walk someplace for dinner."

"It sounds heavenly." Karen smiled.

"Seven o'clock?" he asked.

"Seven o'clock."

She stood, up, daring now to look at her watch. It was three o'clock. Past time to hurry home.

He stood up too. "Let me walk you to your car," he said.

"Oh, no. Stay here and finish your coffee," she said. "I have some stops to make, anyway."

She left the shop and turned toward the river exit. As she began to walk away she caught a glimpse of Chris through the window. He had not moved. The coffee cup was still in his hand. He was looking at her, an excited smile on his face. He looked almost like a little boy.

Eight

When Karen got home, Mrs. Crittendon was still not there. The telephone rang at four. It was the housekeeper calling to say she would not be back.

"My daughter was in a car accident this morning on her way to work. She broke her hip. The doctor says she'll be all right, but there's some internal bleeding. They have to keep her under observation."

"Is there anything I can do?" Karen asked.

Mrs. Crittendon sighed. "Well, I'm supposed to be there with you..."

Karen understood. Mrs. Crittendon was supposed to be at the Belfort mansion keeping an eye on Karen herself.

"Don't worry about that. I can hold the fort," she said, putting into her voice all the obedience she could.

"I suppose you can, at that," Mrs. Crittendon said. "I expect Mr. Marc to call sometime before dinner."

"I'll take the call," Karen said.

"What about your dinner, Miss?" Mrs. Crittendon asked.

Karen laughed. "I'll take care of dinner," she said. "I know where everything is."

"Well, that's nice of you, Miss." In the older

woman's voice Karen could hear her disapproval that she lived with Marc without benefit of matrimony— and also Mrs. Crittendon's loyalty and obedience to the Belfort family. An obedience that went so far as her countenancing Marc's keeping his lover under the family roof, if that was what he wanted.

"Is there anything else I can do?" Karen asked.

"I don't think so. Thank you, Miss."

"You just concentrate on your daughter," Karen said. "I'll take care of things here. I know the house, after all."

"Yes. I guess you do."

For the next hour Karen wandered around the house, enjoying her solitude and her freedom. The place seemed somehow more domestic, more innocent now that both her guardians were gone. She felt a sense of the old freedom she had once taken for granted. She could touch anything she wanted, look at anything she wanted and think anything she wanted. This was a sunlit afternoon in 1996. She could throw open the heavy curtains and let the bright light of this year flood the old rooms. She was free to do as she pleased.

She was still flush with her own spontaneity when Marc called, just after five. She told him what had happened to Mrs. Crittendon's daughter.

"Do you think you can manage all right on your own?" Marc asked.

"Certainly." Karen made a show of hurt pride.

"I guess you can, at that," he said. "I'll call tomorrow at the same time. My broth— There may be some calls during the day tomorrow. Just don't answer. It will only be business.''

"Are you sure? I can take messages.''

"Positive. Just don't answer.''

Karen guessed that Marc did not want certain people to know she was living at the mansion. "How is your trip going?'' she asked.

"Not much fun, but very little time to think about it,'' he said. "Just one meeting after another with people who bore me to tears. How are you doing?''

"Not too bad.'' A bright note had crept into her voice before she could stop it, and she added, "I miss you.''

"I miss you, too. What I wouldn't give to get on a plane for home right now.''

"Well, it won't be too long.''

"I'll make sure of that.''

When they had hung up Karen put on the new outfit she had bought, slipped out of the house at six-thirty and took the streetcar into the Vieux Carré. She got out several blocks from the Royal Sonesta and walked the rest of the way. This time she didn't feel so disturbed by the antebellum aura of the French Quarter. It gave her a sense of adventure.

She met Chris as promised at the Desire Oyster bar, a charming room trimmed in dark wood and marble. They ate oysters and drank white wine, then caught a streetcar and went out to dinner at the Commander's Palace. After dinner they took a long, relaxing walk in the Garden District.

"I'm amazed at this city,'' Chris said. "The old buildings don't look like relics. They seem alive. Almost as though the people who lived in them a hundred years ago were still behind those windows."

Karen looked ahead of her as they strolled down Prytania Street. The Belfort mansion had come into sight, and they were nearing it as they continued their walk.

"I know what you mean," she said.

"I was in Charleston once, when we took a driving tour of the South," Chris said. "That had a similar feel. The houses were so beautiful. But New Orleans is even more interesting because of the mix of cultures. The past is so real here."

They slowly passed the Belfort house on their right.

"That's a beauty, isn't it?" Chris observed. "Just look at those columns."

Karen said nothing. She sensed mute reproach from the house's dark windows. Somehow it looked smaller. With Chris beside her she felt sufficiently free of its spell to wonder how such a quiet old house could have held her soul a prisoner for so long. But by now she knew the answer. It wasn't a house that was holding her in thrall. It was a man.

"I don't think I'd like to live here permanently, though," she said. "The past would weigh too heavily. I think I prefer the suburban life, even if it doesn't have this much charm."

Chris nodded. "You may be right. If I lived in one of these places, I might feel I had to live up to it somehow. I kind of like my own little place back in Evanston—even if the driveway needs resealing and the windows let in drafts and the place could use some aluminum siding."

"At least it's all yours," Karen said.

He glanced at her, his eyes full of a meaning she could not quite grasp.

They turned left and walked to St. Charles Avenue, where they took the streetcar back to the French Quarter. The streetcar was sparsely filled with people who looked as though they were on their way home after a long day at work. Not one of them glanced out the windows to see the sights they were passing. Karen found herself charmed by this atmosphere of fatigue and languor.

"Do you mind if I ask you about your ex-wife?" she turned to Chris.

He smiled. "Not really, no."

"I don't want to pry," she said. "I'd just like to know a little more about you."

"We met in college," Chris said. "I came from out of state. I was majoring in architecture at Champaign. She came from Wilmette. She was an English major. It wasn't exactly love at first sight. I had to pursue her for quite a while. She had several other boyfriends. Better-looking guys than me, with a little more to say for themselves financially, too."

Karen smiled, amused by his self-deprecating humor.

"But I stuck to my guns," he said. "One day I took her up to Chicago to dinner at The Nantucket Cove. At the time I thought that was something pretty special. I ordered her a lobster with all the trimmings, and just as they were putting the bib on her, I said, 'Let's stop beating around the bush. Will you marry me?' She touched her chest and said, 'Well, now that

I've got the bib on I guess I can't say no.' In later years we used to relate that episode to all our friends.''

Karen watched his face. The movement of the streetcar made him seem very boyish and vulnerable.

"What was—is her name?" she asked.

"Susan," he said. "It's a pretty name, don't you think? I always liked that about her."

"Yes. It's a very pretty name."

There was a silence. Karen knew he was going to tell her where the marriage went wrong, and she wasn't sure she should hear it.

"You don't have to tell me anymore," she said.

"No, I want to tell you." He looked down at Karen's hands, then back at her face. "We both went to work after college. We decided to live in Chicago because there was a lot of work there for me, and because Susan's family was there. For a while it was great. We were wrapped up in each other and in being married. We didn't even notice the horrible weather. We went to the movies, we shopped, we took the train downtown to ball games and to the Art Institute.... It was just like real life. Very straightforward, very nice."

"Just like real life?" Karen was struck by his phrase.

"Yes. I meant it as I said it. I think the trouble started just before we conceived Kate. We both wanted children. We talked about it, we got out the calendar, we made the effort—and then Susan was pregnant. But right around that time it dawned on me that we had done it because something was already wrong. I couldn't put my finger on what it was. I just didn't feel sure about us. But I didn't say anything to her. I let myself get carried away by waiting for the baby. Then Katie was born, and you know how that is. Who's got time to think about a marriage when you're feeding an infant at three in the morning?''

They got off the streetcar at Common Street and began the leisurely walk back to the Royal Sonesta.

"After that, things were out of my control," Chris said. "We waited a year, and then Susan got pregnant with Josie. The family had a life of its own. I almost—almost—forgot about my worries. Then, when Josie was two and Kate was four..." His face fell.

"Don't," Karen said, taking his hand. "You don't have to."

He shook his head. "No. I want to." He held on to her hand.

"Then one day, with our little house around us and our two girls sleeping upstairs, Susan just hit me with it. She said there was another man. She said she wanted a divorce. I couldn't stop myself from asking, *Why now? Why didn't you tell me earlier, when there was a chance to do something about it?* And she said..."

"She said she couldn't help it," Karen offered.

He looked at her with a sad smile. "I guess you know something about women."

"Enough."

"Well, you're right. She said she couldn't help it. She said she didn't know at the time how things were really going. But she said she was sure. She wanted out of the marriage." He sighed.

"After that it was the classic divorce situation. Susan moved out and stayed with her parents while she looked for a place of her own. Naturally she was in and out of the house, because of the girls. It was terribly painful to see her, but it couldn't be avoided. The girls needed their mother, after all. She ended up moving in with the other guy, but after a year their relationship ended. She got a place of her own. She still has it. The girls spend two weeks with her, then two weeks with me."

He grimaced. "Sometimes, when I'm feeling bitter, I hope Susan is unhappy. But then I realize I can't allow myself to hope that. I need for her to be happy—for the girls' sake. I even need for her to find a man, a good man, so the girls can have a stepfather when they're with her. Divorce is an amazing thing. If Susan had just died, or disappeared, it wouldn't be nearly as painful. Because of the girls, she's a permanent part of my life, even though I've lost her for good."

Karen nodded. "I understand."

"Do you?" Chris was still holding her hand.

"Of course I do." Karen squeezed his hand. "You've got a lot of pain. But you've also got two beautiful little girls. And one day they'll grow up, and they'll realize what you went through for them."

"Do you think they will?"

"If they have any sense, they will." Karen looked into his eyes. "You haven't wasted your pain, or your courage," she said. "You're doing what you have to do for your little girls."

They walked the rest of the way to Chris's hotel in

silence, smiling now and then at the odd collection of street people intermingled with the tourists. When they reached the hotel, Chris turned to Karen.

"Listen," he said. "I don't have to leave right now. I have business I can do here, at least for a few days. I don't feel quite right about leaving. Not yet."

Karen knew what he was saying. Their brief acquaintance had had a profound effect on him. On her, as well.

"If I were to stay," he asked, "could I see you?"

She thought quickly of Marc and of Mrs. Crittendon. "Yes," she said. "You could."

"I wouldn't want to put you out," he said. "I know you have a life of your own."

"You wouldn't be putting me out." She smiled, the glow from the street lamp throwing a golden light on her features. "I'd like to see you, Chris."

"Are you sure?" he asked. "An old divorcé, with two daughters?"

"I'm sure," she said. And she was.

The next few days were like a dream come true. It was all the more strange and exciting because it was a dream Karen had never had before.

She awoke early each morning. She called Marc at the number he had given her. She called Mrs. Crittendon. She took in the morning paper. She straightened up the house.

Then she went out.

She met Chris at Jackson Square—it quickly became a ritual—and they saw the lesser-known sights of New Orleans. They visited the Mardi Gras Museum, the Botanical Garden, the Metairie Cemetery. They had lunch in charming little cafés and restaurants where local specialties were served. They spent hours simply walking, letting the city's many sights pass them by. And they talked.

An odd entente developed between them. Karen drew Chris out in ever greater detail about his daughters and his past. She wanted to feel that she knew his life. The more she learned about him, the more she respected him.

Chris unburdened himself easily. Talking to Karen seemed to help him put his life in perspective. He had never had a serious relationship with a woman before his wife, he told her, and there had been no women since their separation. He was trying to find a new identity for himself. The effort was exhausting him, but seemed to be making him a stronger and better person.

Karen told him almost nothing about her own life. She thought he sensed that there were secrets she did not want to reveal, at least not now, and he respected this. He seemed to understand that his best chance with Karen lay in not pushing her. So he willingly talked about himself.

He could not know that with each mundane detail of his very American life, he was entrancing Karen, fascinating her further and further. The very ordinariness of it was a tonic to her. She let her eyes rest on his tanned face, his curly hair and intelligent eyes, and she found herself more and more drawn to him.

She got to know his body better, too. Though he was well muscled and naturally strong, he had a gentle way of walking, as though he did not want to draw too much attention to himself. When he thought himself unobserved, a dreamy look came into his eyes, turning them bluer. His hands, with their dusting of freckles, were surprisingly delicate and sensitive. They belied his claim that he was an utter klutz at fixing things.

"Show me a distributor cap and I'll manage to crack it," he said. "I've caused more damage with these hands than either of my daughters have with theirs."

The week passed like a lilting interval of peace, a vacation from reality that soon became a reality in itself. Mrs. Crittendon called with news of her daughter, but was still too busy to return to the house. As for Marc, he called every day.

"I miss you," Karen told him. "When are you coming back?"

"I'm trying to hurry things up," he said. "Tell me, what are you going to wear the night I get back?"

"Whatever you want."

"Make it the silk dress."

"Why?" she asked.

"Because I like the way it comes off."

She felt an odd thrill at these words. "All right."

"You sound different," he observed.

"Do I?" she asked a trifle nervously.

"You must have missed me." There was a smile in his voice.

"You'll find out how much I've missed you."

Karen went through all these motions, took all these calls, always with the knowledge that within hours she would see Chris again. Her guilt over the double role she was playing deepened every day, but she could not control her excitement. For the first time since her return to New Orleans, she felt she had some initiative, some freedom. Chris Carpenter represented that freedom.

On their last night, Chris took her on a carriage ride through the Vieux Carré. They passed the now-familiar sights, which seemed like old friends, creating a wistful mood.

Chris took Karen's hand.

"This isn't an easy night," he said. "I don't want to leave you."

"I don't want you to leave," she said. "But you have your life to go back to."

"It doesn't seem like much of a life," he said.

"Nonsense," Karen objected. "You have your daughters, you have your work...."

"You know what I mean," he said.

Karen nodded.

Chris sighed. "You haven't told me anything about your own life," he said. "Maybe I didn't want to know. I don't want to push you." He put a tentative arm around her and kissed her cheek. "Just tell me whether I should go on hoping," he said.

She looked troubled. "I can't tell you that," she said. "It wouldn't be fair to you."

He nodded sadly. "Then at least tell me you've enjoyed our week," he said. "That will help me."

"It's been a wonderful week."

"And you'll remember it?"

"Of course I'll remember it," she said. "Forever."

"I guess I can hold on to that thought."

He kissed her lips. His kiss was respectful, almost chaste. Not like the terrible penetrating kisses that were Marc's preludes to his possession of her. But there was a diffident charm to Chris's touch that was, in its own way, seductive.

"I'm going to miss you," he said.

"I'll miss you, too, Chris."

The carriage had returned to its starting point. Karen took her leave of Chris. She suspected she would never see him again. But the idea that she might be wrong seemed to sustain her as she walked away into the night.

She got home just before midnight. She found Marc waiting for her.

"I didn't expect you," she said, doing her best to seem calm and breezy.

He wasn't smiling. He stood in the salon with a glass of brandy in his hand, his eyes cold. "I can see that."

Karen knew she was in trouble. Not only was she dressed for her last night with Chris, in a new cotton skirt and top that were worlds away from the silk outfit Marc was expecting, but she had taken great care with her makeup, and the look on her face left no doubt that she had been with a man.

"Did you have a good time?" he asked.

She said nothing.

"I spoke to Mrs. Crittendon," he said. "Her

daughter is doing better. She's coming back to work tomorrow.''

"That's good.''

There was a silence. Karen knew there was going to be a scene. She could not make up her mind how she wanted it to end. The past week had changed her. But Marc was still a dominating presence in her life. The look in his eyes made her knees go weak.

"I trusted you,'' he said.

He spoke softly, but Karen heard something deeper than reproach in his voice. He was acknowledging his own mistake. He should never have trusted her, he was saying. She could not deny this.

And yet all these weeks she had been his slave in mind as well as in body. He would never know how completely she had given herself to him. There was no way for her to explain that now.

"We'd better talk,'' he said. "Come upstairs.''

She was quiet and passive as they went upstairs. She was preparing a speech in which she would tell him that, despite her love for him, she could not continue living as a prisoner. She needed her freedom back. One way or another he would have to accept that about her.

But he did not give her time.

"Take off your clothes,'' he said, looking disdainfully at the new outfit she had bought.

Karen shook her head. "No, Marc.''

"Then I will.''

He was upon her like a panther. He tore the pretty blouse from her, popping the buttons. Her tiny bra, also new, was torn away, as well. He pushed her down on the bed and pulled the skirt down her legs.

He looked at her panties. "So those are new, too, are they?" he asked. "What did he think of them?"

"Marc, stop."

He ripped the panties away with one hand. Karen lay naked, looking up at him through wide eyes. She had never thought him capable of such violence.

"I was lucky I took precautions," he said. "Did you really think you were alone here with Mrs. Crittendon? Did you think my trust in you went that far?"

He looked down at her with scorn, and with a sort of detached interest in her naked body.

"You're a fast worker," he said. "I was gone for one week. You don't let the grass grow under your feet, do you. Is that what they teach you girls up north?"

Nonplussed, Karen stared at him. His rage was like a power source that lit him from within. He almost glowed.

"Who is he?" Marc asked. "Some businessman here for a convention? Or just a tourist, like yourself?"

She suddenly realized what it was. Marc came from generations of men who had fought duels over women, over honor. He had been waiting all his life for this moment. He seemed almost relieved at this opportunity for action. He was prepared to do anything to keep her.

"Marc... We have to talk." Despite her awe, Karen knew now that it was over. She could not go on this way, living in an allegory of possession and honor and obsession. She must return to the real world. If she didn't, she was lost.

"Talk…" His lip curled in contempt. "You don't know how wrong you are, Karen. This isn't the time for talk."

He began unbuttoning his shirt.

"Marc, don't."

His hands were at his belt. His slacks were coming off. His body seemed more powerful than ever before. The lean, matador's limbs had thickened, and he looked frighteningly strong.

He was staring down at her naked body as his pants came off. "So soft," he said. "Soft as velvet, with a heart of stone underneath. I should have known it from the beginning."

His sex was erect, almost more from anger than from excitement.

"I gave you everything," he said. "Everything but this."

There was no love in his touch, but only an assault made all the more terrible by his assumption that the secret places he penetrated now had been exclusively for him until this frightening night. He pinioned her with his strong hands and moved her this way and that on the bed, opening her to thrusts that came from all directions, each more cruel than the last.

"You like variety, then," he hissed. "Try this."

He pushed into her with a long stroke that made her gasp. She was trying to remain aloof from him, to hide behind the armor of new self-respect she had attempted to forge in herself this past week. But now, from the hot core of his anger and of her bondage, the old dependency emerged, the old fainting passivity that made her his slave. She realized she was not as strong as she had thought. His power over her was undiminished.

"Did he do this for you?" Marc asked. "I'll bet he didn't dare."

"Marc, no."

"Come on," he said. "You can't hide from me. I want it all."

He was moving faster, each thrust more knowing than the last.

There was something madly mechanical about him, something inhuman and impersonal that froze her mind while stoking her senses hotter and hotter.

"There," he said. "There."

He saw the tremors shaking her slim body, and he smiled. His hands were on her breasts, thumbs rubbing the nipples roughly. His thighs immobilized her, and he thrust deeper.

"See?" he said. "It's too late for you. You're mine."

He moved faster, sensing that she was ready for the last wave.

"Come on," he said. "Come on..."

The spasm shook her like an earthquake, and she gasped so deep in her throat that he took pity on her in that moment and said nothing more. He held himself hard inside her as the little paroxysms came, an endless series that ebbed with agonizing slowness.

"As black as hell, as dark as night," he said.

Karen was too numbed to speak. She lay on her

stomach unable to move. He savored the sight of her nudity.

"You're mine again," he said. "Say it."

She tried to move, and could not.

"Say it!" he repeated, squeezing her tighter. "Say it, or I'll kill him."

"I'm yours." Karen's words came out against the pillow, a barely audible murmur.

He laughed, a slow, bitter laugh. Then he pulled out of her and left without a word. She lay amid the torn fabrics of her new clothes and the shreds of her resolve to be free.

She heard the door lock behind him.

Nine

Things were different now.

Mrs. Crittendon was not there anymore. Marc had hired a new woman, a dark, stooped creature named Celeste, to cook the meals and keep an eye on Karen. The woman never spoke to her, and simply turned away when Karen tried to speak to her.

After a while Karen realized there were two women. They looked so similar that at first she had not noticed. They must surely be sisters, she thought, for they had the same posture, the same coloring, and even the same way of sighing as they went about their work.

One day, to confirm her impression, she saw them together when they changed shifts. "At least I'm not crazy," she thought. It took her two more weeks to find out that the sister's name was Augustine, and that they both came from a small island in the Caribbean and had six more brothers and sisters in New Orleans.

But the proof that she was seeing straight did not restore the sense of reality she had lost. Life seemed shorn of all immediacy. The hours passed without anything happening. The days were so similar as to be indistinguishable. Each morning she awoke to find the door locked. Celeste brought breakfast, setting the tray on the lowboy without a word. Karen spent the morning alone. She was allowed to leave her room for lunch, but she was never unaccompanied. Then she returned to her room for the afternoon. Marc came home before dinner. Usually he made love to her. Afterward, they ate, and Marc went away, presumably to do some work or reading. Then, in mid-evening, he returned to make love to her again. Once in a while he would spend the night in her bed; usually he left her alone.

There was no love in his caresses. At least, not if love meant sharing and trusting. He handled Karen as though she were a machine on which he was working. His kisses and caresses communicated nothing of himself, nothing but the blunt physical need that brought him to her.

He rarely bothered to converse with her now. He came, took his pleasure and went. She wished he would show some anger, or even beat her, simply to establish a genuine contact. But he never did. He was cold, efficient and inhuman.

In the solitude of her room, Karen sometimes felt her thoughts straying to Brett. She recalled their first times together, when Brett was just getting to know her and his touch was cautious and diffident. Then she thought of the deeper intimacy of their marriage, when he knew how to give her pleasure with sure caresses. And finally of the last times, when sex became an almost desperate attempt to recapture each other as the stresses of life pulled them apart.

Her life with Brett had perhaps been flawed, her closeness with him not always a perfect harmony. But throughout those years of marriage, his touch had meant home to her. Now she was adrift in a strange element where the ecstasy Marc gave her signified precisely the lack of a home. She was outside herself, outside everything. In the silence of her room she waited for the caresses of a man who did not love her, but could not live without her. She had taken leave of the sane world. She wondered whether she would ever see it again.

One night she was sitting with Marc at the dinner table. Outside, the season was changing. There was an expectancy in the cool breeze: autumn was coming. Up north, where Karen came from, there was probably frost already. People must be hurrying to their cars to escape the chill in the air. Down here, of course, the change was gentler.

"Why are we alone here?" she asked suddenly.

Marc looked up from his reverie. "What do you mean?"

"Where is your father? Isn't this his house?"

"I told you. He's in Europe, on an extended trip. He goes every year."

"He's been gone a long time, hasn't he?" Karen asked.

Marc did not respond.

"Why don't I ever see your brother?" she asked.

Marc sighed. "I told you. He would bore you silly. Besides, he doesn't approve of me. It wouldn't be a pleasant encounter."

Karen looked away. "You're lying."

He reddened. "No, I'm not. And even if I were, what difference would it make to you?"

She gave him a long look. "You're right. No difference."

Something about her words had provoked him. He got up and took her by her arms. "Come on. We're going upstairs."

Pulling free of him, Karen got up by herself and went up the stairs in front of him. She sensed him looking at her swaying hips as she walked. She purposefully moved a bit more slowly. At the door of her room he took hold of her from behind, his hands on her breasts. She stood very still for a long moment. Then she opened the door.

Something was very different between them tonight. Rebellion rose within her as she watched him close the door and turn to look at her.

She took off her blouse, unhooked her bra and stood with her breasts bared to him.

"Take a good look," she said.

She felt there was something dangerous about her in that moment as she stood in her long skirt with her hair flowing over slim shoulders to the small, firm breasts. The nipples were hard, her skin very pale in the half-light.

Marc did not move. He was admiring her, she could see that.

"Yankee women," she said, loosening her skirt. "Northern women..."

The skirt fell to the floor. She stepped out of it. Her slip clung to slender hips. The outlines of her thighs, rich and eloquent, stirred under the silk.

"Is this what you want?" she asked, slowly pulling the slip down her legs.

"I wanted..." He looked tormented, his eyes moving over her nervously. "I wanted a woman..."

"You wanted a woman to belong to you," she said, slipping her fingertips under the waistband of the panties. "To take care of you. To see to your every need."

He was breathing hard now. His hands clenched at his side.

"You wanted a woman to be real, as you are not." She pulled the panties down an inch, but left them clinging to her thighs. "A woman with a mind of her own, so she could turn it over to you. You wanted to get off on that. That's what turns you on. Isn't it?"

The panties came further down, her sex peeking out dark and alluring behind the flimsy fabric.

"Isn't it?" she asked. "Not a southern belle, a woman in a painting. You wanted a free woman—but only as your prisoner."

Her hips moved subtly, the panties slipping lower as her hands moved along her legs. Her eyes glimmered in the shadows.

"I wanted love...." He was riveted to the spot, his eyes devouring her.

"I know what you wanted." She pulled the panties down to her knees and stood up straight, letting them fall to her ankles. "What you wanted all along..."

He came to her with a great lunge and took her in his arms. He dwarfed her, a tall man fully dressed holding a tiny, slim woman with no clothes on. Yet she had the power tonight, and she knew it. He moved her this way and that, kissing her. But it was she who drew him on, she who attracted his lips. When he picked her up in his arms, her hands closed around his neck like chains.

He placed her on the bed and looked down at her. She arched her back and spread her hands out against the comforter, posing for him. Her hair made a dark halo around her face, and she moved her legs slowly so he could see her better.

"Take your clothes off," she said.

Her command took him so much by surprise that he did not move. She curled her legs under her and leaned forward to undo his belt.

"No," he said.

She let him go and lay back, raising one knee and contemplating him coolly.

"Take it off." Again she spoke in a mocking tone, her eyes challenging him.

He looked down at her, his eyes burning with rage. Then he tore his clothes off with a groan and covered her with himself. Never had she been so yielding. But every silken tremor of her body was another rebellion, and he could not withstand it. He kissed her everywhere, savoring her escape from his dominion. She held him close, surrounding him with herself, deathly silent as she seduced him to greater and greater excitement.

When her hands found their way to the center of him he gasped deeply and closed his eyes. She stroked him to readiness and guided him quickly inside her, knowing that he had never been this hot, that time was short.

"Come on," she murmured. "Don't be afraid."

His thrusts were frantic and almost insane. He seemed to realize that every token of his power had become her own possession now. The hard hands beneath her back were a thing *she* wanted. The deep urgent thrusts were a thing *she* ordained. He was her creature, his passion her possession.

"Come on," she said, reaching to touch him with soft fingers that knew everything.

"You're a witch," he gasped.

"No. Just a woman."

The last spasm crashed over him like an earthquake. He shuddered madly in her embrace, his whole body on fire. She took him calmly, her hands still holding him, her lithe body silent in its power.

He lay on top of her for a long time, his breath coming in sobs. She petted him and kissed him, but he never looked at her. When he got up and took his leave, without a word, she watched him, her hands clasped behind her head. For the first time she really saw him as a man. Not a figure in a painting or a tapestry, but a human being who had been found out and who was ashamed.

Karen lay naked for quite a while, surveying her surroundings dispassionately. Then she got up and prepared to leave. She made an inventory of all the things he had bought her, and decided to take only essential toiletries with her.

She dressed in the simplest skirt and blouse she could find. She wished she had a sweater; she would need it where she was going. Shrugging, she opened the door. She was not surprised when she did not find it locked.

She went out into the hall. The tall paintings of Belfort ancestors loomed over her, but she didn't bother to look at them. She tiptoed to Marc's door. There was no light in his room. She went down the wide staircase to the front door. No one tried to stop her. She turned the key in the old lock and closed the door behind her.

Standing on the stoop, she turned once to look at the Belfort world behind her. An old dark house, smelling of varnish and very old wood. Not so daunting, after all, she mused. A lot of ghosts with only one another for company.

She skipped down the steps like a young girl and walked briskly away along Prytania Street. Her first thought was to go straight to the airport and catch a flight out of the city. But an instinct somewhere between prudence and superstition told her to try something more unexpected. She caught a bus heading upriver. At the end of the line she got off, asked directions and sat down to wait for another bus.

By now it was very late. A three-quarter moon lit the landscape with a silvery glow. Suddenly Karen realized she was only a mile or so from her old school, the St. Charles Academy. After a moment's hesitation, she set off down the road.

It was strange and oddly restful to see by the light of the moon the landmarks she used to pass during the daytime as a girl. She saw pastures, groves of moss-laden trees, and old houses that had once been part of her lonely year at St. Charles. She even passed

the rutted path between two farms that led to the place
where she had first made love to Marc Belfort. She
was not tempted to go down it.

She ended up on the deserted campus of the school,
ambling among the ivy-covered buildings, finally sitting on the moonlit steps of the Academic Building,
her hands on her knees. She could feel the ghosts of
all her schoolmates haunting the night around her.
She wondered what had happened to them during the
past twelve years—years that had revolutionized her
own life. Were they all like Marc, immured in a past
that would not let them go? Or had some of them
suffered the same shocks that had made Karen into a
woman?

After a while she realized she did not need to
know. Every person's life was a battle between the
past and the future. Under the right conditions you
were able to change, to grow. But sometimes it was
almost impossible to overcome the past. The value
and character of each person were determined by his
or her response to that challenge, the challenge of
growth.

She stayed on the steps for a long time, measuring
her feelings and her memories. Then she walked back
to the highway and headed for town. She remembered
a little café and general store that had also been a bus
station. The sky was light by the time she reached it.
The door to the café was locked, but she saw the
owner moving around inside. She gestured to him,
and he opened the door.

"Morning, ma'am," he said. "We're not open yet.

What can I do for you?" He was looking over Karen's shoulder for her car.

"Is there a bus through here?" she asked.

"Not till ten o'clock," he said.

"Oh."

She could see that he did not know her. But she recognized him very well from her old days here. How strange it was to confront her past this way! It didn't know her anymore. This seemed a blessing.

"But my wife is going to Baton Rouge to see her sister in about half an hour," the man said, taking pity on her. "I think she might be willing to give you a lift."

"Would she really? That would be wonderful."

"Come on inside and have some breakfast."

Charmed by his southern hospitality, Karen followed him through the store to his little house. She sat in the kitchen and drank rich chicory coffee while his wife made breakfast. The newspaper was full of news of the presidential campaign, Bosnia, the illness of Russian President Yeltsin, the crash of Flight 800. Not much of the news was good, but it was all from the twentieth century, so Karen devoured it hungrily.

The café owner's wife started talking the minute they had driven away from the store. She spent most of the trip to Baton Rouge complaining about her two daughters and their good-for-nothing boyfriends. Karen soon gathered that she might not be the most responsible mother. Nevertheless, she felt a profound debt of gratitude to the woman, and thanked her when she let her off at the Baton Rouge airport.

Karen looked for the first flights out. There was a

commuter plane to Atlanta in half an hour. Luckily for Karen there was space.

In the Atlanta airport Karen pondered her options. This airport was a gigantic hub, with flights to every major destination in the nation. She could go wherever she wanted. She let her eye rove over the TV monitors, lingering briefly on Los Angeles, Phoenix, Seattle, New York. Some of her courage ebbed as she reflected that no one was waiting for her at any of these destinations. She had cut herself off from everyone she knew. She was alone in the world.

Then she noticed Chicago. A United flight was leaving in forty-five minutes. Impulsively, she bought a ticket.

On her way to the gate she stopped at a souvenir shop and bought Atlanta Olympics T-shirts in children's sizes. After a moment's hesitation she also bought a Braves ball cap in a man's size. Carrying her purchases in a plastic bag, she got on the plane.

She fell asleep as soon as the plane left the ground, and didn't wake up until the descent to Chicago had begun. Her seatmate, a middle-aged lady in a Chicago Bulls sweater, smiled at her. "You've had a nice rest," she said.

"Yes." Karen smiled sleepily.

"Back to the real world now," the lady said. "We'll be at O'Hare in fifteen minutes. They say it's freezing there."

"Yes." Karen nodded. "Back to the real world."

At O'Hare Karen took a shuttle to a local Holiday Inn and spent the night. The next morning she rented a car and headed for Evanston. She parked her car outside a bank building in the center of town and called the number on the slip of notepaper in her purse.

Chris Carpenter answered.

Ten

Chris was glad to see her. More than glad.

She had called his work number, but he left the office immediately to meet her. He gave her a long hug and then held her out at arm's length.

"I just want to look at you," he said. His face was beaming. He had that little-boy look she had seen on the streetcar back in New Orleans.

"The girls are going to be awfully excited," he said. "I've told them all about you. They're with me this week, so you can meet them tonight. If you want to."

"Of course I want to." Karen smiled.

He shook his head, admiring her, and then held her close again.

"Thank you," he said.

"Nothing to thank me for."

He took the rest of the day off and was home with Karen when the girls returned from school. Karen was surprised by their beauty. The photos Chris had shown her in New Orleans did not do them justice. Josie had strawberry blond hair the color of an autumn leaf, and a bright, energetic personality to match. She was at the age where children cannot stop talking. She told Karen all about her school, her friends, her vacation last summer and her plans for next summer.

Kate, the older girl, was near enough to adolescence to be tongue-tied in Karen's presence. It soon became apparent that she idolized Karen and viewed her as a model of feminine grace. It took a while to draw her out, but in the end she became almost as loquacious as her younger sister.

Karen gave the girls the Atlanta Olympics T-shirts she had brought, and she put the Braves cap on Chris's head. All three insisted on wearing the items. Seeing them this way, Karen could not escape the feeling that the family was rearranging its chemistry to accommodate her. It was an exciting thing to behold and to be a part of. She could not help feeling that she belonged here somehow, that a place had been reserved for her long ago.

She caught a glimpse of herself in the mirror. She looked pretty in a way she had never looked or felt before. She seemed worldly, sophisticated, as though she had been to many exciting places and done daring, sophisticated things. She almost felt herself glow, and she could sense the admiration of the girls and of Chris, as though she brought a breath of exotic air into their little house.

They all made supper together, the girls helping Karen with the salad while Chris barbecued pork chops outside. After supper Karen saw the girls' rooms. They were both neatly kept, and in the closets were cute little dresses and jeans and shirts. The girls were well taken care of, she could see that.

"Their mother does most of the shopping for

clothes," Chris offered. "I just provide a place to keep them."

"I can see you're a good father, Chris."

"I do my best." He smiled. "They need a mother, though."

Karen helped the girls with the dishes. She noticed that they handled the job expertly, fitting the pots and pans into the dishwasher with an adult's foreknowledge of the best places for each item to go.

"How did you girls become such excellent dishwashers?" Karen asked.

"Daddy showed us," Josie replied. "Mom's dishwasher isn't as big. This one is easy. Look—you can even change the height of the shelf if you want."

Karen remembered that Chris was an architect. He probably took an interest in the dimensions of things and the best way to handle them efficiently.

"So your Dad does dishes, too?" Karen asked.

"Yes, but he always breaks glasses. He's a klutz," Josie observed.

"Well, men often are," Karen said.

"Are they?" It was Kate who asked this. She was obviously alert to Karen's familiarity with the opposite sex.

"Pretty often, yes." Karen suppressed her smile.

The girls insisted that Karen kiss them good-night. She felt their eager interest in her as she hugged them. She was not sure whether it came from the fact that something was missing from their lives, or from her own qualities as they impressed the girls. But she did realize that she herself felt at home here already.

* * *

Karen found an apartment that week and began looking for a job. It wasn't difficult, for she had a lot of experience with all the major computer companies and knew all the spreadsheet literature. She found a job with a computer consulting firm the next week, and she settled into a routine that had her working on the northwest side of the city during the day and returning to have dinner with Chris and the girls.

Then the girls went back for two weeks with their mother, and Karen was alone with Chris most evenings. They spent this time getting to know each other better. In a way it was easier with the girls out of the house. At the same time, however, Karen felt she had learned precious and revealing things about Chris from watching him relate to his daughters. He was a sensitive, caring father. It was easy to see that as the girls grew older and faced new challenges, his steadiness and his unpretentious personality would be of great value to them. In the family situation he asked nothing for himself. He only wanted to give. Clearly the girls were deriving enormous benefits from this.

At the end of that first week without the girls, Karen slept with Chris for the first time.

In the beginning, there was nervousness on both sides. Chris did not want to push her. He was feeling uncertain about himself in the wake of his divorce. As for Karen, she felt such a complete dislocation from her recent experience that she was not sure she was capable of intimacy so soon.

But after a few false starts, things happened very sweetly and naturally. Chris was a tender lover who

seemed to care much more about what Karen was
feeling than about himself. His caresses lacked the
hot, penetrating intimacy of Marc Belfort, but they
communicated a warmth and a sense of home that
Marc could never have offered her. In the end she
gave herself with a shock of excitement that amazed
her. She realized that in the arms of Chris Carpenter
she could know passion of a completely different
color than any she had ever felt before.

He held her in his arms for a long time, savoring
the feel of her.

"You're so beautiful," he said.

She snuggled against him gratefully. She knew
things were happening very fast, but she felt an in-
stinctive trust in him that salved her worries and made
her feel excited about the future.

After that night it was understood that their relationship was a serious one. When the girls came back
they found Karen waiting for them. The family pulled
together around her. There was still a lot to learn on
both sides, and some adjusting to do. The process
involved a few missteps, but even these seemed remarkably natural and necessary. Karen was still an
exotic and slightly unreal creature in the eyes of the
girls, so it was important for her to bring herself down
to earth and show them that she was as human as
they were.

Before long she began to cut the figure of a highly
bright and efficient companion, more adept than Chris
with her hands where household tasks were concerned, but very considerate of his judgment in matters of right and wrong, as the girls themselves were.

Karen joined him in disciplining them when they needed it, and took an active part in engaging them in conversation when they were all together.

Karen understood intuitively that both girls were worried about the role they had played in Chris's divorce from Susan. They seemed to feel that they had fallen short as daughters by failing to keep their parents together. The resentment they naturally felt at the breakup of the family was turned upon themselves as guilt. They showed signs, in different ways, that they felt inadequate. Karen quickly learned to lift their spirits with her compliments on their achievements and with her own displays of affection for them. She was not sure whether their real mother was doing all she could in this regard, but she knew it could hardly hurt if she herself made the girls feel precious and loved.

"You're so good with them," Chris observed one evening. "How do you do it? You've never had children of your own."

"I just naturally like them," Karen said. "It's easy when you like someone."

But there was more to it than that, and Karen knew it. For years she had wanted children of her own, and had never succeeded in starting a family. Josie and Kate were made to order for her. They were bright, sensitive, loving girls who needed and wanted her. They were like a dream come true. She had to weigh and understand these feelings to make sure that she treated the girls with the respect they deserved. But there was no doubt about the happiness they brought her.

As for Chris, she felt more at home with him each day. She admired his way of approaching life. He was serious about his work, but far more serious about his family. He saw the importance of enjoying little moments at home, and of being available to his daughters. Obviously his divorce had taught him something about what makes a successful man in a harshly competitive world. It is not his ability to best other men in the struggle for money or power, but his ability to be strong for his children, to give them a home.

Chris was not articulate about this, and perhaps, Karen sometimes thought, not introspective enough even to think it. But it was eloquently clear in everything he said and did. He always came home from work as early as possible when the girls were there, and even saved his weekend work around the house for those odd hours when the girls were either sleeping or busy with their own activities. Often Karen would see him remain in a room with the girls, even if they weren't paying any attention to him. Eventually one or the other would come to his side to show him something she had done, or with one of the countless questions that daughters ask their fathers. At such a moment Karen realized that he had been keeping himself available so that the girls could count on him for his interest and admiration. He had enormous talent as a father.

Months went by. Christmas was coming closer. Karen felt happier with each passing day. Her time with Marc no longer seemed so much a transgression as something necessary and natural, a stage of her existence that she had to go through in order to reach this happiness.

One afternoon, as she was repairing Kate's tape player, Chris said to her, "You know, you are so perfect."

"What do you mean?" she asked.

"Remember in New Orleans, when I said you looked sort of like an athlete or a racehorse when I first met you?" he asked.

"Yes."

"And later I said you looked softer. Like a figure in a painting."

"Yes." She blushed slightly.

"Well, now you just look perfect," he said. "You look as though you've been here forever. And, looking at you, I feel as though I've never been without you. As though I've never known a single moment's unhappiness." He sighed. "I guess this is what it's all about."

Karen said nothing, continuing with her work. But she knew she would never forget his words.

One night Chris asked Karen to dinner.

"Friday night," he said. "I'm taking you to Le Français."

"Le Français!" Karen exclaimed. "We can't go there, Chris. It's too expensive."

"Not for this night. I want it to be special."

Le Français was the most famous French restaurant in the greater Chicago area, one of the most famous in the nation. Karen knew that Chris would never suggest it unless the occasion was special.

The girls would be with their mother in Lake Forest Friday night. Karen and Chris would be alone.

Karen worked hard all week setting up a downtown bank with a software system developed only this year. When Friday came, she left work early and went home to put on her best dress.

As she was getting ready, she looked in the mirror and blushed to see the expectancy in her own eyes. She suspected that Chris was going to ask her to marry him tonight. Nothing could make her happier. She was twenty-eight years old, and at last she was finding herself. Her life was working itself out.

Chris was to call her when he was ready to pick her up. She stood before the mirror in her bedroom, putting the finishing touches on her makeup and waiting for the phone to ring.

When it didn't, she wondered if Chris had been held up in rush hour. It was Friday, after all, and there was a rain falling that might be freezing on the expressways.

Six o'clock came, then six-thirty. Karen called Chris's house. There was no answer. She poured herself a glass of wine and sat down to wait for him.

At seven she tried his house again, and when there was no answer, she got in her car and drove there. The roads were not particularly slippery, though the rain seemed to be changing to snow.

The house was dark except for a light in the kitchen. Karen let herself in and stood in the empty living room, listening.

"Chris? Are you here?" A vague dread made her

hesitate to move from where she was. She had to force herself to look in the den and then go upstairs.

The girls' rooms were empty, of course, and dark. She looked into the master bedroom. It was here, on this bed, that she had first slept with Chris. The warmth of him seemed to reach out to her.

But she noticed that the light was on in the bathroom. She inched toward it, trembling now.

She saw him before she could prepare herself. And yet, as she rushed toward his prone body, she felt something other than surprise. It was a sinking feeling, a confirmation of something terrible that she already knew.

The blood had spread over the tiles beneath his head. His face was turned away from her. But it was the inertness of his hands that was the most terrible thing, more terrible even than the blood.

"Chris!" She fell on her knees at his side. "Chris! Oh, my God..."

She was bending toward the dark place behind his ear when a voice sounded behind her.

"I tried to warn you. But you wouldn't listen."

She turned to see Marc Belfort staring down at her through cool, evaluative eyes.

"Marc! My God..."

Marc was very still, his arms crossed over his chest. He seemed as cold as steel, unmovable. His eyes moved from the lifeless figure on the floor to Karen.

"You have your clothes here?" he asked.

She fought for words. The sight before her took her breath away. "At the apartment," she said at last.

"Let's go."

She clenched her hands into fists as she looked at Marc. "No."

Marc did not move. "Save the little girls," he said. "Come with me."

Her eyes opened wide.

"You wouldn't."

"I did this, didn't I?"

All the strength drained out of Karen at that instant like the air from a balloon. She wilted before Marc's eyes.

"Let's go," he said.

She let him lead her out of the house and to the car waiting around the corner. She looked back, seeing the house recede, and with it her future with Chris.

"Drink this." Marc held out a flask as she sat beside him on the front seat.

She took it and drank. Almost immediately she began to feel dizzy. Before they reached the expressway she was finding it impossible to keep her eyes open.

"Why?" she asked. "Why, Marc?"

"That's a stupid thing to ask," he replied. "Don't ask me. Ask yourself. You did this—I didn't."

Those were the last words she heard. She lost consciousness as the traffic roared by.

Eleven

When Karen awoke, her head throbbing from the drug she had been given, she was lying in Marc's bed as though nothing had happened.

The windowless room gave her no idea of what time it might be. She could not even know what day it was, so profound was her stupor. It took her many minutes to be sure her situation was real, and not a nightmare that had come to disturb her sleep in her Chicago apartment.

But in the end she knew it was real. Or rather, it was the unreality of the Belfort world that had returned to claim her. The real, sunlit world of work, of happiness, of little girls and loving fathers, was no match for this airless place of obsession and silence. In some dark way she had made her choice the night she first gave herself to Marc after the Duchaises' masked ball at Sans Souci. Her fate would not let her turn her back on it now.

A few minutes after she awoke the key turned in the lock and one of the Caribbean sisters came in with a tray of coffee and rolls. So she was being observed, Karen realized. The woman said nothing, but locked the door behind her when she left. Karen poured herself a cup of the strong, chicory-flavored brew. It seemed to revive her, though she could not eat the rolls.

She padded to the bathroom to look for aspirin. Thankfully there was a full bottle under the vanity. She took three tablets and returned to the bed, feeling woozy from her short walk. She drank all the coffee in the pot. A sort of crazed alertness came over her, produced by the caffeine, but it still didn't cure the mental confusion that remained. She sat on her bed feeling her nerves tingle, surveying the room around her.

Nothing had changed. The tapestry still showed the same antebellum lady in her swing. The portrait of Marc's great-great-grandmother still hung across from the bed, and the lady in the picture still bore the same subtle resemblance to Marc himself. All the little knickknacks were in their places, nicely dusted by Marc's maids but looking all the more antique for their polish. The heavy bronze bust of the unknown Belfort lady on the bedside table looked as inscrutable as ever.

Despite the caffeine in her veins, Karen must have drifted off to sleep again, for it seemed only a moment later that Celeste—or Augustine—appeared with her lunch tray. Perhaps out of pity for Karen, the lunch was especially fine: crab salad, cold chicken with a Cajun-flavored *coulis* and white wine. Karen looked at it longingly, but did not eat.

She felt herself getting weaker in the course of the afternoon. Some inner fund of resolve had been taken away from her, and without it there seemed no reason to keep her strength up. Like so many prisoners before her, she was giving up.

Karen watched without interest as the maid returned to take the tray away, shaking her head. Then she fell into a troubled sleep full of dreams of her childhood. When she awoke, a man's hands were on her shoulders. She opened her eyes to see Marc looking down at her.

"You look all in," he said. "Come on."

He helped her to the bathroom where the large tub was full of sudsy, perfumed water. He took off her nightgown and helped her into the tub. She was as passive as a sick child, completely unresisting as he tenderly sponged her naked body.

"Hold your head back," he said, washing her hair with a shampoo that smelled of mangoes and plumeria. "That's a good girl."

When he had finished, he patted her dry with a soft towel and carried her back to the bed. She lay dazed, her body still pink from the hot water. He caressed her slowly, his fingertips moving over her nipples and down her stomach. He kissed her thighs, her knees. Her wet hair still smelled of foreign places and sights unseen.

Finally he took off his clothes and got into the bed with her. She did not struggle or resist as he gently spread her legs and entered her. Small sighs came from her lips as his excitement increased. Neither of them spoke a word. The communion of their bodies made words superfluous.

He finished with a slow spasm that found its echo in her own senses. She shuddered like a bird in his embrace. Glorying in the scent and feel of her body, he lay beside her for a long time. Then he left.

Karen did not move. She did not even dress herself. She lay naked, staring at the ceiling, until somnolence crept over her again. When her dinner was brought, she turned her head to the wall. Celeste—or Augustine—did not bother to leave the tray.

It was late when Marc returned. She could tell by the fact that he was wearing the robe he always wore before bed.

Seeing her nudity, he came to cover her with the comforter. "Celeste tells me you haven't been eating," he said. "You should eat, Karen."

"I'm not hungry." Her voice was very small and faraway.

His dark eyes looked concerned. "You've had a hard time," he said. "It will take you a while to recover your strength. But you can't just give up."

She looked away from him.

"I love you, you know," he said. "More than you've ever realized."

She said nothing.

"All this time I've lived only for you," he said. "You've brought me back to life by coming home. I'm going to make you the happiest woman in the world."

Karen was as still as a statue. The emptiness in her eyes alarmed him.

"Did you love him that much?" he asked.

A small tremor shook her body, but she did not answer.

"However much it was," he said, "I love you a

hundred times more than that. Some day you'll understand what love is, Karen. What it's like to be unable to live without another person. Unable to breathe..."

He removed the comforter and let his eyes move over her naked body.

"Ah, Karen..."

He placed his hands on her thighs and bent to kiss her breast. The nipple tensed at the touch of his lips, and a groan sounded in his throat.

Her hand came from nowhere, wielding the bronze statue with a force that surprised even her. She struck him flush on the temple. Without so much as a cry he slumped unconscious on her breast.

She lay trembling, exhausted by so many hours of concentration on one action. Marc lay like a child, his head on her breast. The moment would have been ironically tender had she not felt his blood dripping onto her skin.

She steeled herself and turned brusquely sideways. His weight slid off her, and she got to her feet. She hurried into the bathroom. An ugly smear of blood ran between her breasts to her stomach. She washed it off and got dressed.

She had planned her moment well. It was late at night. The maids, secure in the knowledge that Marc himself had Karen under control, had gone to sleep.

She put on a dress and tiptoed down the stairs. She turned the key in the front door lock, so slowly that even she could not hear the groan of the tumblers. Then she opened the door and walked quickly away down Prytania Street.

She found a cab at the corner of St. Charles Avenue and asked to be taken to the airport. The corridors and gates were sleepy, almost completely deserted at this late hour. She got on a red-eye flight to Savannah. The plane was three-quarters empty.

She arrived in the wee hours and surveyed the departure screens calmly. There was a flight to Chicago at seven. She looked longingly at the flight number and shook her head. Then she bought a ticket for the first flight to New York.

She was the first passenger at the gate. The airline personnel found her waiting there when they arrived to post the flight number. She did not stir to buy a cup of coffee or read a magazine until the plane had arrived. When it was time to board she was the first in line.

The flight to New York took two hours. At La Guardia Karen saw that there was a commuter flight to New Haven, but she decided on an impulse to take a cab into Manhattan. She bought some new clothes at a Midtown department store and put them on right away, dumping the silk dress into a trash receptacle on Fifty-fifth Street.

She had lunch at the Museum of Modern Art, where she spent a good part of the afternoon. Then she went back out onto the crowded streets, eager for some sense of returning to reality. New York seemed harsh and noisy. It had none of the charm of the busy shopping mall where she had met Chris Carpenter back in New Orleans. But it was, in its own cruel way, real. She let the heavy thump of the traffic and the scream of the sirens penetrate her nerves. She wanted to be uncomfortable. The real world was uncomfortable.

She found her legs getting weak as the afternoon wore on, so she stopped at an espresso bar for a cup of coffee and a pastry. Then she caught a limo to La Guardia and got on a commuter flight to New Haven whose number she had written down that morning.

She got a cab at the New Haven airport and gave the driver her address in Wallingford. The light was fading fast. By the time the cab turned into her street, the sun had set.

She told the driver where to stop. The house was dark.

"Nobody home?" asked the driver.

"That's fine," Karen said evasively. "How much do I owe you?"

She watched the cab pull away before she took out her key and approached the house. The darkness went deeper than the dark windows. The yard looked uncared for. This would have been impossible had Brett been home. He took pleasure in working on the yard on the weekends.

She let herself in through the side door. The kitchen smelled musty.

Karen's heart sank. She knew Brett was gone, had been gone for a long time. How, indeed, could she have expected him to stay?

She turned on the kitchen light, but not the other lights. She peered through the doorway to the little TV room where she and Brett used to watch sports and movies. Everything was cold and deserted.

Sighing, she returned to the kitchen. She found a note on the counter, underneath the pad on which she used to write her grocery lists. The paper was yellowed with age. *If you ever come back,* it read, *you'll know how I feel.*

A sob came to Karen's lips at the sight of her husband's handwriting. Her life with Brett called out to her from the old walls of their modest little house. It had been a good life, she realized. Not an easy life, but, in its way, a happy one. She had been wrong, terribly wrong, to turn her back on it so cavalierly. She wished she could turn back the clock. She should have fought for that life, and fought for Brett.

Slowly she made her way up the stairs to their bedroom. It was silent. She opened the closet and saw the hangers, empty now, that had held Brett's suits, his sport coats and slacks. There was no sign of him now. Only her own things.

"My God. What have I done?"

She lay down on the bed, crying. She felt utterly abandoned. Now she saw the terrible truth of Brett's note. Having returned to the empty house as he had before her, she knew how he felt. She knew how many years of life, of love, he had turned his back on.

She lay for a long time, the cold, dark air settling into her flesh. She sensed that she had reached the end of her journey. She had thrown her life away, and this emptiness was her reward.

She tried to sit up, but the nothingness of her life seized her like a strong hand, pushing her back down.

Why get up? Where could she go now? What could she do? She had exhausted her choices.

Yet she still had sufficient life in her to be surprised and terrified when a voice sounded in the darkness. "So," Marc Belfort said. "You came home."

Karen's grief turned to panic. She tried to get up from the bed but Marc was upon her instantly. His face was a silhouette in the shadows, but she could feel his rage in the hands that pinioned her.

"There's only one way to get rid of a certain kind of woman," he said. "My ancestors knew that. Her hooks are too deep. You can't get them out. Not as long as she's alive."

His hands closed around her neck. He began to squeeze. "Look at my face," he said. "You did this, Karen. You did this."

The breath began to leave her. She tried to scream. His face came closer. She saw the blood on the wound she had inflicted. He wore it like a badge of violence.

"Look at this face," he said, squeezing tighter. "It's the last face you're going to see."

Blackness spread across her vision. He brought his head down toward hers, as if he wanted to finish things by kissing her.

"I love you."

She felt herself floating upward from the bed. The scalding agony in her lungs gave way to a strange lightness. It was ending, she realized. Karen was coming to an end, all her adventures behind her. She wanted to say goodbye, but it was too late. The world was gone from her.

"Karen."

At the sound of her name, she opened her eyes, startled. It was not Marc's face she saw, but the mask of Romeo. The same mask she had seen at the Duchaises' ball, a lifetime ago. Eyes sparkled at her from behind the mask. It came closer, and her lips parted to receive his kiss. The breath had returned magically to her body. She felt alive, safe, even.

The kiss seemed familiar. The taste of her lover was something known to her, as was his embrace. She felt the gentle pressure of his body against hers, and felt herself respond.

"I love you." Were they his words, or her own? She was not sure. The journey back to herself had been so long that she was dizzy.

"I missed you." It was Brett's voice. Amazed, Karen had to fight for breath with which to answer him.

"Brett," she said. "Brett..."

"Are you mad at me?" he asked, holding her close.

"Mad?" she asked. "Why would I be mad?"

"For coming after you this way," he said. "Maybe I was wrong."

She saw the open doorway to the balcony. Charles Duchaise, dressed as Napoléon, was passing by and he paused to look in at her. The walls of Sans Souci had not changed. Everything was the same, including herself. The journey she had taken with Marc Belfort had removed her neither from this place nor from this night. It had been just her imagination.

Charles tactfully closed the door, a faint smile on his lips.

Brett took off his mask. The familiar dark eyes and the freckled skin were there before her like a gift.

"I couldn't leave it the way it was when you left," he said. "I got to thinking about us, and I just had to see you."

Karen looked up at the wall. She saw the portrait of the handsome young man in riding boots, with his dark eyes and his haunted air. A forgotten Duchaise ancestor, no doubt. Earlier the look in those eyes had fascinated her. Now it looked remote and rather quaint, like the painting. A fantasy of romantic yearning from a bygone era.

"I should never have let you get so far away," Brett said. "From now on it will be different."

"Far away…" Karen looked over his shoulder at the portrait. Then she held him closer. "Yes," she said. "From now on it will be different."

National Bestselling Author

JOANN ROSS

does it again with

NO REGRETS

Molly chose God, Lena searched for love and Tessa
wanted fame. Three sisters, torn apart by tragedy,
chose different paths...until fate and one man
reunited them. But when tragedy strikes again,
can the surviving sisters choose happiness...with
no regrets?

Available July 1997 at your favorite retail outlet.

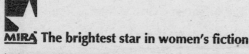

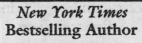

New York Times bestselling author

LINDA LAEL MILLER

Two separate worlds, denied by destiny.

THERE AND NOW

Elizabeth McCartney returns to her centuries-old family home
in search of refuge—never dreaming escape would lie over a
threshold. She is taken back one hundred years into the past and
into the bedroom of the very handsome Dr. Jonathan Fortner,
who demands an explanation from his T-shirt-clad "guest."

But Elizabeth has no *reasonable* explanation to offer.

Available in July 1997 at your favorite retail outlet.

MIRA The brightest star in women's fiction

CATHERINE LANIGAN

the bestselling author of
ROMANCING THE STONE* and *DANGEROUS LOVE

Searching—but (almost) never finding...

Susannah Parker and Michael West were meant for each
other. They just didn't know it—or each other—yet.

They knew that someday "the one" would come along and
their paths would finally cross. While they waited, they
pursued their careers, marriages and experienced passion
and heartbreak—always hoping to one day meet that
stranger they could recognize as a lover....

ELUSIVE Love

The search is over...August 1997
at your favorite retail outlet.

"Catherine Lanigan will make you cheer and cry."
—*Romantic Times*

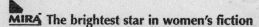

MIRA The brightest star in women's fiction